UNSCREWED

UNPLUGGED

UNZIPPED

One Hot Mess

Lois Greiman

A DELL BOOK

ONE HOT MESS
A Dell Book / April 2009

Published by Bantam Dell
A Division of Random House, Inc.
New York, New York

This is a work of fiction. Names, characters, places, and incidents
either are the product of the author's imagination or are used
fictitiously. Any resemblance to actual persons, living or dead,
events, or locales is entirely coincidental.

Dell is a registered trademark of Random House, Inc., and the
colophon is a trademark of Random House, Inc.

ISBN 978-0-440-24477-6

Printed in the United States of America
Published simultaneously in Canada

www.bantamdell.com

OPM 10 9 8 7 6 5 4 3 2 1

To Robert James Daun, a hero in the making.
Thanks for being you.

1

Luck is merely a product of the happily delusional mind.

—*Chrissy McMullen, Ph.D.,*
in one of her more maudlin
moods

SENATOR!" I SAID, bracing my leg kittywompus across my back door lest Harlequin bound down the stairs and into Miguel Rivera's nattily attired crotch. It was eleven o'clock on hump day, too early for a nap, too late to legitimize a meal involving bacon. "I . . ." I glanced past the senator's smooth-suited shoulder at the septic guy, just recently arrived to drain the pit in my yard. I'd called SuperSeptic nearly a week ago when my toilet had rumbled eerily upon flushing. It had been a particularly distressing moment, since I treat my system with all the sensitivity reserved for a high-strung, fair-haired child. Since the growling incident, however, I had become even more cautious, reserving my bathroom for mirror time and emergency peeing.

Fourteen additional calls to SuperSeptic had produced a "waste-removal associate" immaculately attired in sparkling white coveralls with a red double S emblazoned across his chest. He'd arrived not ten minutes ago, merry as Robin Hood, saving me from violating the Clean Air Act and/or murdering the SuperSeptic guys.

The senator's sleek good looks struck me as somewhat incongruous against the backdrop of my dusty yard and the whistling septic man.

"I wasn't expecting visitors," I said. And even if I had been, I certainly wouldn't have expected Miguel Rivera. He dined in restaurants I couldn't afford to drive past and owned property beyond my capacity to fantasize about, including a modest rancho called Alba Rojo, nestled somewhere in the Santa Monica foothills.

Three years earlier he'd been a senator for the state of California. Currently he was merely Lieutenant Jack Rivera's estranged father. Jack, on the other hand, was another story entirely. Kind of a cross between a pit bull and a really top-notch aphrodisiac. Powdered rhino horn maybe. Not that I would know. I need an aphrodisiac like Colin Farrell needs sexy lessons. But don't get the wrong impression; I no longer harbor any adolescent fantasies for those foreign bad boys.

"Ms. McMullen . . ."

I am, after all, an intelligent, independent woman and a certified shrink to boot. Still, that kind of snockered Irish accent had, in earlier days, been known to pump my estrogen into overflow, effectively drowning my brain cells and floating my imagination into steamy flights of fancy involving . . .

"Ms. McMullen." The senator's voice yanked me back to

the present. *His* accent wasn't bad either: a rich cappuccino of political clout and Latino masculinity that, oddly enough, reminded me of François, one of my newest but dearest friends. "It is good to see you."

"Yes, I—" had no idea where I was going with that statement and was more than happy to be interrupted.

"When I saw the septic truck parked near your house, I thought, perhaps, you would be in your backyard. Might I come in?" he asked.

I drew back a half inch and refrained from shrieking like the village idiot. But the truth was, I wasn't quite prepared for a visit from a political icon. It was Wednesday morning. I wasn't due at my office until one o'clock, giving me all morning to ignore my housework. Hence, my living room looked as if it had been struck by an ill-humored poltergeist. I wasn't particularly well dressed, either. In fact, I was a little understated for the SuperSeptic guy. But he'd kept me waiting for most of a week and I thought he deserved whatever he got. Including the tornado-victim hair.

"I'd love to visit," I said, and pushed Harlequin back with my knee. Harlequin's a dog. He's a cross between a Great Dane and . . . something equally large but not necessarily canine. "I'm afraid this isn't a very good time though, Senator. I—"

"*Miguel* . . . please," he said. "I am sorry to interrupt your morning ablutions. Truly I am, but I will not take up so very much of your time."

"Ablutions." The word threw me, juxtaposed as it was against the sight of the SuperSeptic man hoisting the lid from my apocalyptic pit.

"I would not have arrived unannounced if my visit were not of the utmost importance," the senator added.

His dire expression snagged the image of Farrell as defiant sex slave right out of my mind, replacing it with a sketchy, leftover nightmare in which the senator's son lay facedown on the concrete. I'm not generally prone to dark dreams, but the one I remembered from the night before was a doozy.

"Jack," I rasped. "He's not—"

"May I come inside?" asked the senator.

I bent, grabbed Harley's collar, and held him at bay while my guest stepped elegantly past us into my living room.

Harley and I followed, shuffling and panting. But the senator was too well bred to mention my heavy breathing.

"What a cozy home you have here," he said, barely glancing at the detritus that had somehow accumulated on my furniture since Thanksgiving. "When Rosita and I were first wed, we lived in a humble but comfortable—"

"Has something happened to Jack?" My voice sounded a little croaky, which might, in the wrong circumstances, cause the uninitiated to believe I cared about Rivera Junior.

The senator watched me for an instant, then shook his head. "Gerald is quite well."

"Quite well? What does that mean? Has he been injured? Is he—"

"No." He smiled his thousand-dollar-a-plate smile.

If I were ten years older or one dateless night more desperate, that smile might have convinced me to trade in my favorite late-night companion for something with a pulse. But François, as I call him, is a decent lover, for someone who lives in my bedside drawer and runs on batteries. Unlike more conventional boyfriends, he never leaves the toilet seat up or hogs the remote. Of course, he never pays for dinner, either, but there are pros and cons to every relationship.

"So far as I know, my son is in excellent health, Christina. You needn't worry on his account," said the senator.

I felt my lungs deflate but didn't verbalize my relief. Rivera and I have had a bit of a tumultuous relationship for the past . . . well, from the moment we first met over the body of a formerly illustrious football player named Andrew Bomstad. The Bomb had been rather rudely chasing me around my office desk before dropping at my feet, dead as a salami. Lieutenant Rivera had subsequently accused me of his murder.

"I cannot tell you what it means to me that you are so concerned for Gerald's well-being," the senator said. "He is lucky indeed to have a woman such as yourself."

I wondered rather obliquely if I should take umbrage at his implication. After all, I was not Jack Rivera's woman. We had dated a bit, teased a lot, and fought like badgers. Rivera isn't the sort of guy you pick out china patterns with. He's more the sort to throw china *at*. Still, he has the kind of shivery allure that tends to make women go weak in the head. I had been known to do the same. But I'd never been jelly-brained enough to climb into bed with him. After seventy-some failed relationships, I was taking it slow, playing it smart, communing with François, and studiously avoiding the stupid zone.

"So this has nothing to do with your son?" I asked.

"Well, in a manner of speaking . . ." he said, and let the

sentence dangle as he motioned toward my couch. "The past few days have been rather taxing. Do you mind if I have a seat?"

"No. Of course not." It seemed wrong to say yes, even though, in fact, I did kind of mind. My hair was greasy, I was dressed like a down-on-her-luck stripper, and politicians tend to make me nervous, even when they're not my pseudo-boyfriend's prestigious sire.

The senator sat like he did everything—with a kind of polished panache. I tried to do the same, but Harlequin has ruined many of my grandiose gestures. Pulled off balance, I plopped into my La-Z-Boy like a kid on a trampoline, grateful that my T-shirt was long enough to compensate for my shorts, which were rigorously true to their name.

Wrestling the beast back under control and myself into an upright position, I stared at the senator. He looked as calm as a table leg. I, on the other hand, felt like there were Pop Rocks in my abbreviated pants.

"Can I get you anything to drink?" I asked. It was approximately five hundred degrees in the shade and had been for days, despite the fact that Thanksgiving had come and gone. Hence the practically nonexistent shorts and my growing suspicion that L.A. would, once again, be bereft of a white Christmas. "Water, soda?" I felt as dehydrated as pumice. "An IV drip?"

He smiled. "I'll take a bottle of water if you have it."

I didn't. Elaine Butterfield, best friend and staunch tree-hugger, had warned me against the evils of plastic. One and a half million barrels of oil wasted annually on PET and all that. "Is tap water okay?"

He assured me it was, so I locked Harlequin in my solitary bedroom with his squeaky toy, Lucky Duck, then pattered into the kitchen for the proposed beverage. It was lukewarm and a little brown, but I handed it over and sat back down, determined to look classier sans giant dog.

"Now, what can I do for you, Senator?" I asked, crossing one nearly naked leg over the other. I have pretty good legs, long and relatively slim. It's my torso that tends to resemble a steamer trunk—well stuffed and sturdy.

He sipped the drink, somehow refrained from making a face, and stared soulfully into my eyes.

"You are an intelligent woman, Christina."

I waited. In the past, such statements have generally been followed by *"So why the hell are you acting like such a twit?"* A query that has been posed with the regularity of the setting sun.

"Articulate, well spoken, intuitive," he added.

"Well . . . I wouldn't say—"

"You would be an asset to any organization." He took another drink and nodded, staring ruminatively off into middle space.

I narrowed my eyes a little. "What organization do you have in mind?"

He shifted his gaze back to me and smiled as if just remembering I was there. "Tell me, Christina, have you ever considered becoming involved with politics?"

No. But I'd never really thought about having a dentist drill directly into my brainpan, either. "I'm afraid I have my hands full with my practice," I said. My response sounded as diplomatic as all hell to me.

"I am certain you do," the senator replied, diplomacy obviously not lost on him. "You are, after all, a successful businesswoman in your own right."

Success is a matter of opinion, I suppose. The truth is, I

rent a little office in Eagle Rock, where I counsel the good, the bad, and the gorgeous. I had once been a cocktail waitress in the greater Chicago area but thought that getting a Ph.D. might provide a better income whilst allowing me to display a bit less cleavage as I ministered to the mentally unfortunate. I was partially right; my décolletage is almost always above my nipples these days. But while I could afford to buy a peanut buster parfait pretty much whenever I wished, I couldn't manage to pay for a new septic system. Thus SuperSeptic's third visit of the year.

I refrained from fidgeting while the senator continued. "Well educated. Intelligent." He scowled a little and seemed to stare through my left eyeball and into the world beyond.

"Are you feeling all right, Senator?" I asked. Usually, when conversing with Miguel Rivera, it felt as though every other woman on the planet had mysteriously disintegrated. Perhaps it was that single-minded focus that made him so successful in the political arena. That and the fact that he looked like a slow orgasm in Armani.

He shifted his attention back to me with an apologetic smile. "I always wanted a daughter, Christina. Did you know that?"

No I didn't know that. In fact, according to his only son, Miguel Rivera should have been rendered impotent at puberty, but maybe that was a biased opinion. Most children have them. I myself have often compared my mother to a burying beetle, which, if the spirit moves it, will eat its young.

"Someone like you," he added. "Bright, resilient."

Was he hallucinating? "Listen—" I said, but he interrupted again.

"Practical, yet instinctive."

"Ummm. Thank you."

"Not to mention beautiful." His smile brightened a little. He took a deep breath and leaned back, intensifying his focus by a couple hundred watts. "Any man would be lucky to have you," he added, his voice soft and speculative.

"I—" I began, but suddenly the realization hit me like a linebacker on steroids: He was coming on to me. I jerked to my feet. It wasn't as if I hadn't fantasized about the good senator a time or two, but having your X-rated ideas reenacted in your living room is a little different than simply playing them through your mind when it's just you and your high-amp Frenchman. "I know Jack and I generally seem mutually homicidal," I yammered. "But really, we're—"

"Good for each other."

I let the rest of my intended monologue hang unspoken in the cranked-up silence. "What are you doing here?" I asked finally.

He looked mildly confused, then his eyes widened and he rumbled a good-natured laugh. "Surely you did not think that I was...that I was propositioning you, Christina."

It took me a moment to catch my breath, longer still to zap my brain waves back on track. "Of course not," I said, and stomped down my politically incorrect irritation. I mean, apparently I'm bright and beautiful and all that other crap, so why the hell *wasn't* he coming on to me? "Why *are* you here, exactly?" I asked, managing—quite successfully, I believe—to disguise my annoyance.

"I came to beg your help," he said, and stood. Suddenly

his voice was darkly dramatic and as enticing as hidden calories.

Sometimes my late-night conversations with François began similarly, but I didn't think this was going to be that kind of interlude. "My help?"

He held my gaze. "There has been a death."

I flinched. My own life had been threatened on more than one occasion during the past year. It tends to make a person a little squirrelly.

"The police have not determined the cause, and I feel in here"—he placed a perfectly manicured hand on his chest—"that the mystery must be solved or there will be dire consequences."

"What kind of consequences?"

"Unthinkable ones."

The hair at the back of my neck crept upward like tiny fingers. "Such as?"

He watched me in silence as if wondering how much to say, then: "I, too, am intuitive, Christina," he said. "It is a gift from my mother's side."

"Uh-huh. But what does this have to do with me?" I was trying pretty hard to act casual, but my heart seemed to be a little bit stuttery in my chest.

He gave a brief shrug. "Perhaps nothing."

"Perhaps?"

Stepping forward, he took my hand in both of his. They felt warm and strong. "I did not mean to frighten you. It is simply that . . ." He paused. Emotion flashed through his ever-earnest eyes. Regret, sorrow, fear. Or maybe he was just a really first-rate actor. "I, too, am fearful."

"Of . . ."

He drew a fortifying breath. "The truth is this: Last night I was visited by a dream," he said.

I waited, but he failed to continue. "Is this a version of Dr. King's speech or . . ."

"About Gerald."

"Oh?"

"As you know, he and I have had our difficulties."

In fact, "Gerald" had at one time accused his old man of murdering the woman whom they'd shared as a fiancée—a long, twisted, and somewhat perverted story.

"But he is my only son. My heir," he said, and fisted his hand against his chest. "The produce of my loins."

Whoa, I thought, and wondered if it was time to swoon like a wilted lily.

"I have no wish to see him hurt."

I shook my head.

"In my dream . . ." He spread his fingers and swept his hand in the air between us, as if seeing the scene in panoramic color. "He was lying on the concrete. Eyes open, face pressed against the cold cement."

Despite the theatrics, I felt my heart slow dramatically. My own dream last night had been similar, although in mine, there had been another body beside Rivera's—an unidentified woman. I took a deep breath, steadying myself. "What does this death have to do with Jack?" I asked.

"As of yet . . . nothing."

"Then why—" I began, but he pulled a Polaroid from his breast pocket.

I reached for the photo with some misgiving, peered at the image, then turned it right side up and looked again. It took me a minute to determine the logistics. Longer still to realize that the thing I was looking at had once been human. "Holy shit!" I rasped, and, jerking back, dropped the snapshot.

There was a moment of silence, then the senator stepped forward to retrieve the photograph. "I am sorry," he said.

My hands were shaking. "What was that?"

"At one time that was a woman. Her name, I believe, was Kathleen Baltimore."

I pulled my gaze from the picture to his face. "Why are you telling me this? Showing me this?"

"Because my dream also revealed *her*."

The shattered images of my own nocturnal imaginings jolted through me like a cruel electrical current.

"She lay on the concrete beside my son's unseeing body." He paused. I said nothing. I felt too sick to my stomach to remind myself that I didn't believe dreams were the harbingers of evil to come. Neither did I set much store by the boogeyman or extraterrestrials. "So you see why answers must be found. Before it is too late," he said.

"But who is she? How is Jack—"

"So far as I know, Gerald does not know Ms. Baltimore."

"Then why—"

"Neither is he acquainted with most of the victims with whom he becomes involved. And yet he is put at risk with each new tragedy. Therefore, we must do something. For her as well as for him. Before my dreams become reality. As they so often do."

I shook my head again. Thus far it wasn't helping the situation a great deal. And it was something I was good at.

"The LAPD is a huge department," I said. "Are you sure Jack is even involved?"

"I believe my son has yet to review this case."

I turned my head a little, maybe believing it would help me think. Couldn't hurt. "You got the picture before he did?"

He paused for a second. "In truth, Ms. Baltimore died in Edmond Park."

"Edmond Park! That's—Is that even in California?"

"It lies some miles northwest of our fair city."

"Nowhere near Jack's jurisdiction."

"Maybe it would not be quite... *kosher* for Gerald to become involved in this tragedy, Christina, but he is a strong-willed man. A *stubborn* man. A man bent on justice, and I feel in my heart, in my *soul,* that he will become embroiled for some reason, and..." He shook his head, seeming to subdue a shudder. "My dreams of late have been quite vivid, filled with evil. With death. How would I forgive myself if something were to happen to him, my only son, before amends were made between us?"

I remained mute for a moment, trying to separate honest emotion from calculated sensationalism. But he was a politician. Perhaps the two had blended into one quixotic toxin years ago. "Listen, Senator," I said, "I appreciate your concerns, but I don't know what this has to do with me."

"It was you who solved the mystery of Andrew Bomstad."

"That was different." And quite personal. Bomstad had been determined to rape me before he dropped like a slapped housefly at my feet. It hadn't seemed quite fair that I might be held responsible for his death.

"What of Robert Peachtree?" he asked.

"Sorry about that," I said, but it probably wasn't my place to apologize. Old Peachtree, had, after all, murdered the senator's fiancée, Salina Martinez, and *tried* to do the same to me after I'd learned the truth. I know it seems unlikely—a nice person like me—but these things happen . . . repeatedly.

"I am not above begging," the senator said.

"I'd like to help you. Really I would, but—"

"All I am asking is that you look into the situation. Learn the truth about her death before Gerald becomes involved. I would consider it an enormous favor."

"I wish—"

"Indeed, you would be a hero to the great state of California. A shining example of feminine ability."

"That's nice, but—"

Someone rapped a happy beat on a window not six feet from my head. I jumped, shoved my heart back into the too-tight confines of my chest, then excused myself to open the back door. SuperSeptic Guy stood there. His coveralls were still gleaming, as was his smile.

"Are you finished already?" I myself may have been a little more on the scowly side.

"I'm afraid you've a bit of a problem," he said.

My spleen knotted up despite his toothy expression. "A problem?"

"It looks as if your pipes may need to be replaced."

"Replaced." My spleen did a free fall, waving dismally to my stomach as it headed toward my knees. "Which pipes?"

"All of them. It appears as if you're going to need an entirely new system."

"I can't—"

"And the sooner the better." He turned away, one happy little camper.

"Wait," I said, stepping onto my dry, crackly lawn. "There must be something else you can do."

"'Fraid not," he said, and was already whistling as he disappeared around the corner of my house.

I followed him, intent on verbal persuasion or bodily intimidation or both, but in that instant, the senator spoke from behind me.

"I'll pay," he said.

I turned in a haze.

He stood framed in my humble doorway, well dressed, polished, and as serious as a coronary.

"I am quite a wealthy man, Christina," he said. "If you help me save my son, I shall pay you handsomely."

2

Excrement happens.

—SuperSeptic Associate

CORRECT ME IF I'M WRONG, but isn't there some sort of governmental department that handles things like, say, the prevention and investigation of crimes?" Laney asked. Elaine Butterfield has been my best friend since the fifth grade. Back then she was called Brainy Laney—later she was called a lot of other things, several of which had to do with her cup size. Brainy Laney Butterfield is as watch-me-as-I-sink-into-depression beautiful as she is smart. Currently she was on location, filming segments of *The Amazon Queen,* an admittedly hokey series that had garnered millions of fans.

As for me, ten hours after the senator's visit, I was snuggled up on the couch with an oversize dog, cell phone pressed to my ear. Following work, I had changed back into my tattered shorts ensemble, considered going shopping for Christmas gifts, and promptly fallen into a post-Thanksgiving coma from which the phone had awakened me.

"The senator said the murder was in a different jurisdiction, in Edmond Park," I explained.

"So crimes committed in other parts of the state can no longer be solved without involving Christina McMullen, Ph.D.?" she asked.

"I guess he's worried about Rivera."

"His son Rivera?" she asked. Her tone was a little dubious. Laney has a tendency to cut through bullshit like a snowplow through whipped cream. Though she herself would never call it bullshit. Or eat whipped cream. Nothing but self-harvested seaweed sprouts and moon juice for Laney. "The son whose fiancée he was sleeping with?"

I rubbed my eyes. "The same."

"The son whose fiancée he planned to marry?"

I refrained from sighing. "I never said the Riveras were normal."

"Uh-huh. How exactly is he worried about his son?"

"He said he had a nightmare about him."

"About Jack." Her tone had gone from dubious to don't-even-go-there.

"Yes." I didn't tell her I'd had a similar dream. It was, after all, probably just a coincidence. But I'd had other dreams about Rivera. Less horrific ones, but just as vivid. They had revealed that he was . . . well, quite favorably endowed. And if I remembered correctly how he'd looked stepping out of my steamy shower some months ago—

which I thought I did—the dream had been startlingly correct. I didn't tell Laney that, either. I needed some time to think things over before voicing the words aloud. "Saw him facedown on the concrete and felt it was a premonition. Something destined to take place if he became involved in this investigation."

"Well, he *is* an investigator," she said. "Which, lest you forget, you are not, Mac."

"I know, but . . ." I pulled a blanket over my legs. I felt a little chilled despite the fact that the temperature still hovered near triple digits. Must be my minuscule body weight. "You didn't see the picture."

"There was a picture?"

"Of the murder . . . of the *victim*."

"How did he get a picture?"

"I don't know. He was in politics. He can probably pull a rabbit out of a hat, too."

"That's great, if you need a rabbit. Do you need a rabbit?"

"Not so much."

"Then I'd be careful. This sounds kind of fishy to me. How did he even learn of a death in Edmond Park? Who is this woman? And why does he care about her? I don't like the idea of you getting involved."

"With a murder investigation?"

"With a politician."

I grinned a little, happy just to hear her voice. "But maybe I could help."

"You asked for my advice. I'm giving it. Stay out of it. Please. For my sake." She sounded just like she did in the seventh grade when she'd asked me not to meet Jeremy Jackson in Zocher Park after curfew. I hadn't listened then, either. I'd ended up having to cover for the two buttons missing from my parochial-school jumper. Jeremy, on the other hand, had been forced to explicate a broken nose.

"I'll think about it," I said.

There was a pause, then a sigh. "You already agreed to help him, didn't you?"

I hesitated. Lying to Brainy Laney is like trying to con the pope—foolish and morally prohibitive. "Did I tell you about the SuperSeptic guy?"

Silence. Then: "I'm trying to divine if there could possibly be a segue here."

"He said my pipes are broken. Or something."

She hesitated. "And you felt that was the universe's way of telling you to risk your life by investigating the death of a woman you've never met."

"I felt I don't have enough cash to pay for toilet-bowl cleaner much less a whole new system."

"The senator offered you money?"

"Said he had only one son."

"Mac, if it's just money, I can wire you some—"

"No." It was tempting, so tempting that I felt a need to interrupt her before I crumbled like my aging pipes. After all, I still owed her for the last loan, which had been given to me on account of my fundamentally deranged brother. Word of advice: If your fundamentally deranged brother says he needs twenty thousand dollars, jab a nail file in his eye and run like hell, even if the money is to repay a loan from a cowboy-wannabe mobster who has something of a crush on you. I think there might be a bumper sticker to that effect. "I appreciate it, Laney. Really. But I'll be fine. There are a lot of crazies here in L.A.; business is brisk."

"Maybe that could be your logo: *L.A. Counseling, where crazies come to roost.*"

"You think it'd help business?"

"Depends. How crazy are they?"

I laughed, but just then there was a knock at the door. The laugh froze in my throat. It was well past nine o'clock in the evening. I have three really good friends—I was currently speaking to one, another was drooling on my leg, and the third was lying in vibratory preparation in the little drawer next to my bed. That just left rapists and somnambulists roaming the streets.

"Mac?"

"I think there's someone at my door," I said.

"Look and see who it is. I'll stay on the line."

I traipsed to the kitchen window and peeked between the curtains. I'd bought them on sale at JCPenney sixteen months earlier. It'd just be a matter of time before the wrinkles hung out.

"Damn it," I said.

"Who is it?"

"Rivera."

"Junior or Senior?"

"Junior." I slipped the curtains shut, but at that exact moment he turned his head toward the window. "Oh, crap."

"What happened?"

"I think he saw me."

"Good. Go talk to him, get his opinion. See if he thinks it's wise to look into this."

"Yeah." I was hiding behind the wall. But I was pretty sure he could see through it. Like Superman. But without the cape. And the Speedo. And tights. "Yeah, that's a good idea."

There was a momentary pause. "What'd you do, Mac?"

I made a face but decided on the truth. "It could be I told the senator I'd keep this a secret." I was whispering now, though I was pretty sure Rivera would have to have Superguy's super ears to hear me.

"Why?"

"Because he offered me a crapload of money," I hissed.

"So he *is* paying you."

"I haven't said I'd do it yet, but the man's richer than Zeus."

"I didn't even know they had an established monetary system on Olympus."

Rivera rapped on the door again. "McMullen," he called. "Open up."

I stood thinking in silence for a moment, pretty sure Laney had heard him. "Do you ever wish I weren't an idiot?" I asked finally, and she laughed.

"Never."

"McMullen!" He rapped again, louder this time.

"You'd better let him in, Mac. Doors are expensive."

"You'll be home soon?"

"Before the next attempt on your life," she promised.

"You'd better hurry," I said, and hung up.

"God damn it, McMullen. Either that was you at the window or there's an intruder in your house. In which case I'm going to break—"

I opened the door before he could complete the sentence or activate the intent.

"Lieutenant Rivera," I said. My tone was ultra-controlled, but seeing him generally makes my ovaries emit some kind of supersonic whine heard only by bats and insects. "How nice to see you."

Harley tromped past me, skidding to a halt in front of Rivera, who rubbed the dog's ears and scanned the interior of my domicile, possibly looking for desperadoes and expatriates.

"You okay?" he asked.

Those were generally the first words out of his mouth. Like "hello" to nonpsychotics.

"I'm fine." I gave him my most charming after-nine smile. "Thank you for asking."

"You were damn slow at opening the door," he said, and glanced through my foyer to my living room. A misplaced lamp shade and a pile of magazines could be seen from where I stood. He handed me a grocery bag and moved into the bowels of my house.

"What's this?" I asked, peering into the bag.

"Have you been burgled?" He moved into the living room, surveying the damage of my survival.

"What's with the flour?" I asked.

"Did you see the guys who did this?" Tossing my latest romance novel from the La-Z-Boy onto the couch, he took a seat not far from where his father had been just that morning.

"I didn't think the LAPD was allowed to be so hilarious," I said, and, following him into the living room, set the bag on the arm of the couch. There were approximately six food items inside. One was shrimp. They looked gray and unusually uninviting. "Normal men bring chocolates."

"I brought a recipe, too."

"Why?" I asked, pulling a carefully printed index card into the light.

"Give a woman a fish and she'll eat for a day," he said. Reaching beneath him, he came up with a comb and two ink pens. "Teach her to cook . . ." He tossed the pens beside the paperback. He looked good. Tired but rugged, dressed in faded blue jeans and a bone-weary T-shirt that knew what to do with a man's chest. "She'll make a man happy without getting naked."

I dropped the recipe back in the bag. "You wish you'd ever been so happy."

He watched me. The devil was shining in his eyes. "You sure you're all right?" he asked again, but slower now, studying me.

"Just frustrated."

His brows rose hopefully. "Yeah?"

I gave him a look meant to scathe. "About my septic system."

"Still peeing at your office?"

"I prefer the term 'micturition,' " I said, but I didn't really. I grew up with three brothers. If I had used that word on any one of them, they would have laughed until their kidneys fell out.

Rivera snorted and rose to his feet. "That's not even a word."

"Isn't it kind of late for you to be irritating me, Rivera?" I asked.

"You have dinner yet?"

"I had a late lunch with a friend."

"How is Mr. McDonald?"

"Oh ho." I held my sides, faking laughter. "You are one funny man tonight."

He crossed the floor toward me. His movements were panther slow, his dark eyes steady as he stepped up close, caressing my arm and pressing his body lightly against mine. "That's not my defining characteristic," he said, and suddenly I could feel his erection through his jeans. I swallowed. I mean, it's not like I hadn't wanted to do the lance dance with him since the first moment we'd crossed proverbial swords, but I'd sworn on a stack of ex-beaus that I would play it smart this time.

"I thought we were taking this slow," I said.

"There's slow and there's dead," he said, and bending down with mind-numbing intensity, he kissed me.

It was the kind of kiss one reads about: hot and endless and full of spine-tingling promise. My endocrine system lit up like a switchboard, blazing through my mostly dormant body and tingling all the way to my toenails.

"And you're not dead," he murmured.

But one more kiss like that might kill me. On the other hand, *he* might kill me if he knew I was conspiring with his old man. They didn't exactly see eye to eye. Hell, they didn't even see eye to ankle. "Listen, Rivera..." I took a couple of fortifying breaths and tried to remember the less productive uses for lips. "Good kiss, by the by..." I sounded a little like I'd taken a heavy hit of nitrous oxide. "...but... I have to work tomorrow."

"Me, too."

"I should get to bed."

The scar-nicked right side of his mouth tilted up a quarter of an inch. "Just what I was thinking."

I could feel the rumble of desire in his chest and wondered rather fuzzily how my hand had become planted there.

He kissed the corner of my mouth.

"Maybe this isn't a great idea," I said, though every single body part I possessed screamed in synchronized disagreement.

"Something wrong?" he asked, and, slipping a few strands of hair back from my cheek, found that must-be-kissed area under my jaw.

I stifled a moan. *Maybe.* "No. I just—" I began, but in that moment he kissed me again, open-mouthed, until I thought I might pass out. I was now sprawled against the wall behind me, breathing hard and barely holding my sizzling instincts at bay.

He drew back a scant few inches, watching me. "Anyone trying to kill you?" he murmured. His breath shivered against my skin.

"Not until now," I managed.

He laughed. The sound was lovely and quiet and shimmied along my crackling nerve endings like a rogue electrical current. "I'm not trying to kill you," he said, and kissed me again.

"Yeah?" I felt limp and hot and desirable. Not unlike fresh-cooked linguini. "What *are* you trying to do?"

"If you haven't figured that out yet, I'd better feed you first. Let you build up your strength," he said. After watching me for a few more heart-pounding seconds, he kissed me again, then took the bag from the couch and disappeared into the kitchen.

Harlequin and I followed him in something of a haze. He had an ass like a middleweight's, narrow and lean and as firm as eggplant. I found I wanted, quite badly, to grab it with both hands, but I forced myself to stop and lean a shoulder against the doorjamb, watching him.

"Maybe I'm expecting a hot date," I said.

Bending, jeans stretched tight over his plum-ripe rear, he took a frying pan from beneath the oven. He glanced at me from a cockeyed angle for an instant, eyes gleaming, then grinned.

I gritted a smile. "What's so funny?"

"Nothing. Come melt some butter," he said. If the desire in his eyes wasn't naked, it was at least indecent.

I sauntered over casually, making sure my hips were on a roll. They're what flowery amorists would call "generous," so I have to be careful, 'cuz sometimes when I get them going it throws the earth off kilter.

He handed me a bowl with a half pound of butter inside and amped up his grin. "Nuke it, will you?"

I turned away with a scowl, a little irritated, a little confused, a lot horny. And that's when I saw my reflection in the microwave. I opened my mouth to scream, but no self-respecting noise would come out. My mascara had headed south, making me look like a shocked raccoon, and my hair! One side had somehow exploded, while the other was crushed to my skull like luncheon meat gone bad.

"Holy crap!" I gasped.

He chuckled, then took the bowl from my numb fingers. "Electrical outlet or lightning?"

I combed my fingers through the frizzled tresses Clairol had optimistically called Rosewood. They were brown. "I thought you wanted that stuff melted."

Another chuckle as he dumped the butter into a pan. "Just wanted you to see your reflection."

"You been short of perps to torment at the station?"

"Perps?" He glanced over his shoulder at me, and there

was something about the way he did it—with his mouth tilted up in beguiling mischief and his whiskey-dark eyes gleaming past the midnight fringe of his hair. It made me want to skip the meal and jump to the main course. "You been watching *CSI* again?"

"Maybe I could send you some houseflies to torture."

"Came here instead," he said, and twirled the butter in the pan with a knife. "Just to keep in practice."

"I'm not really in the mood right now."

He slid his gaze down my body.

"For that, either," I lied, and he laughed in that sexy way that makes my hair tingle.

"Good thing I brought the makings for fettuccine, then?"

Screw my ovaries. My stomach suddenly felt like it had been awakened by a wet dream. "With Alfredo sauce?"

"Just because I'm a cop doesn't mean I'm stupid."

"What can I do?" I asked, and shouldered in beside him at my cracked little counter. From then on I didn't care that I looked like a lightning victim or that my shorts were practically nonexistent or that he had the sensitivity of a sledgehammer. Turns out, sledgehammers can cook like the devil. We did a kind of primitive dance around the kitchen, slicing, chopping, mixing. Eventually he stood behind me, his hand over mine, his crotch pressed to my backside, supposedly demonstrating the best way to sauté shrimp. In less than fifteen minutes he was feeding me Alfredo sauce from a wooden spoon.

"How is it?" he asked.

I refrained from swooning. "Not bad."

"Not bad as in 'it'll do' or not bad like 'forget the damn sex, it's already too late'?"

"I gotta tell you, Rivera..." I gave him a sleepy glance through my lashes. "You'll know if I come."

"If?" he asked, cocky as hell, and fed me more sauce. Seeing his fingers against the spoon, broad and dark and masculine, almost really did make it too late. In fact, for a second I nearly forgot that I'd give my left lung for anything Italian.

A drop of sauce plopped onto my chest just above my frayed neckline. He glanced down, eyes blazing. I held my breath, and then he reached out with ridiculous slowness and wiped it away with his pinky. The feel of his skin against my breast was almost more than I could handle. But he was already offering me the sauce. I took his finger in my mouth, sucking hard. His lids lowered dramatically, his face hardened. I smiled as I drew back and licked my lips.

"Want to get some plates or should we just clear the table and have at it?" His voice was no more than a low growl.

Estrogen was sluicing through my system like go-juice. I wanted nothing more than to ride him like an untamed bronc, but if the truth be known, there is nothing that makes a woman so attractive as her would-be partner's unsated desire. I turned away to get the plates, knowing how my legs looked from behind, and even though those same legs were a little unsteady, we were eating in a minute. In five I was done and leaning back to watch him finish up. He ate with careful deliberation, the muscles in his arms flexing impressively with each movement.

"If you want help cleaning up, you might not want to look at me like that," he said, and settled his fork onto the edge of my country-blue stoneware, abandoning eight noodles and a quarter cup of sauce. That's what drives me crazy about him. It isn't the lightning-quick temper or the way the scar at the corner of his lips dances up with anger or humor. It's the control. Taut. Crisp. Until it lets loose.

"You look tired," I said.

He shrugged, an economical lift of tight-packed shoulders. "Not too."

Was every line suggestive or was it just my hormones shouting lewd suggestions? I rose to my feet, reminding myself I was not going to sleep with this guy. This guy had accused me of murder, had stood me up, had made me look at my reflection in the microwave.

I picked up my glass, placed it on my plate, and rose to my feet. "What's going on at the precinct?"

Another shrug. He was watching me. I could feel the heat of his attention down to my funny bone. It wasn't laughing. "Been a fairly quiet week. Why do you ask?"

"Just making conversation," I said, and turned toward the sink.

"So you don't jump my bones?"

I glanced over my shoulder. "Your bones are perfectly safe with me."

"Shall I worry on behalf of my other parts?"

I smiled from the kitchen doorway. "Feel free."

He rose to his feet and gathered his dishes. Maybe it was my imagination, but every movement seemed darkly erotic, every glance suggestive.

As he stood beside me at the sink, the soap suds on his maple-syrup fingers made me think how it would feel to have him washing his hands over my shoulders, down my arms, over my . . . I shut off my X-rated thoughts, but I was already feeling flushed.

"You okay?" he asked.

"Of course."

"You look a little flushed," he said, handing me a plate. Our fingers brushed. His lips twitched as if he knew every lurid thought that raced through my overheated mind.

"Anything exciting going on at work?" he asked. He wasn't a big fan of psychology. Maybe like an STD patient is wary of hypodermic needles.

"Not much," I said.

"Yeah?" His arm slid against mine. I reminded myself that arms are not anywhere near the sexy zone. "Everybody cured?"

"What can I say?"

"Give me those other dishes," he said.

I handed him the dirty breakfast crockery. A corner of a Pop-Tart resided in the middle of the plate. I'd left a smattering of frosting, too. Self-control. I've never been more proud.

"Nutritionally balanced as usual, I see," he said.

"Has anyone told you that you're much more appealing with your mouth shut?" I asked, and snuck last night's dinner dishes into the sink.

"Most women think I'm better with my mouth open," he said. Slipping a soapy arm around me, he pulled me against him, kissing me open-mouthed and hard.

"What do you think?" he murmured finally, so close I could feel his thoughts inside my cranium. They were hot and smutty.

"About?" I could barely force out the word.

There were pinpoints of black in the dark-whiskey irises of his smoldering eyes. "Enough wooing?"

"Is that what this is?" Somehow, his right thigh had become lodged between mine. I resisted riding it like a romance-novel love stallion.

"The new and improved version."

"That must be why I didn't recognize it."

He ran his hand down my back. I shivered down to my platelets, let my eyes fall closed, considered swooning.

"I think things are going pretty well between us," he said. "We haven't found any new corpses lately."

"What more can we ask?" I breathed. He slid his hand lower, pulling me close. His erection shifted a little. My lips felt dry. I licked them. He followed the movement with his eyes, then leaned in and kissed my lower lip. I was panting like a greyhound. His kisses moved down my neck. He shifted my tattered T-shirt aside with careful fingers.

"You haven't threatened to decapitate me for almost a month."

"Always a favorable sign." It was difficult to remember how to form complete sentences. He tugged my saggy shirt lower and kissed the top of my left breast. I felt the corresponding side of my brain go numb, while my right side began firing off impractical but creative scenarios. God, I love the right brain.

"And I haven't threatened to incarcerate you." His kisses slipped lower. I couldn't decide if I should be happy that I wore such a cleavage-friendly bra or pissed that it was in the way.

"Thank you for that, by the way," I said.

"My pleasure," he murmured, and, cupping my breast, somehow managed to coax it out of its container and rain kisses near the nipple.

I rolled my eyes toward the ceiling and grabbed fistfuls of his shirt.

"You've kept your nose clean," he said.

"While the rest of me is dirty as hell," I rasped.

"Jesus, McMullen!" He paused, staring at me with lightning-bright intensity. "I'm trying to logically justify why we deserve to have sex."

"Oh." Jesus God. Sex! "Yes." Why wasn't there more oxygen in the room? What had happened to the damn oxygen? "Of course. Carry on."

"I've been gentlemanly."

I made some kind of unidentifiable noise in my throat. It might have been a snort or a moan or a gasp. God knows.

"For a cop," he said. He was holding both breasts now. I didn't look down, but I knew the nipples were perched on the top of my bra. He licked one.

I shrieked something inarticulate and bucked against him.

"While you've been"—he was breathing hard—"so damn sexy I can hardly—"

I grabbed a handful of hair at the back of his head and smashed in for a kiss.

After that, all hell broke loose. He was on my nipple, suckling. I think I screamed. He moaned and tore my shirt over my head. My shorts were simply gone, probably disintegrated like wet toilet paper. And suddenly I was perched on the counter, legs spread, bra AWOL. His shirt looked like it had lost a battle with a wolverine. His belt defied me for one frantic second, but finally I mastered it. And then his cock burst free.

I think I might have taken the Lord's name in vain at that point, but it might have been him.

And then someone knocked on my door.

I gasped, wondering wildly if outsiders could see us. I slammed my gaze to the window above the sink, but my blinds were closed fast.

"Screw that!" I breathed, and kissed him, searing his lips with my own.

He was as hot as sin against my core. His hands crushed my butt, drawing me nearer, pulling me onto him.

"Christina," called a voice from the far side of the door. "I am sorry to bother you."

I froze. Rivera froze. We stared at each other. Inches apart. Hearts hammering. Stuff throbbing.

"McMullen," Rivera murmured.

"Yes?"

"Why is my father on your stoop?"

3

You're just lucky blood's so hard to get out of the carpet.

> —Connie McMullen,
> mother of Chrissy and her
> three primeval brothers—
> enough said

*M*Y GAZE WAS WELDED to Rivera's face. "Your father?" My voice sounded as if my throat had been exfoliated with sea salt.

His cock throbbed between us. I throbbed right back. Nobody ever called me a piker. I was absolutely stark naked and happy to be so.

But he drew back, pulled up his jeans, buttoned them in place.

I'd like to say on my behalf that I didn't shed a single tear. Though, in truth, I might have whimpered a little.

"The senator," he said, and stared at me.

"Senator?" I cleared my throat and straightened. I felt cold suddenly. I wouldn't say that Rivera hates his father, but . . . well, he *hates* his father. "What makes you think it is he?"

He stared at me askance. Maybe it was my phraseology. Sometimes people are uncomfortable with proper sentence structure.

"*Him,*" I amended.

"Christina," called the senator again.

"Were you expecting him?"

"No." My voice squeaked. I disciplined my expression and vocal cords. "No. Why would I be?"

His brows lowered, he backed up a pace, putting distance between us, canting his head slightly, eyes narrowed. "When you mentioned a hot date I didn't think you meant my old man."

My jaw dropped. "I *didn't* mean him."

He was still watching me, eyes dead steady. "No?"

I grabbed my shirt from the counter beside me. "What the hell's wrong with you?"

"Then why is he here?"

Yanking my shirt over my head, I jumped off the counter, pulled my shorts out from under his foot, and actually considered biting his ankle on the way up. "How would I know?"

"He didn't—"

But suddenly the back door squeaked. I gasped even before he called my name again. "Christina, are you here?"

Rivera jerked toward the door, pushing me behind him as he did so. I was pulling on my shorts and swearing and panting all at the same time. I'm a real humdinger at multitasking.

"I do not mean to bother you." I could hear his footsteps in my living room. "But—" He stepped into the kitchen just as Rivera Junior pulled on his shirt. I threw my underwear in the nearest drawer, zipped my fly, and jerked my head up just in time to see their gazes clash.

"Gerald!"

"Senator."

There was a moment of hot silence, then: "I am sorry. Christina's door was left unlocked. I worried that something was amiss," said the elder of the two.

As for me, I was peering past Rivera's arm like a tipsy cockatiel.

"That why you came by?" he asked.

They stared at each other. "As far as I am aware, there is no law against me visiting a friend."

Rivera glanced back at me. "You two buddies now, are you?"

I stepped out beside him, cleared my throat, and resisted checking myself to make certain my garments were firmly in their allotted positions. "Hello, Senator."

"Good evening, Christina." He gave me a stately nod. "I am sorry to disturb you. As I said, I worried that your door was unsecured and thought I had best check on your well-being."

"Oh." I wondered a little dimly if it was possible for a face to burn right off its head. "That was very thoughtful of you, Senator."

He made a dismissive motion with his hand. "It was nothing. I was in the neighborhood, after all."

"Really? Well, it's so nice of you to worry on my account, but as you can see, your son was kind enough to—"

"Cut the crap!" Rivera snarled. "What the hell's going on here?"

I shifted my eyes from one to the other, a million thoughts cruising drunkenly through my hormone-washed head. I didn't want to cause more problems between them by blurting out the senator's earlier proposition to me. Neither did I want to break a trust with the older Rivera, and I wasn't all that crazy about the idea of admitting that I had agreed to horn in on a situation that some might consider the business of the police department. "Nothing's going on," I said. "Your dad just stopped by to—"

"You sniffing after her, too?" Rivera asked, turning to his father. "That what this is about?"

The senator's back stiffened. "I'll not have you using that profane—"

"Wasn't Rachel enough? How 'bout Salina? Hell, you got her killed. I would think that would just about—"

"You blame *me* for her death?" The senator's voice was deadly low.

Rivera laughed. The sound was coarse and nasty. "She sure as hell wasn't *my* fiancée anymore, was she?"

"Still looking for others to blame, aren't you, Gerald? It is so like you to be unable—"

But suddenly Rivera launched forward, grabbed his father by the lapels of his blazer, and thrust him up against the wall. "What the hell are you doing here?"

They glared at each other, eyes spitting, lips snarling.

"My whereabouts are none of your concern," rasped the senator.

"They are if you're in this damn house."

"I believe Christina can decide which of us—"

"Oh, for God's sake!" I said, stepping forward and grabbing Rivera's fist. He had a death grip on his father's coat, but adrenaline or just plain pissiness made it possible for me to pull his hand away. "He just came by to ask me for a favor."

"Christina!" hissed the senator, but I ignored him.

"Yeah?" Rivera's mouth jerked. "Is this the kind of favor where clothing is optional?"

"What are you?" I asked. "Twelve? He wants to talk."

A muscle jumped in his cheek. "About what?"

I faltered.

"We have a mutual friend," said the senator, and smoothed his jacket into place. "I but came to inform Christina of her condition."

"Really." Rivera didn't turn toward his father but kept his whiskey-burn gaze on me. "What friend is that?"

My lips moved. My mind was absolutely immobile.

"I do not think that is any concern of—" the senator began, but Rivera interrupted again.

"What's her name?"

The image of a dismembered corpse flashed through my mind. "Kathleen," I said.

"Kathleen what?"

"Cahill," lied the senator.

"What's wrong with her?" Rivera asked.

"I have sworn to keep her condition quiet so that she is not bothered by those—"

"What's wrong with her?" Rivera asked again, and turned his glare on his father.

The elder man lifted his chin with arrogant defiance. "If you must know . . . the young lady is with child."

"Yeah?" Rivera smirked. "You gonna be a daddy again, Senator?"

"She is the daughter of a dear friend who has—"

"So was Salina. It didn't stop you then."

Silence plowed into the room, then: "Still bitter that you cannot keep a woman for yourself, Gerald?"

"You goddamn bastard," snarled Rivera.

"Stop it," I said, and grabbed his arm, but maybe I was trying to restrain the wrong Rivera.

"Are you so weak that you cannot accept a little competition?" asked the senator.

Rivera's lips twisted into a grin, brows lowered over deadly eyes. "You want competition, old man, let's—"

But at that moment I pulled a plate from the sink and slammed it against the counter. It crashed into a hundred satisfying shards.

The jerks jerked toward me in unison.

"What the hell is wrong with you two?" I gritted, and slammed my gaze from one to the other.

"He—"

"He—"

"Shut up!" I ordered, stabbing a finger somewhere between them.

The senator recovered first. "I apologize for my son," he began. "I see he has not yet learned—"

"We don't have a mutual friend," I said, and turned my gaze from the older to the younger Rivera. Usually, runaway honesty isn't a problem with me, but the blatant lies of father to son had frayed my nerves. "The senator has asked me to investigate a death."

Rivera's brows jerked into his hairline. "What the hell are you talking about?"

"Just informally, of course. He thought the police department might be too—"

"What death?"

"That's not the point here," I said, tone calculated to soothe the wild beast. "It simply—"

"What fucking death?" Rivera growled.

I straightened my back. "Kathleen Baltimore's. But I believe her death took place well out of your jurisdiction."

He stared at me a second, then threw back his head and laughed. "Jesus, McMullen, who do you think you are? Columbo?"

"No." I may have mentioned before that I hate to be laughed at. But being laughed at by a braying clod like Rivera makes my blood hurt. "I realize—"

"You're lucky to still be breathing after that last fiasco."

"Well . . ." I could feel my temper rising toward the boiling point, but I diluted it with common sense. Two irate idiots were enough in one kitchen. "Thank you for your profound—"

"You damn well better thank me. I've saved your ass more times than a fucking firefighter."

"I don't think it proper that you speak to a lady in that tone," said the senator.

"And you!" Rivera rounded on his dad with a sharp snort. "What the hell are you thinking? You got some hot deal cooking? Maybe one of your asshole friends offed another of your asshole friends and you want to know what's what? Decided McMullen here is expendable?"

"A woman has died," the senator said, tone stiff and holier than hell. "I did not know her, but I feel in my heart that it was not—"

"Heart!" Rivera laughed again. The sound was about as pleasant as the rumble of a road grader. "You don't have a fucking heart."

"Rivera," I said, but he turned toward me, spewing vitriol.

"So you were willing to lie for him, too, huh?"

Emotion was splashed across his face like acid—anger and hate, but there was more. There was hurt, injured hope.

"I didn't lie," I said, voice quiet.

"So you had no idea why he might be stopping by."

It had been such a small lie. The littlest fabrication, engineered to keep him calm. I opened my mouth, perhaps to say something to that effect, but maybe my lips knew better than to spout something so asinine.

He stared at me for an eternity, then he turned away.

"Rivera," I said, but he just kept walking, through my foyer and out of my life.

4

You're gonna sit down. You're gonna shut up. And
by the grace of God Almighty, I ain't gonna kill you.

—*Esse Goldenstone,*
upon discovering a pack of
Camels in her grandson's
backpack

MICKY GOLDENSTONE took a seat on my therapy
couch at 8 a.m., and settled his right ankle over his left
knee. He was lean and black with a smile that could light
up the universe and a glare that could stop your heart. I
suspected both were employed with some regularity on
the fifth-graders he taught at Plainview in Tujunga.

"Hey, Doc, how goes the rat race?" he asked, and
watched me as he settled back against the cushion. He'd
been a client for just under a year, but we'd covered some
pretty rocky ground in that time.

"Pretty well," I said.

"Yeah?" His teeth were aligned like little white soldiers.
"You winning, then?"

I crossed one leg over the other and smiled. I liked Micky, had since the moment I met him. "Pretty even odds, actually," I said.

He shook his head a little. "Then you're ahead of the game."

"Trouble at work?" I asked.

"No." The answer was straightforward, solid. Our gazes struck and locked. I braced myself. I have clients who come in to chat about their acne or their hangnails or their difficulty paying the mortgage on their million-dollar homes. Micky Goldenstone wasn't one of them. "I found her old man."

I drew a careful breath through my nose and pushed my own suddenly minified troubles behind me. Yes, Rivera had acted like an ass, I had had to force the senator out of my house, and I was still peeing at the office, but I didn't have burn scars from my father. I didn't wake up screaming in the middle of the night, and I didn't have guilt so deep it ate my soul like battery acid.

"The man Kaneasha was living with," I said.

He didn't bother to nod. He was already immersed in the past. Immersed and sinking deeper. I could tell by his expression, his darkening dialect.

"Cig," he said, and sat in silence for a moment, eyes narrowed.

"Did you speak to him?"

He remained silent, looking at nothing.

"Micky," I said.

He drew back almost seamlessly. "Yeah. Yeah. I talked to 'im."

"And that's how you learned—"

"He's a—" He stopped himself, gritted his teeth, making

a muscle bunch in his jaw. "They ain't together no more." He nodded. "She left more'n a year ago. Maybe 'cuz he beat the crap out of her." He shrugged. "Maybe not."

I had a thousand questions, but so did he. I let him run.

"He admitted it. I didn't ask. Hell! I didn't wanna know. But he was proud. Fuckin' crackhead can—" He burst to his feet and twisted away, raw energy tightly bound. "Can—"

"Micky," I said, soothing.

"Can beat the shit out of woman half his—"

"Micky," I said, raising my voice.

"What!" He turned toward me, hands fisted, eyes burning.

"Sit down please."

He did so, but his eyes were still burning, his hands still fisted.

I watched him, letting him calm. *Hoping* he'd calm. "Her abuse at the hands of her boyfriend is not your fault. It was—"

"That's bullshit!" He watched me, then inhaled deeply, making his nostrils flare. "I was the one that raped her."

I kept myself from wincing. "Yes."

"She was just a—" He jerked to his feet again. I let him go. "All elbows and knees and—" He stopped, turned abruptly toward the window. "Eyes." He said the word so softly I could barely hear him.

"From what you've told me, her family life was not particularly stable. Her mother was a cocaine addict, isn't that correct?"

He didn't respond.

"And her brother—"

"Gone. Just fuckin' gone. Shi's dead. Terrence's in the

pen. In prison." He said it almost wistfully. I pulled the conversation back, making a mental note to consider his tone later.

"Her father abandoned her. She had no grandparents and—"

"Yeah." He turned on me with a snarl. "She had a shitty life. Did that give me the right to fuck her like she was some—"

"Sit down," I said.

"Don't tell me—" he began, but if I had learned anything as a scantily clad cocktail waitress, it was when to ask and when to demand.

"Sit your ass down!" I ordered.

He did so.

"You raped a girl," I said, leaning in.

He stared at me, face blank.

"A thirteen-year-old child."

His cheek twitched, but nothing else showed in his expression.

"It was a heinous crime. Cruel. Unspeakable. She trusted you and you hurt her."

He swallowed, but I didn't stop.

"Who's to blame for that, Micky?"

"God!" He squeezed his eyes closed, pressed his nails into his palms. "They should have fuckin' killed me."

"Who's to blame?" I repeated.

He opened his eyes, pursed his lips. "I am."

"Yes." I waited an instant. "Did you make her use drugs?"

He didn't answer.

"Did you?"

"No."

"Did you make her live with an abusive man?"

"I think the rape was enough." He smiled a little, but the expression was gritty.

"*Did* you?" I demanded.

"No."

"Then why do you want to accept blame for more?"

He waited half a lifetime before he spoke. "Because she's got a kid."

I felt my stomach drop toward the floor, but I'd learned to play poker with three brothers who cheated like Irishmen. Nothing showed. "Is it yours?"

He waited again, as did I.

"I don't know," he said finally.

I exhaled carefully. "How old is the child?"

He shrugged. The movement was stiff.

"The boyfriend didn't know?"

"Said the kid didn't live with them. Only saw him once or twice."

I nodded.

"Once or twice," he repeated. "In two years."

I kept my expression as impassive as his. "What are you going to do now?"

He stared out the window. "Put a gun in my mouth?"

I kept my hands relaxed in my lap. "That'll never work."

He glanced at me, brows dropping.

"You're never going to suffer enough if you're dead."

He snorted and sat up straight. "You wasn't raised by your grandma, was you?"

I stared.

"Grams was a big believer in hell."

From what I had heard, his grandmother had also saved his life. "Are you going to hell, Micky?"

"I think I might be there already."

"Then you might just as well continue to live."

He pushed himself backward in his chair and stared at me. The tiniest smile tickled his lips. "Jesus, woman, does the board of shrinks know you dish out this crap?"

"You can always kill yourself, Micky," I said. "You might as well wait."

"Not if I'm a chicken shit."

I shook my head. "You're not."

Our gazes clashed. "Why would I wait?"

"That's what Esse would have wanted."

He stared at me. "She tied me to the radiator once. Did I tell you that?"

I shook my head.

"I says I was goin' out with my dogs. She says I wasn't. I says no one owned me and she could go . . ." He paused, almost smiled. "Next thing I know I was flat on my face with my hands cranked up behind my back and her sitting on top of me. All ninety-two pounds of her. Spent the night listening to her read Scripture. The whole fuckin' night." I could hear him inhale, feel him think. "What if the kid's mine?"

I had no idea, but I kind of loved Esse Goldenstone. "Then you'll have to make some decisions."

"Can I off myself then?" Maybe it was a serious question, but there was a light in his eye again.

I tented my fingers and leaned back in my chair. "It'd look bad on my shrink record," I said.

"Jesus." He brushed one palm across his close-cut scalp. "More fuckin' guilt," he said.

And I laughed for the first time all day.

5

If it looks like a cat, walks like a cat, and has whiskers like a cat, it's probably a damn cat. But if it eats your groceries, messes up your kitchen, and makes you want to rip out your hair by the roots, you either married it or gave birth to it.

—Shirley Templeton,
who should know

"HEY."

I glanced up from where I was supposed to be updating records but was really just staring into space. My temporary secretary, Shirley Templeton (don't laugh, I didn't name her), was glancing around the edge of the door, mug in hand.

"You okay, honey?" she asked.

"Yes." I straightened with military professionalism. "Certainly," I said, but I was lying. The day had been a killer. After Micky, there had been a kleptomaniac, a pathological liar, and a man. Not a normal egg in the clutch.

Shirley came in. She was on a one-day-flu loan from my regular secretary, the Magnificent Mandy. In fact, she was the Magnificent Mandy's aunt. I wondered a little hazily if that made her the Magnificent Shirley, then decided it probably didn't since she was the antithesis of her niece. Where Mandy was small and thin and as scattered as confetti, Shirley was broad and round and solid. She was also as black as a broker's power suit. She waddled a little as she approached my desk, and I noticed she carried a small paper bag in her left hand.

"Thought you might need a little pick-me-up," she said, and set the bag on my desk.

If my olfactory system didn't fail me, and it rarely did when considering copious amounts of calories, there was something filled with chocolaty goodness in the bag. But following my post-Thanksgiving binge I had finally screwed up my nerve and stepped onto the scale. Subsequently, I had sworn off goodness of all sorts.

"That's very kind of you," I said, "but I should get these records taken care of."

"You working on Mr. Goldenstone's?"

I glanced up. Maybe I shouldn't have been surprised that she was familiar with my client list, but Mandy of the magnificent caliber had never quite gotten a single name right. The last time, I believe, she had referred to Micky as Mr. Nugget.

"Yes. As a matter of fact, I am."

She nodded, just a couple of superfluous chin wobbles. Shirley Templeton was not an attractive woman. But then, according to her niece, she had gestated a baker's half dozen kids, and that can't be gentle on anybody. "Poor fellow, carryin' around that load of guilt."

"Shirley!" Granted, I didn't know her well, but she didn't seem like the type to eavesdrop. "I don't mean to be rude, but you cannot listen in on my sessions with clients."

"Listen in," she said, then chuckled a little. "Now, why would I do that?"

"Well . . ." That was a good question. Still, her niece had done so until her ears grew into cauliflowers. "You seem to know more about Mr. Goldenstone than is easily explained. I just assumed you—"

"Oh." She waved a dismissive hand. "That." Shaking her head, she bent with some difficulty to retrieve a little geometric metal shape from the floor and stuck it back on its magnet sculpture atop my coffee table. "I've seen enough troubles, honey. Don't need to hear nobody else's."

"Then what made you think Micky was guilty?"

"I didn't say he *was* guilty," she explained. "Said he carried around a load of it is all."

Maybe there was a difference there, I wasn't sure.

"How do you know he carries guilt?"

"I don't know." She shrugged shoulders wide enough to make a linebacker wealthy and an ox useful. "Maybe I got a nose for it."

"You can smell guilt?"

"Can't you?"

Maybe I gave her a look like she'd lost her marbles, 'cuz she chuckled again. "Not *smell* smell. But, you know, sense it."

I wasn't sure I did, but I nodded. Maybe my nose was good for other things, because the chocolaty goodness emanating from the bag was becoming a little distracting.

Her eyes went serious. "It's a good thing what you're doing for him."

I peeked into the bag. I'd been right. Little chips of

goodness all over the top of a dessert bar. Possibly goodness all the way through. "How do you mean?"

Going to my mini-fridge, she pulled out a carton of milk and set it beside the bag. I glanced up in surprise.

"You don't wanna mess with no osteoporosis. Mama—she's bent over like a candy cane. Thing is..." She narrowed her eyes, getting back on track. "Mr. Goldenstone needs help. You're helpin'."

"You think so?" I was feeling insecure and a little gooshy, so I took the goodness out of the bag and broke off a piece. "Sometimes I feel like I'm just..." I shrugged and tasted, sending my salivary glands into a hastily choreographed version of *Riverdance*.

"Just takin' their money?" Shirley said. "Well, don't you be thinkin' that. You're helpin'. And not with the kind of sugar water some folks hose ya with. You're giving him the hard stuff, but he's drinkin' it down."

I took another bite and heard a taste-bud chorale join the dancers. "Really?"

"Some folks take some hard knocks, but if they got the right person helpin' 'em, they can still get set right before it's too late."

"I don't know." I stifled a weak-ass sigh. "Some days it feels like I should just pass out cookies and go home."

"Well..." She chuckled. "Cookies don't hurt, neither, but you keep doin' what you're doing and things'll get better."

I studied her a moment. There was wisdom in her eyes and strength in the set of her jaw. Turns out she was kind of pretty.

"Thank you," I said, and she nodded, all business suddenly.

"I tidied up my desk, confirmed tomorrow's appointments, and rescheduled today's no-show. Anything else you want I should do before I head home to my brood?"

Marry me? "No," I said. "Thank you. That'll be fine. It's been really nice working with you."

"Pleasure's been mine," she countered.

After she left I sat there alone, ate my *Riverdance* bar, drank my milk, and wished, to my chagrin, that the Magnificent Mandy had never darkened her mother's womb. Aunt Shirley was so much better, and maybe she was right. Maybe I was doing some good. But maybe there was more good that could be done. Perhaps I should look into Kathleen Baltimore's death, regardless of the fact that Rivera was already spitting tacks. Maybe she was one of those people who just hadn't been given the right chances. Just because the senator had offered to pay me didn't mean it was the wrong thing to do. And just because his son insisted it was the wrong thing to do didn't mean it was. In fact, chances were good it meant the opposite. Rivera might not own the stupid market, but I'd say he had a pretty good share.

Turning to my computer screen, I Googled Kathleen Baltimore.

After fifteen minutes I had learned several things: She had died on Tuesday in Kern County, the hummingbird capital of California; she was survived by a single daughter; and the police had determined her death was an accident.

I shut down my system and headed home.

Harlequin met me at the door like an overwrought lover. Large, excited, and a little drooly.

We had dinner together on the couch while watching

Grey's Anatomy. I don't see a lot of television—except for Laney Brainy as the Amazon Queen, of course—but Harley has a thing for McDreamy. I went to bed with dreams of my own and found *myself* a little drooly.

But even thoughts of Patrick Dempsey couldn't steam the memory of Kathy Baltimore's photo out of my head. I wondered how the senator had gotten that photo and why he was so sure that she was the woman from his dream—especially if the police thought her death was accidental. In the morning my mind was still mulling.

I dressed in an apple-green shift with a strand of pearls and sexy cork wedge sandals. Classy as hell, but late. Grabbing a glass of milk and a granola bar, I jumped into my Saturn and lurched onto Foothill Boulevard. Five minutes later I had cut two people off on the 210 and was trading hand signals with the locals. At 8:57 I screeched into the parking lot, ready to throw open the L.A. Counseling doors before my first clients could arrive and be instantly offended by Mandy's magnificence. But, to my fantabulous surprise, Shirley was already manning the desk.

"My niece asked me to fill in one more day," she explained.

I refrained from dancing. "Still not feeling well?"

"Terrible bug, I guess. Say..." She reached under her desk and brought out a white cardboard box. "I stopped at the Donut Hole on the way here and got a couple a caramel rolls. Ate one 'fore I got here, but Lord knows if I pack another ounce of fat into my arteries, they're going to have to come up for air. You take the last one."

I took the box, protesting weakly. I love caramel more than sin. "I don't think—"

"Oh . . ." She waved dismissively. "Don't you go telling me you can't eat it. Scrawny little thing like you don't have the strength to lie. Here." She picked up a card that was propped with its kindred in front of her. "Your first client. Daryl Ellingson." She put it on top of the box. "He should be pulling in any minute now. Your three o'clock canceled on account of she has to work, and a woman name of Celeste Friedman called in a panic. Wanted to get her daughter right in. An emergency, she says. I told her you didn't have no time 'til this afternoon, but that conflicted with her Pilates class."

I refrained, quite professionally, from rolling my eyes. "So I shouldn't be expecting her?"

Shirley gave me a "what's that?" glance, accompanied by a sassy tilt of the head. "Course you should. After I borrowed a little of that guilt that's been rolling around in here, she decided to take your free three o'clock."

"Guilt?"

"I just asked if little Amy was her only daughter or if she had a spare—just in case things don't work out."

I stared in silent admiration.

"You get goin' now. You better start in on that roll or Mr. Daryl'll show up and you'll have caramel on your teeth," she said, and shooed me down the hall.

But she opened my office door before I'd had a chance to slip into a glucose high. "I forgot to tell you that a Senator Rivera called."

"Oh?" I glanced up, immediately nervous.

"He's got a mighty sexy voice for a Republican." She scrunched up her face a little when she said it. I was going to have to guess she voted for the other side.

"What did he want?"

"Asked that you call him soon as you get a chance." She glided into my office like an angel and set a note beside the roll. "Home phone, cell phone, pager," she said, and left.

Unfortunately, I didn't have time to be floored by her efficiency. Back-to-back clients kept me on my toes until nearly noon, at which time curiosity took me by the throat. I set my records aside and called the first number on the list.

"Caring Hands," said a chipper voice.

I glanced at the phone. "Um . . . I'm sorry. I was given this number for Senator Rivera."

"The senator? Hang on a minute." She covered the receiver, but I could hear her clear as vodka. "Hey, Emmy, is the senator still here?"

The answer was out of my range, but in a minute Chipper was back on the line. "I'm sorry. We can't seem to find him right now. I thought he was serving lunch, but maybe he's helping on the floor."

I blinked. "We're talking about Senator Rivera, right?"

"Yeah. If you want to leave a number I can try to get him a message, but my shift's done here in fifteen."

"Senator *Miguel* Rivera?" Somehow I couldn't quite see him dishing up reconstituted mashed potatoes in his Armani suit.

"Yes, ma'am. If you want to come see him yourself, he'll be here until five or so."

I hung up the phone a moment later and wandered out to the reception desk a little after that.

Shirley was alphabetizing the files and possibly curing cancer in her spare time. "What do you know about Senator Rivera?" I asked.

She wrinkled her nose. "He was against offering condoms to high-school kids."

"I take it you're an advocate for contraceptives."

She snorted, jerking her head back a little. "I'm forty-one years old. I got seven kids, five grandkids, and an ex I ain't seen since before Dion come screamin' into the world. Far as I'm concerned, they should be injectin' birth control into them kids' Tater Tots."

I sat down, watching her work. "What else do you know about the senator?"

She shrugged. "Good-looking fella, if I recall. Got into trouble with the ladies some time—" She stopped, lowered her brows, gave me a sassy oh-no-you-don't expression. "He ain't snooping 'round you, is he?"

"No. No. He just . . ." Where to begin. "His son and I . . . Jack is . . . Lieutenant Rivera and I are . . . friends," I finished poorly.

"His boy's a cop?"

I cleared my throat. "Yes."

"And you two been seeing each other?"

"I guess you could call it that."

"Well . . ." She scowled. "Ain't life a kicker."

"It is."

"So if you're hangin' with the boy, why you askin' me about the old man?"

I considered telling her that I respected her opinion, but it sounded too mushy even with the sentimentality of Christmas looming over me like a bad-tempered gargoyle. "I was just wondering about your perspective."

She nodded. "Well, there's a sayin'," she said. "You swim in Shit Crik long enough, some of it's gonna get in your ears."

6

Give me your tired, your poor, your huddled masses.
And I'll give you a neighborhood where there ain't a
white family within a five-mile radius.

—*Micky Goldenstone*

IT'S HIGHLY POSSIBLE that I should have stayed at
work and never made the trip over to Caring Hands, especially since I was undecided about whether or not to
agree to the senator's proposal. But my last client left at
4:50, and I thought if I hurried and no one tried to kill
me, I could see for myself whether the stylish Miguel
Rivera really *was* hobnobbing with the down-on-their-
luckers in one of L.A.'s high-crime areas. Besides, I had a
secret shortcut across town. At 4:58 I joined a zillion
cranky commuters who seemed to be in on my secret, but
finally I arrived at a listing brick building on the corner of
134th and Wilmington. Leaving my Saturn in the donors'
parking lot, I walked in the front door and up the railed

ramp. A dining area opened at the top of the incline. It was filled with a couple of dozen long tables that teemed with shuffling diners. At the far side of the room, volunteers dished meals onto paper plates.

Making my way through the crowd, I ran into a dark-haired woman whose name tag proclaimed her to be Helen. She had somehow dodged the hip spread generally associated with middle age, and I tried not to resent her for that. My efforts weren't tremendously successful, even though she was perfectly civil in a harried sort of way and didn't ask me if I was humping the senator when I inquired about his whereabouts. Pointing vaguely toward the shifting mass of humanity, she hurried off, but a moment later I spotted my quarry dishing up mashed potatoes to a bearded fellow in saggy trousers.

Miguel Rivera wore wrinkle-free blue jeans and a small-plaid button-down shirt. The sleeves were rolled back from perfectly manicured hands and he wore no tie. I figured his working-man ensemble had cost more than I bring home in a week; if there's one thing to be said about the senator, it's that he knows how to dress for every occasion.

The bearded guy moved on, followed by an African American woman with a little girl. Vaguely, I could hear the senator commenting about her cornrows. But after a minute the middle-aged woman sans fat hips caught his attention and directed it toward me. Our gazes met with a little spark of recognition and he smiled.

Subsequently, the hipless woman took over his job and he came my way, wiping his hands on a napkin.

"Christina." He smiled. The expression was still top shelf, a little self-deprecating, a little flirty, as effective here as at any lavish banquet in Pasadena. His handshake, however, was the real showstopper. Warm and personal, squeezing my fingers intimately between his slightly calloused palms. "What a pleasant surprise. What are you doing here?"

Excellent question. "My secretary gave me your message, but when I called I got this number."

He shook his head and looked embarrassed. "I must have given her the wrong number. How foolish of me. But you needn't have come all this way. I only called to . . ." He sighed mournfully. "To apologize. Both for my behavior and for my son's. We were . . ." Another head shake, accompanied by a vague scowl. "What is the word?"

"There are a lot of them," I said, remembering the stunning stupidity of the other night. He looked at me and laughed.

"You see, this is why I like you so very much, Christina," he said. "You do not stand on ceremony. In fact, that is why I stopped by. I knew you would have the integrity and intellect to get to the bottom of this."

"The bottom of what, exactly?"

He gave me a curious glance. "The cause of Ms. Baltimore's death, of course."

"Uh-huh." Two days and a conversation with Laney had stirred up a few doubts about the good senator. "If you don't mind me asking," I said, "why do you care?"

"Despite the troubles between Gerald and myself, I am still his father and I still wish to protect him."

I was only more confused. "And you think he's in danger because . . ."

"I am beginning to suspect that you are not a great believer in premonitions and dreams, Christina."

I shrugged, feeling a little guilty for my lack of faith. "I don't think I would bet a new septic system on either."

He laughed. "Perhaps it is my heritage that makes me more prone to believe. Or perhaps it is my age. In my many years I have seen a great deal that cannot be explained."

"Like your dream."

"Yes."

"About that—how did you know who the victim was when you saw her in your dream?"

"I did not," he said, and motioned toward the back. I moved in that direction.

"Then why—"

"As it happened, I read an article regarding her death just after . . ." He shuddered. "After that horrible dream."

"An article?"

"Online."

"And it had a picture of her?"

"Taken just weeks before her demise."

I nodded. I could hardly disprove it. One could find anything online. "Okay," I said, deciding to let that go for a minute. "But why not hire a professional if you're so set on investigating?"

He sobered handsomely. "May I be honest with you?"

"Does this suggest that you haven't been in the past?"

He laughed again. "As you know, I was in the political arena for a long while. Indeed, I may yet be again."

I stared at him, not sure where he was going or how long it would take him to get there.

"Having the media connect me with an unsolved death would do me no good," he added.

Something knotted in my stomach. "*Are* you connected?"

He shook his head like a sad warrior, wearied by the world. "The truth rarely has any bearing in matters such as these. Once the paparazzi learn I have paid to have a death investigated, they will insist on knowing why."

"Why not tell them about your dream?"

His smile suggested I might be kind of naïve. "The citizens of this great country are wonderful people, Christina. Strong. Resourceful. But they—like you, perhaps—do not set a great deal of store in things they cannot touch. Cannot prove. You see, I have no desire to make my constituents believe I am easily spooked. Neither did I wish for my son to think less of me. I was certain I could trust *you* to be discreet. Still..." He motioned me toward a hallway. It was narrow and poorly lit. Three doors lined the wall on the right. One stood open. Inside, piles of paper were stacked on the desk. "I realize now that I was wrong to ask," he admitted, and motioned to a green plastic chair. "To put you in such a position. I know how you feel about my son."

Well, I thought, surveying the room, that would put him way ahead of me.

"I'd like to apologize, too," I said, and, smoothing my apple-green shift against the back of my thighs, classily took the proffered seat. He closed the door and sat in the chair across the desk from me. "I didn't mean to call you a liar. Especially in front of your son. It's just that... he and I... we've had enough trouble between us without added fabrications." That's what I like to call lying if the lies are propagated by me. "But I'm afraid I may have only made things worse."

He scowled, looking concerned. "What do you mean?"

"He was obviously a bit ... upset." That's what I like to call rabid when referring to someone I had recently considered screwing. "When he left."

The senator leaned back a little. "But surely you've spoken to him since."

I didn't reply but studied the endless piles of paper.

He stared at me a moment, appalled, then shook his head. "My son, he is a stubborn man."

"Really?" I tugged my attention back to him and gave him my first-string smile. "I hadn't noticed."

He looked startled for a second, then laughed. "Perhaps love makes you blind, yes?"

"I—" My mouth opened but nothing else came out, and he laughed again.

"Give him time. He will call. He thinks a great deal of you."

"Does he?" I didn't mean to sound pathetic. But sometimes ... well, I'm pathetic.

"Christina," he said, tone soothing. "Surely you do not doubt that."

"Uhh ..."

"Have you not looked in the mirror?"

I remembered seeing myself in the microwave that night and stifled a shudder. "No more than necessary."

He shook his head. "Could it be that you truly do not realize how attractive you are?"

I was sure I should think of some snappy comeback to that, but nothing came to mind.

Nevertheless, he smiled, warm and toasty. "I am truly sorry to cause trouble between the two of you."

I shrugged, determined not to act like a weak-kneed

ninny. "About Kathleen Baltimore," I said. "Why didn't you tell me the police determined her death was an accident?"

He sighed and sat back, studying me. "Sometimes the police are wrong, Christina." His eyes grew intense, thoughtful. "I simply wish to ascertain that this is not one of those times."

I watched him, trying to read his expression, his body language. "You believe she was murdered," I said.

"That is what I had hoped to find out."

"Because you believe Jack, a Los Angeles police officer, might somehow become involved with an accidental death that took place in another city." My tone might have reflected my skepticism, because he drew a deep breath and pursed his lips, studying me for a moment.

"Christina," he began, and suddenly his eyes were filled with parental zeal. "I realize that, being as of yet childless yourself, you cannot fully understand the agony and ecstasy of bringing children into this world. But as a father, I feel it is my—"

"Senator," I said. He stopped, brows raised. "Let's try the truth," I suggested. "Just this once."

He opened his mouth, closed it, then gave a nod. "My apologies again," he said. "At times your beauty causes me to underestimate you."

Perhaps Rivera wasn't *too* crazy for thinking his father was propositioning me. But more likely the senator treated every woman like she was a sex bomb about to explode. "How did you know her?" I asked, taking a stab in the dark.

He looked surprised at my attack. "As I told you earlier,

I had a dream and simply wanted to make certain her death would in no way endanger Gerald."

I stared at him a moment, wondering if he could possibly be telling the truth, but then I remembered his occupation and stood up. "Well, I'd best get back to the office," I said. "I have an eight o'clock appointment. I hate to miss it for a sack of lies."

He watched me for a moment longer, then smiled a little and leaned back in his chair. His eyes were gleaming. "I never doubted that you would be good for my son. But until this moment I did not realize that you are exactly what he needs." He nodded. "Someone to cut through the murk of misinformation. To—"

I picked up my purse.

"My apologies," he said, and, blowing out a reluctant breath, motioned to my chair again. "Please. Sit. I shall tell you the truth. Nothing but the truth."

I stared at him, cynical and a little pissed.

"The whole story," he added.

I sat reluctantly, perching on the edge, as if I might fly away at the flutter of another lie. "Story?"

"The truth is . . ." He drew a slow breath, as if fortifying himself. "I did know Ms. Baltimore."

Perhaps I was about to speak, but he hurried on. "It was long ago, early in my political career. In truth, both she and her husband worked on my first senatorial campaign. Kathy was young and enthusiastic. As was I." He smiled nostalgically. "Those were good days, filled with hope and—"

"Did you sleep with her?" I asked. I really didn't have an evening appointment, but I hadn't had dinner yet and hated to miss out on all those empty calories for a bunch of bullshit.

His eyes opened wide as if shocked by my assumption, then narrowed in seemingly earnest affront. "I don't know what my son has told you, Christina, but I assure you, I am not so immoral as he would make me seem."

I considered apologizing, but then I remembered Salina, the senator's late fiancée. When I had first seen her, she was dead, but she was still astonishingly beautiful. Her eyes, as wide as fishbowls, were dark and sightless as she stared at the senator's freshly painted walls. She had previously been involved with Rivera Junior before ending up with the senator. As had one of her contemporaries. "Did you sleep with her?" I repeated.

For a moment his brows dipped dangerously toward his eyes, but finally he relaxed. "I suppose I cannot blame you for possessing the very qualities that I admire. It is that same forthright nature that brought me to your door. Indeed, that, matched with your intelligent—"

"Holy crap!" I said, and pulled my purse strap against my shoulder, ready to leave.

"Wait!" he said, and held out a hand as if to restrain me. "Very well." He sighed again. "No. I did not sleep with Ms. Baltimore."

I stared at him askance.

"I swear it on Mama's grave," he added.

I settled back in my chair. For a moment I considered asking if he'd even *had* a mother, but it seemed best to stay silent on that account. If his son was any indication, Latino men were a little touchy where their mamas were concerned.

"She was happily wed," he said. "As was I. Gerald was

still in his teenage years. And if I remember correctly, she had a child. A daughter, I believe."

I heroically refrained from asking if he'd slept with the daughter.

"So why do you care what happened to her after all these years?" I asked.

"As I said, she was instrumental to my career when I was still young and inexperienced. I feel responsible."

"Are you?" I asked.

"What?"

The question was out now, and it seemed worthy. "Are you somehow responsible for her death?"

"I did not mean it literally."

"How did you mean it?" I asked, then hurried on, trying to soften the sound of it. "That is, over the years there must have been hundreds of people working on your campaigns. Why are you concerning yourself with her?"

He remained silent for a moment, watching me. I felt my nerves crank up tight, sensing something big.

"Is it the truth you want, Christina?"

"It might be a nice change." It was a quote straight from Rivera Junior, but the senator only nodded, not recognizing his son's words.

Straightening slightly, he looked me directly in the eye. "I want nothing to stand in my way," he said, "when I make my bid for the presidency."

7

Every morning I read the obituaries. If I ain't there I make myself a cup a tea and carry on like I have for the past century or so.

—*Ella Brady, Chrissy's*
maternal grandmother,
age unknown

ON THE FOLLOWING MORNING, as I lay in bed and considered the dust motes floating aimlessly in a slanted beam of sunlight, my head was still reeling. Senator Rivera was planning to run for president, his son still hadn't called me, and I had to pee something terrible.

It was Saturday. I dressed in a pair of only slightly stained sweats, packed Harley into the Saturn's abused backseat, and headed to Yum Yum Donuts, where they fry up reasons to go on living. I used their bathroom and, being the health-conscious nut that I am, ordered a milk with a side order of apple fritters.

While Harley romped with a dachshund the size of my left ear, I ate my goodies and considered the day ahead.

I can't really tell you what possessed me to finally head west. But I arrived in Edmond Park in a little less than a full lifetime and called directory assistance for Kathleen's address. Despite Kern County's claim to fame, there wasn't a hummingbird in sight. Still, it was a pretty town, quiet and considerably cooler this close to the mountains.

A few minutes later I was parked beside a three-story Victorian. It was painted yellow, had gingerbread trim and a matching detached garage, which managed not to detract much from the overall ambience. Above its door was a wooden sign that declared it to be *Kathy's Cave*.

Harlequin was snoozing jerkily in the back, boxy snoot squished against the door, paws drooping over the edge of the seat. Apparently his dachshund buddy had worn him out. I debated waking him to make it appear as if I were just out for a stroll with man's best friend, but after some deliberation I left him to his frolicking dreams, crept out of my Saturn, and made my way up the driveway to the garage. I have no idea what I thought I might find, but let me say, I fully understand the curious cat's plight.

There were no windows on the garage door, so I went around to the side and tried the knob. The door was locked. But the house was only—

"Can I help you?"

I jumped guiltily and turned. "Oh, yes, hi."

The woman who came toward me said nothing. She was about my height, dressed in blue jeans cinched tight at the waist. She had a runner's physique and a skeptic's gaze. I judged her to be in her early fifties, though not a strand of gray could be seen in her hair. It shone in the sunlight, a deep chestnut hue set in waves that looked natural to my untrained but generally jealous eye. Her face was lightly lined with wrinkles that were somehow attractive, and her eyes were red.

Kathy's sister, I guessed. I had seen pictures of the deceased on the Web, and they looked alike. Both athletic, handsome women aging with panache. There had also been photos of the deceased with her daughter, standing in front of their wooden wares at a craft show.

"I just . . ." I motioned toward the garage and wondered a little desperately what the hell I was doing there. "I just stopped by to see if Kathy was around."

Pain chased anger across the woman's well-maintained features and was gone.

"She's not." The words were solid, matter-of-fact. "What can I do for you?"

"Oh, well, I . . ." I glanced toward the garage again and noticed the other sign. The one that listed wooden items for sale. "I had ordered a . . ." I tried to read the list, but it seemed imperative that I look the woman in the eye, so I turned back toward her before ascertaining shit. ". . . a piece from her some time back. I just stopped by to pick it up."

She was watching me pretty closely. It gave me the willies. "Now's not a good time."

"Oh. I'm sorry. Shall I stop by later?"

She drew a deep breath. "If you put down a deposit, I'll make certain you get a refund. What's your name?"

The question caught me off guard, but I refrained from starting like a particularly stupid deer and tried to kick my mind into gear. "There's no problem, is there?" I asked. "I was hoping to get my . . ." Still couldn't read the damn sign. ". . . *piece* today."

"What's your name?" she asked again, and her eyes narrowed a little.

"Uhhh, Bea," I said. I don't know why I chose that particular lie. Possibly because I'm deranged. "Beatrice Ankeny."

"How did you know Kat?" she asked.

"Kat?" I was stalling—and possibly very stupid.

"You work with her at the plant?" She took another step toward me.

"No, I . . . I never met her, actually. Just her . . . I think it was her daughter . . . at the mall in Chatsworth. I ordered through her."

"You never met her?" She seemed to relax a little, but I wasn't that optimistic.

"No. Just her daughter. Jessica, wasn't it?" I watched her, looking for clues, hoping she wouldn't try to kill me. "She was sure a pretty girl."

"Jess?" She pursed her lips, nodded. "Yeah. Pretty, just like her mom." She choked up a little. "She woulda done anything for that kid."

"Well, that's—" I began, and stopped myself short, as if shocked into silence. "*Would* have? What do you mean? Has something happened?"

She cleared her throat, glanced toward the street. A car drove by at a leisurely pace. Small-town life. Crazy. "She's dead."

"Dead! No! What happened?" Oscar material right there.

Her eyes narrowed. "I don't really know."

"You don't know! You mean . . . she's missing?"

She glanced toward the street again. "The coroner said she died from loss of blood. In her workshop."

I gasped. If I hadn't felt so guilty I would have been proud. "How'd it happen?"

"They say she passed out, fell into the saw."

"Oh my God, that's horrible. Did she have a history of seizures, or why—"

"What did you say your name was?" she asked, and took another step toward me. There was something in her eyes, something that stopped my brain entirely. I searched my mind for my fake name, but it was gone, entirely gone.

"Who are you?" she gritted, and pulled a pistol from behind her back.

8

When in doubt, shoot first and ask questions later.
But avoid the head, 'cuz they're a lot more likely to
answer if they're not dead.

—D, *Chicago mob boss and
pretty good friend*

*M*Y HEART WAS BEATING like a wild bunny's, but my
brain had stopped dead in its tracks. "Hey!" It was the
only word I could come up with on such short notice.
"What are you doing?"

"Who are you?" she repeated.

The pistol was short and black, but I'm told guns can
kill you no matter what their size and ethnic background.

"My name's . . . my name's Beatrice," I said, and found
that for the literal life of me I couldn't remember my declared surname. Damn it!

"You're lying," she snarled, and leaned toward me. The
gun muzzle wavered a little. "What are you doing here?
Who sent you?"

"What? No one sent me! I just—"

"Why can't you leave her alone? Why couldn't everyone just leave her alone?" she blurted, and suddenly she was crying, sobbing like a heartbroken child. She lowered the gun muzzle and wilted to the ground. I glanced toward my Saturn and considered making a dash for it. It seemed like the sensible thing to do. But my would-be attacker had slumped onto her elbows, weeping into the perfectly manicured bluegrass.

"Hey," I said again, voice tentative enough to suggest I really wasn't nuts. "You okay?"

"No." She was shaking her head. "No."

I glanced toward my car again, thinking Harley was probably crazed with the need to save me, but not so much as a whisker showed through the window. "Can I do anything? Get you a glass of water? Call a friend?"

She glanced up, face etched with sorrow. "He sent you, didn't he?"

I chanced a careful step closer. "Who's he?"

"Her old man. She was married for..." She choked a laugh. "Jesus, for twenty years. 'Til Jess went off to college. She stayed with him 'til then, but even after that—" She shook her head.

I eased cautiously onto the grass beside her. "After that what?" I asked, but maybe she didn't hear me.

"I was always so proud of her. Smart, pretty, successful. Always wanted her to be proud of me, but..." Her voice trailed away.

I was nodding. I don't know why. "Do you think he had something to do with her death?"

She blinked at me, eyes shiny with tears. "What?"

"Her ex. Do you think he had something to do with your sister's death?"

She stared at me a full five seconds, then laughed out loud. The sound was choked and watery. She wiped her nose on her wrist, leaving the gun on the grass as she settled back on her haunches. "Who are you and what do you really want?"

I pondered that for a moment, glanced at the car, and decided I was more likely to be rescued by a swarm of wild bees than my ever-faithful hound. "I just . . . I was hoping to find out how this happened." I motioned weakly toward the garage. "Kathy's death."

She staggered to her feet. "You a cop?"

"No." I rose, too, thinking it might be a good idea to be upright in case she started taking potshots at me.

"A private investigator?"

"I'm a psychologist," I said.

"Are you kidding me?"

"Sometimes it surprises me, too," I said.

She scowled at me for an instant, then turned away and walked into the house, leaving the gun on the lawn and the door open behind her.

I stood there for a good three minutes wondering what a normal person would do, but I hadn't encountered a lot of normal in the past . . . well, lifetime, so finally I picked up the gun between my forefinger and thumb, turned, and followed her inside.

The house was as cute as a Cabbage Patch Kid. Carefully framed period photographs graced the entry. The walls of the kitchen were papered with tiny rows of flowers. Geraniums bloomed in the window above the sink.

The woman with the chestnut hair sat sprawled on a slat-back chair near the table, face blank, hand wrapped around a coffee mug.

"You take yours black?" she asked.

It took me a minute to catch up, but when I did I set the gun on the counter. "I don't drink coffee," I said.

She glanced up as if startled from her sorrow. "Ever?"

"Not unless it's banned by the Diabetes Foundation."

The shadow of a grin crept across her haunted face. "Who sent you?"

I pondered that for a second. "An old friend of hers asked me to look into her death."

"So you really didn't know her?"

I shook my head, and she laughed a little.

"She always said I was too damn jealous, but she was so . . ." She drew a deep breath and gazed into the living room. The hardwood floor gleamed like honey. An untrimmed tree looked strangely naked against the bay window. ". . . so amazing. I told her I'd have to be crazy not to be jealous."

I don't know why it took that long for the lightbulb to flash on, but it finally did. "So you were her . . ."

She waited for me to finish the sentence. I floundered around like a beached mackerel for a couple of stupid lifetimes and finally came up with ". . . partner?"

Her snort was neither ladylike nor polite. Standing up, she went to the coffeepot and refilled her mug. "God, that's a stupid term. It sounds like we were in harness together. Kat and Queenie." She chuckled. "Not bad names for draft horses."

She was babbling.

"I'm sorry. I just didn't—" I began lamely, but she was waving it off.

"It's all right. No one could figure out what to call us, even if they knew. And hardly anybody knew." She was gazing past the geraniums through the spotless window.

"Why not?"

" 'Cuz of Shithead."

"Her . . . ex?" I guessed.

Taking a long plastic container from the refrigerator, she removed the cover and set it in front of me. Rows of shortbread stared back at me.

"Who's the friend?" she asked.

"I'm sorry?" I said, startled from my observation of the cookies. Shortbread's almost good enough to turn me Scottish.

"The friend who sent you—who is it?" she asked.

I didn't know how much to say, but she had been kind enough to refrain from shooting me. "His name's Miguel."

She took a cookie, sat back down, and nodded as she ate. "Do you think I'm psychotic?"

"What?"

"I'm relieved that it's a man." She sighed. "You're a shrink, right? Does that make me psycho? That I still care even . . ." Her voice watered up. She cleared her throat.

"I think you've been through a terrible shock." When in doubt, spout gibberish.

She nodded again, jerkily. "The neighbor found her. Should have been me. I should have been around when she was in the shop, but she was usually so careful. Wore a face mask. Kept the blade shields in place." She winced, fighting tears.

"Were the shields still in place?"

She cleared her throat. "No. She must have been having trouble with the saw again. Must have thought she could fix it herself. Could..." Her voice broke. She fought for control and won. "I should have been here, but she... she didn't want to live together. Said her daughter wouldn't understand. But it was really because of Shithead."

"Her ex." It would be nice to have one solid answer.

She nodded.

"Was he causing her trouble?"

"He used to—you know, name-calling, lots of yelling. But things have been quieter lately. She said she wanted to keep it that way, for Jess. Didn't want to cause a scandal. Like this is the Middle Ages or something." She winced. "Kat hated confrontations."

While this woman had no qualms about pointing a gun at a perfectly nice, if somewhat deranged, stranger. Love's funny.

"How long had you and..." I paused, stumbling over the words again.

"We were lovers," she said.

"Of course. Yes." Geez, I was a trained professional. And an adult. And generally not retarded. "How long were you lovers?"

"Six years."

Wow. And I thought it something of a wonder that Harlequin and I were still together after a few months.

"I wanted to get married. Skip off to Vancouver and make it official, but she thought the announcement might show up in the paper. I told her if she loved me she'd do it. But I know she loved me." Her brow wrinkled. "I know it."

Doubt showed in her eyes. I wondered, perhaps uncharitably, if she had doubted enough to kill.

"So her relationship with her ex was pretty serene?"

"Nothing overt, but he always resented the fact that she'd ruined his perfect life."

"How so?"

"They were the ideal family. Him a"—she made quotes in the air with her fingers—"real estate tycoon. She the perfect wife, the perfect mother. Then she ups and files for divorce."

"How long ago was that?"

"Seven years. The town was abuzz."

"Did you know her then?"

"I'm from Frisco. Just moved here after Crazy Bet."

"Bet?"

"My ex."

I nodded, wondering about Bet's gender but managing to keep my curiosity to myself.

The kitchen went quiet. The cookies watched me. The gun did the same.

I screwed up my nerve. "Do you think her ex-husband was somehow involved in her death?" I asked.

She stared through me. Tension bloomed like Canadian thistles. Her lips twisted up in a smile, her eyes narrowed. "God, I'd love to see him swing." She said the words through gritted teeth with enough venom to make my skin crawl, but finally she drew a breath and focused on me as if just remembering I was there. "No," she said. "It was bad luck. Just dumb, bad luck."

9

He's just a flash in the pants.

> —The Magnificent Mandy,
> whose quotes were
> sometimes more confusing
> than magnificent

I HAD RARELY SEEN more vitriol stamped on another's face, and yet Queenie had been certain her lover's death was an accident. Why? Had Kathy had some sort of medical condition that made such an incident more likely? Or was Queenie simply unable to consider anything more heinous?

Questions roamed around in my head as I pulled away from the big Victorian. I told myself to head home, to let it go, but I found myself, instead, at a McDonald's. A sign on the door spoke of employment opportunities and promised to build the leaders of tomorrow.

Harley and I shared a Big Mac. I ate most of it; I've seen *Super Size Me* and try to be a responsible mom. But he was still hungry after the burger, so we decided to share a cone. "Hey," I said to the leader of tomorrow who was slumped behind the counter. I was banking on the fact that small-town folk would be acquainted with one another. "Do you happen to know where Kathy Baltimore lives? I ordered a chair from her a couple months ago and was hoping to pick it up today."

I was blindly fishing for information, but she just stared at me with all the energy of a catatonic loggerhead and shrugged. Tomorrow, I decided, was in big-ass trouble.

I returned to my Saturn, where Harley and I continued our lunch. I ate the ice cream. He had the cone. Neither of us ate the paper wrapper.

After our meal, we turned toward home, but I couldn't quite force myself to leave town. Instead, I stopped at a little shop called Flower Power. I roamed amongst the greenery and fake rocks for a while, wishing my thumb wasn't as black as a politician's soul, until a gray-haired lady with appropriate-size hips finally ran me to ground.

"Can I help you?" she asked.

"Ummm, yes, how much is this..." I pointed to the nearest plant but couldn't think of a word for it.

"That's a dracaena," she said.

"That's right," I agreed, and nodded judiciously. "It'd look just perfect on the oak stand I ordered from Kathy Baltimore."

Her face froze. "I hope somebody already told you."

I gave her my Oscar-winning blink. "Told me what?"

"Kathy passed away just a few days ago."

"No!"

"I'm sorry. Did you know her well?"

"Not at all. I'd just ordered the one piece from her."

"It was a terrible shock for everyone."

"How awful."

"It was. A terrible tragedy. She was such a lovely woman. Had a beautiful house on Parsley Street. Fixed it up herself. Filled it to brimming with geraniums and old turn-of-the-century photographs."

"How did she die?"

"Well, you know she had the shop."

I nodded.

"They said she fell into her saw. Just passed out and all of a sudden toppled forward."

"Oh God."

She shuddered. "It makes me just sick to think about it. Fran says there was blood everywhere."

"Fran?"

"A neighbor."

"Don't tell me she found her."

"Oh, no. Eldred Ernst found her. He lives next door to her. Said the saw had been running for a week. Probably went to complain. Eldred's..." She shook her head. "Well... I don't like to speak poorly of anyone."

"So she was dead when he found her?"

"Oh, my, yes."

"When was that?"

"Tuesday night. I didn't find out until Wednesday morning."

"And the saw had been running for a week?"

"That's what Eldred said, but he's such a... Well, I don't like to bad-mouth anyone, but he once called the police because Maxie ran through his yard. Called the *police*. Said Maxie was a menace."

"And Maxie is..."

"My schnauzer. Wouldn't hurt a flea."

"So how long had the saw really been running?"

"I can't say," she said. "But it's a terrible shame. A terrible shame."

I moved on. Everyone I met agreed it was a terrible shame, except tomorrow's leaders, of course, who were catatonic.

Remembering Queenie's words about Kathy's marriage, I looked in the housing section of the local paper. Kevin Baltimore, real estate tycoon and shithead, had four properties listed. I circled the picture of a humble little split level and drove to his office.

It was easy as tinkling to talk his secretary into letting me meet with him.

"Ms. Ankeny," he said, arm extended, a hundred teeth gleaming as he hurried across the floor. "I'm sorry to keep you waiting." He was fifty pounds overweight, as heavy in his face as he was in his belly, and smiling like a picket fence. "It's very nice to meet you."

If he was mourning his ex-wife, I'd have to give up my Oscar. *"Mrs.,"* I corrected.

"What's that?"

"It's *Mrs.* Ankeny," I said.

"Ahh, so you and your husband are looking to buy in our area."

"Considering it," I said.

"Great. Well, you'll love Edmond Park. It's very peaceful here."

"That's what we thought," I said, "but I heard there was a murder."

"A murder!" He drew back, appalled.

"I was told a woman was killed in her home just the other day."

He stared at me a moment, then shook his head. "You must be talking about Kathleen?"

"I'm not sure what her name was. They said she was working in her wood shop and—"

"No, no. That was just an accident," he said. "She passed out, landed on her saw. It was a terrible thing. But just an accident."

"Passed out? Did she have some sort of medical condition or—"

"No." He was shaking his head. "Not that I know of, that is, but they think her heart stopped."

"How awful."

"A terrible tragedy."

I almost mouthed the words with him.

"But, as I said, it was just an unfortunate accident. Our little town is as peaceful as Mayberry."

I tried a few more questions, but he kept steering the conversation back to real estate. By the time I squeaked out of there, I was considering buying a little fixer-upper near the golf course. The man could have sold dentures to crocodiles.

My last stop before leaving town was the police station. I walked in, mind spinning.

An officer in uniform straightened from his conversation with a woman twice his age. She was laughing as if his stellar wit was surpassed only by his good looks, and I could see why. He *was* pretty. Six-one in his stocking feet, he had gold-blond hair and a smile that had probably kept his mother fretful for most of sixteen years. I casually checked his left ring finger. It was notably nude.

"Can I help you?" he asked.

"I hope so. I was wondering if I might get a little bit of information."

"Regarding?"

I considered lying. But sometimes cops take offense to creative fabrications. I've learned that the hard way.

"It's of a private nature," I said.

He looked interested. His secretary looked like she'd hatch an egg to know. The trip to his office was short, appropriate for the size of the entire building. His office was simple, tidy, small. A metal desk occupied the majority of the space.

"I'm Officer Tavis." He had traditional Celtic good looks. Sparkling eyes. Dimples. The kind you read about in those lovely smut novels where the women look orgasmic even precoital. Slap him in a truncated kilt and he could be the Highland Rogue himself. "What can I help you with, Ms. . . ."

Again I debated lying. But maybe I'm learning.

"McMullen," I said.

"Is that Scottish?"

"Irish."

He shook his head and tsked. "Ahh . . . I'm sorry to hear that."

"I carry on as best I can."

He laughed. It was a nice sound, soothing, honest. If he had sported a wee bit of a burr in his speech, I would have taken him down right there and then. "What can I help you with, Ms. McMullen?"

I took a deep breath and jumped. "I was hoping you could tell me about Kathleen Baltimore's death."

"You a friend of hers?" he asked.

"Not exactly," I said.

He nodded. "Want some coffee?"

"No, thank you."

He poured himself a cup and sat down. "A relative?"

"No."

"Then I feel compelled to inquire about your interest in her death."

"I'm looking into it for a friend."

"And your friend's name?"

I paused. Honesty is all well and good, but you don't want to take it too far. "I think he'd rather I didn't divulge that information at this time."

He didn't comment. "Are you a private investigator, Ms. McMullen?"

"I'm a psychologist."

"Really?" He canted his head and smiled a little. I wasn't sure if I should be insulted or flattered.

"Yes."

"Where do you practice?"

"L.A."

"Yeah? They as crazy as we like to believe?"

I considered that a minute. "Probably."

He laughed. "What can I tell you?"

The question floored me. If I had wandered into Rivera's office asking questions about a case, he probably would have had me interrogated, handcuffed, and strip-searched by now. I opened my mouth but failed to speak.

"We don't have a lot to hide here in Edmond Park," he explained, apparently unsurprised by my surprise.

"So you don't think she was murdered?"

His brows raised a little, but that was the extent of his dramatics. "Do you have some reason to believe she was?"

"Like I said, I'm just checking into it for a friend."

"Whose name you don't wish to divulge."

"Sorry."

"Well..." He smiled and stood up. "In the hopes of making your friend believe we're not just a bunch of booger-flicking hicks, I'll say this: There was no sign of a struggle. Ms. Baltimore wasn't an Amazon, but she was fit. Took jujitsu classes from Carl Franken on Tuesdays and Thursdays. There was no blood but her own at the scene. I had it tested. No flesh under her fingernails. No spare hairs that the sweepers could find."

"Fingerprints?" I was grasping at straws. I had no idea what I was talking about.

"There were other fingerprints, of course, but none that came up suspicious."

"Which means what? That whoever was in her workshop hadn't been convicted of a previous crime?"

"Hasn't been accused. Can I ask what your friend's interest is in Ms. Baltimore?"

"You *are* an officer of the law," I said.

"Oh, that's right." He grinned. "Then you'd best tell me before I get out the thumbscrews."

"Thumbscrews?" I said.

"We're not against progress here in Edmond Park, but we don't want to rush into anything," he said.

"He worked with her years ago," I said.

"He?"

"As I said, I don't think it prudent to mention his name."

He nodded. "But your friend's a man."

"I know several," I said.

He laughed. "I was just curious."

I studied him for a second. Something told me he might not be quite as retiring as he seemed. "Because Ms. Baltimore was a lesbian?"

He watched me a little closer. "So you know that."

I didn't respond.

"Not everyone does," he said.

"So I'm told."

"By whom? Or is that classified, too?"

"I spoke with Queenie."

He nodded, saying nothing.

"Was it monogamous, do you think?"

He shrugged. "Ask any citizen in this town, ninety-nine out of a hundred will tell you Kathy Baltimore was as straight as a T square."

"*Are* there a hundred citizens?"

"Five thousand nine hundred and thirty-two," he said. "According to last year's census."

"Holy cow," I said.

A dimple peeked out. "She didn't flaunt her sexuality," he said.

"And what about Queenie?"

"I think she would have done anything Kathy asked her to do short of murder."

"So they were in love," I surmised.

"I'm told it happens sometimes."

I wondered if it had happened to him, but I didn't ask. "What about *Mr.* Baltimore?"

"Kevin?"

"Yes."

He shrugged. "What about him?"

"Any reason he might bear her ill will?"

"Well . . . they were married for twenty-odd years."

"How odd?"

"It's just an expression."

"What does it mean?"

"I take it you've never suffered marital bliss."

"And I take it you have."

He laughed. "I have no reason to believe Mr. Baltimore would have harmed her. Nor do I believe he did."

"What about Queenie?" I asked.

"You spoke to her."

I nodded.

"Did she seem to be faking her distress?"

"Not unless she missed her calling."

He raised a well-there-you-go hand.

"So you think Kathy's death was truly accidental."

He stared at me a second. "I filed a report to that effect," he said.

Which wasn't quite an answer.

"Thank you for your—"

"Can I ask *you* a couple of questions?" he asked.

"You're still a cop," I said, and smiled, but the grin had dropped from his golden retriever face.

"Why does the senator care about Ms. Baltimore?" he asked.

10

Honesty's the best policy. But insanity's a hell of a
lot more effective in court. So you're set, McMullen.

—Lieutenant Rivera,
always comforting

WHAT MAKES YOU THINK—" I began, but Tavis interrupted me.

"Eldred Ernst saw you talking to Queenie. Said there
was a disturbance."

"What does that have—"

"Ran your plates," he said. "Christina McMullen, Ph.D."
He watched me. I watched him in return, still a little
breathless but for different reasons now. "A few months
back, you were on the scene when the senator's fiancée
died."

"I didn't have anything to do with her death," I said.

"What are you doing in Edmond Park?"

"I told you, I just want some questions answered."

He stepped closer, forcing me to take a step back. "I'm the police in this little burg," he said. "If there are answers to be had, I'm the one who will have them."

I straightened, reminiscent anger firing up. "I'm a citizen," I said. "Doesn't that give me a right to ask a few questions?"

We glared at each other for a couple of seconds and then he laughed. "Yes, it does. You're kind of feisty, Ms. McMullen."

I felt dazed, unable to keep up with his mood swings.

But he dropped into his swivel chair, unconcerned about my confusion. "I've always wanted to play good cop/bad cop. It's not easy alone."

"What's wrong with you?" I asked.

He laughed. "I was just having a little fun. If you have more questions, please..." He lifted a hand toward me. "Ask away."

It took me a moment to gather my composure. "Did Kathy report any disturbances recently?"

"No."

"No scary noises? No security issues?"

"Nope."

"And you would know?"

"I would know."

"Who were her confidantes?" I asked.

"Well... Queenie, of course," he said, and shrugged. "Her daughter, I suppose. I'm not sure who else. Far as I know, everyone liked her. Why does Senator Rivera believe it was murder?"

"I didn't say he did."

He smiled.

"She worked on one of his early campaigns," I said, and

wondered why I was defending him. "He feels responsible."

"Is he?"

"I don't think he would have asked me to look into her death if he were."

"Maybe it's all a ploy."

"What kind of ploy?"

He shrugged. "People are peculiar. I mean, it doesn't seem as if your relationship with the Riveras has always been smooth sailing. I believe the lieutenant accused you of murder at one time."

"Where do you get your information?"

He laughed. "You'd be surprised what you can find on the Internet."

"Or appalled."

"Well, yeah, that, too."

"Listen, Officer . . ."

"Tavis," he supplied.

I paused midthought. "Is that your last name or—"

"It's my given name," he said. "We don't like to stand on ceremony here in Edmond Park."

"Officer Tavis," I said, beginning over. "I didn't kill anyone."

He laughed again—the jolliest cop I have ever met, but maybe avoiding L.A.'s daily ration of homicides brightens one's outlook. "I never thought you did. We're not quite so suspicious as some," he said. "You still dating Rivera?"

"Do you have a different Internet than I do?"

"I didn't have a lot to do this morning."

"No kidding."

"You didn't answer my question, and I *am* an officer of

the law," he said. "I could lock you up for suspicious behavior."

"No, you couldn't."

"Oh. Well, then you should answer just because."

"Because?"

"I'm bored. And I have dimples." He pointed at them.

"I don't believe my relationship with Lieutenant Rivera is any of your concern."

"That bad, huh? He accuse you of murder again?"

Actually, he had, but I didn't think it necessary to say it out loud. "It's complex," I said.

"Okay, then how about if we keep our relationship simple. How do you feel about casual sex?"

My ear bulbs stood up and took notice, but I was still sure I'd heard him wrong. "What?"

"It's a small town," he said. "I don't get the chance to meet a lot of single women I'm not related to."

"Are you serious?"

"Serious as a hard-on," he said.

I was still on my feet, though I wasn't really sure how I was staying there. "I take it you guys haven't talked much about sexual harassment out here in . . ." I gestured a little wildly. "Nowhere."

He shrugged, grinned, didn't stand up. "I'm not feeling harassed *yet.*"

"Holy crap!"

"You're an attractive woman," he said. "I didn't think to check your stats, but I'm assuming you're over the age of consent."

I wasn't sure if I was expected to respond, but it was out of the question anyway.

"I'm fair to middlin' in bed," he said. "Willing to try almost anything once so long as it doesn't involve condors. I don't like scavengers."

"I see." My voice had gone weak.

He smiled. "I have references."

I blinked.

He widened his grin.

"Well, think about it," he said, and, rising to his feet, crossed the floor and opened the door.

I collected my mandible from the floor. Outside his office, his secretary was staring with owlish eyes.

"It was nice to meet you, Ms. McMullen," he said.

"Yes," I muttered, voice as hazy as my mind. "You, too."

11

Breaking up is hard to do. But bustin' him in the head ain't all that easy, either.

—*Shirley Templeton,*
discussing her husband's
ill-advised infidelity

LANEY." I felt breathless and a little hallucinatory by the time I was in my car and on the phone. "I was just propositioned by a cop."

"So things are pretty much par for the course?" I could hear someone yammering at her in the background, but someone was always yammering at Laney. Especially since she had morphed from struggling actress to Amazon Queen.

"No. A different cop," I said.

"Rivera's different."

I was exasperated, harried, horny, and confused. "One I hadn't met until a few minutes ago."

"Well . . ." She paused. I could imagine her mulling

things over in her Amazonian brain. "You're gorgeous." Then, "Tell them I'll be right there," she said quietly. Back to me: "Of course guys are going to come on to you."

"He asked if I was interested in casual sex."

"Which you are."

"Well, yes, but I didn't think it was culturally acceptable to admit that to a total stranger."

"You're growing up so quickly." I could hear someone muttering about makeup and camera angles. I think someone else might have been proposing marriage. Generally speaking, there was always some guy proposing marriage where Brainy Laney was concerned, but I had her full attention now. "Was he off duty?" she asked.

"That's the weirdest part. Not only was he in uniform, he was standing in the middle of his own police station."

"What were you doing at the police station?"

I opened my mouth and paused. As it turns out, Laney doesn't like it when people attempt to murder me, so she sometimes tries to discourage me from doing things that might precipitate that eventuality.

"Mac?"

"Oh, I was just . . . asking a few questions."

"About what?"

"We're running out of daylight," someone said. He sounded impatient and a little gruff. I didn't think it was the proposal guy. They usually sound dreamy and a little high.

"One minute," Laney responded. "Are you in trouble, Mac?"

"No. Absolutely not."

"Why were you talking to a policeman?"

"Listen, L . . . you seem . . . breaking up," I said, using a ploy I've implemented a hundred times with my mother. "I'm afraid—"

"No, I'm not, and no, you're not," she said. "Why the policeman?"

"You're running out of daylight," I said, a little peeved.

"We'll run into it again. How'd she die?"

"Who?"

"The woman the senator asked you to investigate."

I sighed and wished I wasn't stupid.

"How'd it happen?" she asked.

"That's what I'm supposed to find out."

"And?"

"I think it was an accident."

The world went quiet for a full fifteen seconds before she spoke again. "You know what happens when you lie to me, Mac." I did. In fact, I couldn't help but scratch my neck a little at the memory. When we were twelve we went to Camp Woodhollow together. I had subsequently snuck out of our cabin for a nocturnal visit with a boy called Tadpole. When Laney inquired about my whereabouts, I lied like a . . . well, like a man. The rash covering me from nose to nipple the following morning made me look like a burn victim. The camp nurse thought it was poison ivy, but I knew better; it was retribution.

"Honest to God, Laney, I think it was accidental," I said, and forced myself to stop itching.

She let me hang up after I promised to be careful. She would be returning to L.A. in a few days and apparently hoped to see me alive. I kind of hoped so, too, but as I drove home, the radio reporter droned on about a hundred depressing stories, and I couldn't help wondering why a guy with Highland Rogue dimples would proposition a woman wearing stained sweatpants and dog drool.

I was still wondering when I reached home, but my observations were cut short when I saw Rivera sitting in his Jeep beside my curb. Remembering the scene with him and his father, I actually considered zipping past as if I were just another commuter, but he had already seen me. I knew it, even though he wore dark glasses, so I parked in front of him. A moment later he stepped out of his vehicle, all cool slow motion and somber expression. I hadn't seen him since nearly having kitchen sex with him, and he looked good. His hips were lean and synchronized to my heartbeat, his arms were tight-muscled and dark beneath the sleeves of his T-shirt. Something fired up inside me at the sight of him, but I casually opened my door, buying myself a little time as Harlequin tromped over me on his joyous way out of the car.

By the time I exited the vehicle, I was almost over how Rivera's biceps bunched prettily below his faded sleeves, and I barely noticed that his jeans rode low and loose on his tight-assed hips.

"McMullen," he said.

"Rivera," I responded. Cool as an eggplant.

He looked past me to my Saturn. "You in Sespe?"

"Where?" I scowled. The place almost sounded familiar, but I couldn't quite place it and nothing showed on his face.

"Where, then?" he asked.

Lies come so readily to a girl who has survived three

perpetually moronic brothers, but I stifled them. "Edmond Park," I said.

He nodded, glanced past my car toward the Al-Sadrs' immaculate lawn, then: "I'm going to have to give up," he said.

My throat felt tight, my knees stiff. I knew what he meant. He was angry—about his father's visit, about the fact that I would consider getting involved with the senator's shady dealings, but I asked the question anyway. "On me?"

He removed his sunglasses. His eyes were dark and intense. Emotion shone in the gleaming depths. "It's been an interesting ride."

I didn't want to beg. Or cry. Begging and crying are sometimes misconstrued as weaknesses. Still, I felt the tears and the pleas bubbling up inside me like the goop in a lava lamp. So I painted on a smile and went for humor. "But we haven't even gotten to the part where we rush downhill screaming with pleasure yet," I said.

He glanced away again. A muscle jumped in his jaw. "I don't think it's that kind of ride."

I nodded crisply, but my words were less controlled and wobbled a little. "You could be wrong."

His lips tilted the slightest degree. "It's happened before," he said.

"Never thought I'd hear you admit it."

He grinned, but the expression was dark. I felt my heart squeeze up tight in my chest. "Any possibility you'd take some advice?" he asked.

I cleared my throat. It felt painfully tight, but I was not going to cry. "It's happened before," I said.

For a minute I thought he'd argue, but he didn't. That,

more than anything, made it all seem horrifically final. "Stay away from my old man," he said.

And suddenly a thousand unchecked excuses rushed to my lips. "Listen, Rivera, I just went to Edmond Park to—" I began, but he held up a hand.

"I can't do it." His throat tightened, the tendons standing out for a moment beneath his tanned skin, then relaxing. "I can't wonder what you're up to every minute. Worry—" He paused, glanced away, brows lowered. "Maybe I'm getting too damn old. Maybe the job's taking its toll, but I've got to keep my head in the game or I'm going to wind up dead."

I swallowed a lump the size of a walrus. "I don't want you dead," I whispered.

"Yeah?" His voice was raspy. His eyes burned with emotion, but he bunched his jaw and failed to reach for me like I hoped he would. "I don't want you dead, either, McMullen. That's why I'm warning you."

I was floundering in confusion and sadness and hopelessness. "About?"

"Jesus. Don't you ever—" For a minute I thought he'd explode. That I'd explode back. That we'd make up and start anew. But none of that happened. "Maybe you think I'm jealous of my old man. And maybe I am. Shit . . ." He laughed. The sound was coarse. "God knows he has more money, more power, and more . . ." He drew a deep breath through his nostrils. They flared slightly. "You can't trust him, Chrissy."

"Trust him? Why are you talking about . . ." I paused as a thousand thoughts scrambled through my head. "You don't actually think he had something to do with Baltimore's death!"

He didn't answer, but his brows lowered another fraction of an inch.

"Do you?" I asked.

"The murder's out of my jurisdiction," he said, and, turning, walked out of my life.

I went running Sunday morning. Four miles. It was the longest six hours of my life. When it was finished I scoured the sinks, scrubbed the floors, washed the windows, and shambled out to collect the mail I had neglected on Saturday. More bills. The whole day was like a finely sliced little sliver of hell.

By five o'clock in the afternoon I had convinced myself that it was all for the best. I shouldn't be wasting my time on guys like Rivera, anyway. I needed someone mature and giving and open-minded. He was childish, selfish, and opinionated. It was good that he dumped me.

I poured myself a glass of Asti Spumante, then added another cup to convince myself of my it's-all-for-the-best theory. Maybe it wasn't a stellar idea, because booze makes me weepy in the best of circumstances. This wasn't even close: I hadn't had sex in a millennium, and it didn't look like that was going to change anytime soon unless I was brain-numbed enough to take the offer of a guy who had known me for approximately thirty seconds; I had gained two pounds since Shirley began working for me; and I could have bought a new Porsche for the cost of a new septic system.

But, hey, things weren't so bad. I took another slug of wine and gave myself a little pep talk. I was, after all, a healthy, intelligent woman who still had all her teeth.

Setting my glass aside, I riffled through the mail on the immaculate table. Everyone wanted money. Except... I came across a handwritten envelope, read the return address, then read it again. *Gerald Miguel Rivera* was sprawled across the upper left-hand corner. Holding my breath, I opened the envelope and pulled out the enclosed card. It was embossed with the senator's initials. A piece of paper fluttered to the floor, but I left it for a moment as I read the note: *Dearest Christina, please forgive my crass behavior of some days past. The sole purpose for my late visit was to apologize for my former actions, but I fear even the best of intentions are often waylaid when emotions flare. Thus I say now, it was wrong of me to involve you in problems that are not your own. You must put the death out of your mind, for I could never forgive myself if something untoward happened to you.*

That was it, just *another* apology for the nocturnal visit that had so rudely torn me from the precipice of ecstasy and thrust me back into the abyss of celibacy. Not that I was resentful or anything. But if he didn't want me to investigate, why hadn't he said so at Caring Hands?

I scanned the rest of the card for more, but there was nothing else. Just his grand, sweeping signature. I read the words again, though, and noticed that the word "death" was a little blotchy, as if he had altered it.

Mulling, I bent to retrieve the fallen paper. It was a check. For ten thousand dollars.

My heart jolted. My eyes popped. I lowered myself to a kitchen chair and did a little careful breathing.

After that I did a lot of pacing—through the spanking-clean living room back to the spanking-clean foyer. Into the spanking kitchen, back to the foyer. But no matter how many times I looked, the check was still there.

It was mine for the taking. What would it hurt? Rivera wouldn't care. He had already dumped me. There would be no impassioned speeches about accepting money from the devil. No explosive arguments about my bad judgment. No absurd questions about where I had been.

Sespe. I shook my head. What on earth made him think I had gone to . . .

But suddenly my mind clicked away from sprawling notes and mouth-watering checks.

Sespe, Rivera had said. I had heard something on the radio about a death in a little town called Sespe.

And the senator's note—it almost looked as if it had originally said *deaths* instead of *death*.

Holy shit, I thought, and quit my pacing.

Someone else had died.

12

They say love makes the world go around....I
haven't been dizzy for a long time.

—Mr. Howard Lepinski,
willing to take a spin

I DIDN'T GET TO BED until well past three a.m. that
night. But even then I couldn't sleep.

There had indeed been another death. A drowning. It
had taken place in Sespe, a sleepy little town best known
for its production of a work boot called Ironwear. It was
fifty miles from where Kathy Baltimore had died.

Emanuel Casero had been on his way home from the
pub on Wednesday night. Friends said he was a bit inebriated. They had offered to drive him home, but he opted
to walk, as he always did. This time, however, he never
reached his destination.

A passing jogger had found his body facedown on

Sespe Creek's rocky shore at 5:47 on Saturday morning. There was no sign of foul play.

No. No sign. Just a drowning. Everyone had liked Manny. He was a joker, a good time. He'd been a member of the Yellow Jackets bowling team and a staunch supporter of the Republican Party.

Uncomfortable thoughts rolled around in my head like fractious bottles of nitro.

A staunch supporter.

Although I had searched the Internet for some time, I found nothing to suggest that Casero had worked for Senator Rivera's campaign. Still, it seemed spookily coincidental.

I stared at my ceiling, willing myself to sleep and failing miserably.

It has been said that there are no coincidences. On the other hand, there must be thousands of "staunch" Republicans in California. Eventually they were likely to die. Casero's death probably had nothing to do with Kathy's.

But if that was the case, why had Senator Rivera sent me the note?

Was it really to apologize? Or had he sent it with the express purpose of dropping a hint about the second death? Perhaps he knew of my difficulty in leaving well enough alone. After all, he certainly had been privy to my idiocy involving other crimes. Despite advice to the contrary, it had seemed physically impossible for me to ignore the death of his fiancée. Neither did I quite manage to let the police handle the investigation of the Viagra-induced linebacker who had so rudely expired in my office.

I sat upright abruptly, waking Harlequin, who lifted his enormous head for one instant before flopping it back onto my legs like a fifty-pound bag of flour. But I barely noticed.

Maybe the senator had given me the check as added incentive, thinking I would then feel obliged to see my mission through to the end. Maybe he thought I was too moralistic to accept payment for a job not completed.

I snorted at the thought.

Harlequin twitched an ear as if I were a bothersome fly.

Scrubbing my eyes, I wished I had never gotten involved with a cop. Or, if I had to do something so idiotic, why couldn't I become enamored of someone like Officer Tavis? On the other hand, what kind of cop encouraged people to call him by his first name? Not the Los Angeles kind of cop, that was for sure. I was always surprised the LAPD guys didn't have monikers like Officer Rage or Lieutenant I'll Tear Your Head Off.

I refused to think about it anymore. No more thoughts of dismembered bodies. No more thoughts of blue-tinged faces being nibbled on by crayfish.

But I knew I was fooling myself. What kind of person could put those kinds of gruesome images behind her and fall into blissful slumber?

My kind.

I was asleep before I was horizontal. Dreaming before Harlequin even started to snore.

I'm thinking about getting married," said Mr. Lepinski.

"What?" I jerked as if electrocuted. In my fatigue-induced imaginings there had been cops. Two of them. One dark and one fair. Both horny as hell and both wearing handcuffs.

I straightened in my chair and chastised myself sternly. I had made a solemn vow to forget about men completely and focus with singular concentration on my career.

Howard Lepinski was lying on my therapy couch. For the first several months of our acquaintance, he had barely relaxed enough to remain inside his own skin, but he had unwound considerably since then. I eyed him now, wondering if he had changed more than I realized. He had come to me as bony as a supermodel. Did his arms seem a little less stringy? Was his expression a little less stressed?

"Married," he said, glancing toward me, his eyes luminescent behind his hefty wire-rim glasses.

I forced myself to focus, even though the cops in my dreams had been wearing nothing but their duty belts . . . well, and the handcuffs. "To Penny?"

He nodded shyly, and then, to my amazement, his face quirked into what I thought might be a grin. Though in actuality I had no reference point. Lepinski wasn't known for his sparkling personality.

"How long have you and Penny known each other now?" I kept my tone steady, using my best shrink voice. It was designed to make him remember that his wife of twenty-some years—who I assumed had, at one point, also made him smile—had recently done the fornication fandango with the deli guy. Which, in turn, had precipitated Lepinski's visits to me. Though I had needed half a box of NoDoz to get to that point.

He sat up and looked at me.

"Three months and twelve days," he said steadily, but I didn't relent.

"How long did you know Sheila before you wed?"

He blinked, just a little reminiscent of Mr. Magoo. "Two years and twenty-seven days," he said. Mr. Lepinski is an accountant. Numbers are his sanctuary.

I nodded sagely. "Perhaps it might be wise to wait, then, and make certain—"

"I don't set an alarm anymore," he said.

I mulled that for half a second and came up empty. "I beg your pardon?"

His eyes were shining again. "Since Penny," he said. "I can't wait to get out of bed in the morning."

"Maybe you're just getting adequate sleep." While in connubial bliss, the former Mrs. Lepinski had been known to wake him during the night to discuss his shortcomings.

"She calls me first thing in the morning, just to make sure I'm all right."

"That's nice," I said, tone coolly professional. "But I want you to keep in mind that it is often considerably easier to live with someone when you don't actually *live* with them." The truth was, I didn't want to see him hurt again. He was a strange little man, but I had figured out fairly recently that he was a pretty good egg, and I was sure my caveat had nothing to do with jealousy on my part. Even though I myself am awakened each morning by a dog with a bladder the size of a threshing machine.

"She says it's okay if my voice is all scratchy and funny from sleep."

"She's a photographer. Is that right?" I asked, unnecessarily checking my notes.

He nodded. "Portraits. That sort of thing. To pay the bills, you know. But she likes nature shots. Wants to start her own gallery someday."

A-huh! So she was just looking for some poor sucker to finance her hobby! She was a gold digger. Okay, Mr. Lepinski probably didn't have a lot of gold to dig, but it was safe to assume that he had more than a portrait photographer with an artistic bent.

"An artist," I said. "That must be a very different life from that of an accountant."

He scowled a little. "I suppose so."

I held his gaze, imparting skeins of wisdom. "You're quite a . . . pragmatist, Mr. Lepinski. Some might even say you're set in your ways."

"I suppose so," he said again.

"Do you think you're ready to cohabitate with someone who might . . ." I shrugged. "Store their peas near their carrots?"

He blinked and pressed his knees together, mannerisms reminiscent of the early days of his therapy, but then he drew a quiet breath. His lips twitched again.

"She makes me laugh," he said.

And I couldn't think of a damn thing to complain about.

*H*ey, Pete," I said.

I was still sitting in my office when I made the call to my brother. The day had been filled with problems regarding family and loved ones and friends, making me wish I had some of each.

My kin live a couple thousand miles to the east in a strange, windy land called Chicago. Pete is the middle of my three brothers. Usually I have a rather unfavorable adjective in front of the word "brothers," but not tonight, which tells us all a little something about my current mood.

"Hey, sis," he said. "How's it hanging?"

"All right. How's little Christianna?" Some months previous, he and his wife of approximately two minutes had named their newborn after me. Maybe because I had saved his sorry ass from a bevy of "friends" who were intent on killing him.

"She's great." There was enthusiasm in his voice. "Cute as a bunny."

"Yeah? Put her on the phone."

"I realize you wouldn't know this, Christopher," he said, "but babies can't talk."

"I just want to hear her breathe," I said, and then wished I could haul back the words; I didn't want to hear babies breathe. I didn't even like babies.

"You okay?" Pete asked.

"Yeah." I sighed, a little touched by the concern he didn't bother to hide. It wasn't as if I were nostalgic for a more traditional Christmas or anything. But I had heard that a Santa-garbed bell ringer had recently collapsed from heat exhaustion outside the Macy's in Pasadena, and maybe I secretly thought God intended Santa to be cold. "I guess I'm just tired."

"You sure?" he asked. " 'Cuz you sound kind of sappy. Like you're human or something."

I scowled into the phone and wished I'd called Jack the Ripper instead. "Let me talk to Chrissy," I said, and he laughed.

"She's in bed."

"At six o'clock in the evening?"

"She's not a CPA, you know. She can sleep whenever she wants. Besides, she was driving me crazy, so I put a little Budweiser in her bottle."

"You did not!"

"I been at the station all day and I still got night class."

"Put Holly on the phone!"

"Couple of sips and she was out like a fat first baseman."

I was breathlessly appalled. "You don't even deserve to have a house plant."

"Hey, I didn't hear her complaining."

"I'm calling Mom," I said, and he laughed again.

"Shit, Christopher, what's wrong with you? You really think I gave my baby beer? Holly'd put my balls in a vise."

I gritted my teeth and glanced out the window toward the coffee shop. The midmorning haze had burned off, leaving the afternoon hot and windy. "You're an ass," I said.

"Yeah, but I'm the father of your only niece."

"How is she really?" I asked.

"Loud, funny, chubby. Hey, kind of like you," he said.

I hung up after I'd called him a few relatively creative names, but I still felt kind of out of sorts. My family may be nuttier than Skippy brand, but they're still family. If the truth be told, I even missed Chicago in a strange sort of masochistic way. The smog, the gritty wind, the Mafia.

Which made me think of Dagwood Dean Daly. I'd first met him just a few months earlier—while saving Pete's sorry ass.

D, as he liked to be called, was a card-carrying member of the mob. Involved in drugs, prostitution, and politics, but kind of charming, in a break-your-kneecaps sort of way. Well, actually, Pete had said he was better known for stealing livers. I've never known what that meant exactly. Maybe it was just a euphemism. Kind of like "steal your heart." Or maybe not, I thought, but my mind trickled to a halt.

Politics. D was involved in politics. Which maybe meant that he would know something about Miguel Rivera, especially if the senator had presidential plans.

I bit my lip, tried to talk myself out of being an imbecile, and dialed the phone.

13

Tequila—a sure cure for monogamy.

> —Chrissy's brother Michael,
> who wasn't exactly riddled
> with the disease in the first
> place

NOT ANOTHER INCIDENT with your fuckwit brother, I hope." D didn't believe in long salutations, such as "hi."

"No," I said, feeling breathless and ridiculously flattered that he'd not only remembered me but recognized my phone number. Which could, if one thought about it, be considered a good thing or a somewhat deadly thing. Depending on how fond you are of your liver.

"It's good to hear your voice, Christina," he said. A chair squeaked as if he were leaning back, putting his endangered-species boots up on his polished walnut desk.

"Ummm..." I was never quite sure how to talk to a crime boss. One who dressed like a Garth Brooks wannabe and had framed photographs of himself with

Disney characters was even more confusing. "It's good to hear yours, too."

"Yeah? Did you miss me?"

I straightened, remembering to be professional. "Do you have a minute, Mr. D?"

"*Mr.* D," he said, and laughed. "Does someone have a gun to your head or something?"

I glanced around a little nervously. No one did. "Not at the moment," I said.

"Don't I remember telling you my life story?"

"Maybe a piece of it."

"I think you're a hell of a shrink."

"Why do you say that?"

"Most people don't even know my name."

"Isn't it Mr. D?"

I could hear his smile. "I missed *you*," he said.

Sentiment sometimes makes me fidgety, even when it doesn't involve a liver-stealer, and I tend to cope by employing humor, some of which is not very humorous. "I was hoping your aim hadn't improved," I said.

He chuckled. "That might be funny even if I *weren't* a thug."

I swallowed, realizing for the first time what a truly bad idea this was. "I thought you hired out that sort of thing."

He laughed. "What can I do for you, Christina?"

I closed my mind and tried to act sane. It didn't go well. "I have a favor to ask," I said.

I dreamt about Rivera again that night. Again he was lying on the concrete. But this time there were *two* bodies beside him.

I awoke at three in the morning, breathing hard and telling myself it was just a dream. But the image of his sightless eyes was clear enough to make my hands shake.

Pushing Harlequin aside, I stood unsteadily and made my way to the bathroom. The mirror above the sink was not kind. I looked pale and haunted. Dark crescents hollowed my eyes. Sleep lines were etched like scars into my face. I tried to scrub them away and assured myself that everything was fine. The deaths were, after all, outside Rivera's jurisdiction. He had said so himself. Everything was fine. He could look out for himself. Just as I could.

And just then I had to pee so badly I ached. Glancing at the toilet, I sighed, turned, then pattered from the room and out the back door. The night was cool and quiet and dark. The dust felt soft against my bare feet. I peed in the shadows near the corner of my house and went back to bed, falling almost immediately into dream-shrouded slumber.

The following morning wasn't much better. I tried to forget about my troubles and focus on work, but it was no use. My last client of the day left a couple minutes before five. I paced nervously around my office for a while, then tromped out to the reception area.

Shirley was dusting the leaves of our resident rubber tree. It looked shocked but happy. Two days ago she'd brought in a ficus and a jade as big as Buddha. They looked giddy.

But the Magnificent Mandy was to return from her sick bed on the following day, and that spelled trouble for all living things. I stifled a sigh.

"I can't tell you how much I appreciate all your hard work," I said.

Shirley glanced up. "What? This? This ain't hard. You oughta try nursing a baby while frying bacon and cleaning toilets." She settled back in her chair. It heaved a little under her weight. "Lucky you don't have to pay me by the pound, huh?" she said, and sighed as she tucked her rag away in the bottom drawer. "How was Mr. Mozer tonight?"

"All right."

"Yeah?" She canted her head. "Then what's the problem?"

I considered denying there was one. It didn't seem worth it. "If someone gave you a check . . ." I paused. "For no particular reason—would you cash it?"

"Was it . . . like a gift?"

I scowled, not really sure how to answer that. "I guess so."

"Then yeah."

"It's quite a sizable check."

"Then *hell* yeah," she corrected.

"What if there are strings attached?"

"Are those strings likely to land you in the maternity ward with a baby the size of a watermelon stuck in your woo woo?"

A bevy of questions screamed through my mind, but I tried to remain focused. "No."

"Killed?"

"I hope not."

She squinted her eyes at me.

"No," I corrected.

Her heavy brows lowered. "You can't keep peeing in the backyard."

I started. "How did you know—"

"Seven kids. I've seen everything."

"I *do* need a new septic system," I said, "but maybe it'd be wrong to take his money."

"Honey..." she said, and, standing up, came around the corner of the desk like a road mender on a mission. "You got a good head and you got a good heart. I'm sure you'll use the money wisely."

"Really?"

"Of course. Besides, if it's from some man, he probably deserved to lose it anyhow."

"Yeah?"

"Cash the check," she said, "then go get yourself some sleep."

I took her advice. Well, I cashed the check. But then, when I least expected it, my car missed the turn onto Sunland Boulevard and sped west toward Sespe.

Happy Daze Pub looked like any other bar anywhere in the country. It was small, dingy, and quiet, even for a Tuesday night. Christmas lights were strung haphazardly above the door. I took a stool near the corner, where I could get a panoramic view of the place.

The occupants were a manila lot. Blue-collar workers mostly, with a businessman thrown in for color. The bartender was a woman. She had good-sized arms, which flexed mightily as she leaned against the hardwood.

"What can I get you?" Her voice matched her arms. My guess was steroids and a good healthy disgust for anyone sporting testicles.

"I'll have a strawberry margarita."

"No blended drinks," she rumbled.

"A vodka cranberry, then," I said.

She nodded and moved away. I was a little insulted at

her haste. I mean, I'm a firm heterosexual, but at least she could have flirted a little.

"A margarita?" someone said, and I turned.

The man who approached the bar was carrying a drink of his own. He was twenty soft pounds overweight, had curly hair, and wore a diffident expression.

"What are you thinking?" he asked.

I gave him one haughtily raised brow. I'd learned while serving drinks to the inebriated populace of Schaumburg, Illinois, not to take too much guff. "That I like strawberries?"

"I think they serve them at the Dairy Queen. Do you mind?" he asked, and indicated the stool beside me.

I shook my head and he sat, setting his drink down in front of him. It looked like a gin and tonic.

"This isn't the kind of place with fruit?" I asked.

He took a swig of his drink. "This is the kind of place where people come after their shifts at the plant."

"To get drunk?"

"By the shortest possible route."

"You work at the plant?"

"For twenty years."

I looked him over. He couldn't have been much older than thirty. "That's a long time."

"I'm generally the first one here," he said.

"Hey, Mac." A man in a khaki work shirt gave him a nod in passing.

"Hey," answered my companion, and took another swig.

"Your name's Mac?" I asked.

"That's what they call me. How about you?"

"They call *me* Mac."

"You're kidding."

"Wish I were," I said. "So, you've lived in Sespe a long time?"

He shrugged. "Old man loved work boots."

"So you do, too?"

"Took too much effort to love anything else. How about you?"

I glanced around the room. California had gone smoke-less in the '90s, but judging by the haze, Sespe might not have gotten the memo.

"I'm a cocktail waitress," I said.

"Yeah? You meet Lyda here?" he asked, as the bartender returned with my drink. She set it in front of me and nodded.

"Hey, Mac," she said, then to me: "Four-fifty."

"I got it," he said, and lifted his almost-empty glass in a well-understood signal. She gave him a near smile and moved down the bar to fulfill his wishes.

"Thank you," I said.

He shrugged. "Friday's payday."

"No point letting all that potential money go to waste."

"Almost be a sin," he said. "Where do you work?"

"L.A."

"Yeah?" He jiggled his ice. "I heard of that place."

I smiled and tasted my drink. It wasn't bad, maybe a lit-tle heavy on the vodka.

"What are you doing *here*?" he asked.

Honesty may get you to heaven, but a couple of handy lies will get you answers. "I was visiting my brother. Just on my way home."

"What's his name?"

I took another sip. "What?"

"Your brother. Could be I work with him."

"Oh. No. He lives in Santa Barbara. Just had a new baby."

He smiled a little. Lyda replaced his drink. "Babies are nice. New life and all that," he said, and gazed with melancholy at the bottle-lined wall in front of us.

It seemed a perfect segue. "I heard a guy drowned here the other night."

He drew a deep breath. "Weird."

I felt my stomach cramp. "How so?"

He took a swig. "Manny liked the water. Could swim like a fish, or so he said."

"So you knew him."

He shrugged.

My heart was racing. "Did you work with him?"

"He got himself fired a few months back."

His answers seemed strangely succinct after his former verbosity.

"I'm sorry. Were you two close?"

"Me and Manny?" He glanced at me. He had kind eyes, pale green, a little sad.

"Evening," said an aging man in a sport coat.

"Hey, Milt," he said, then sipped some more and shrugged. "Actually, I don't think he liked me very much."

A blue-jeaned man in a sweatshirt paused in passing. "Hey, Mac. Me and Garrett are goin' to Burley's come Friday. Wanna come?"

He nodded. "I'm driving this time, though."

Garrett's friend laughed and moved on.

"You seem like a pretty popular guy," I said. "Why would anyone dislike you?"

He sighed, glanced at the bottles again, then looked at

me. "You must be tired of listening to people's problems all day."

I drew back a little, wondering wildly how he had known my true occupation.

"Delivering drinks," he said.

"Oh, yes. Well..." I tried to relax, but tense was becoming so comfortable. "I like talking to people. It's kind of...therapeutic."

He smiled. "You get a lot of drunks where you work?"

"It's not uncommon."

He nodded. "Manny was an okay guy."

"Just okay?"

He took a sip of gin. "Were your parents really mean or do you have another name besides Mac?"

He seemed like a nice guy. But other guys did, too, and sometimes they tried to kill me. "Truth is," I said, "I'm a little uncomfortable about giving out my name."

He watched me for a minute, then: "I'm sorry," he said.

"For..."

"Whatever made you skittish. Sometimes life kind of sucks."

It was one of the wisest things I'd heard in weeks. "Sometimes."

"Manny's wife left him 'bout a year back."

"The guy that died?"

"Yeah."

"Do you think it was suicide?"

"There's talk, but..." he said, and shrugged.

"He got fired. Lost his wife. Sometimes people get depressed."

"They do indeed."

"But you don't think that was it."

He shrugged again.

"Why?"

"Word was he might be expecting some money."

"Money? What kind of money?"

"He was suing Ironwear for a . . ." He nodded at his unspoken thoughts. "A hefty sum."

"For what?"

"Racial discrimination."

"And he had won the suit?"

"Guess it's a moot point now."

"A hefty sum should have put a smile on his face."

"It's the last thing he needed."

"What do you mean?"

"Nothing," he said. "Sorry. What do I know?"

"Mac," someone said in passing.

"Woods," he responded, lifting a hand.

"I thought everyone needed a . . . hefty sum," I said.

He smiled, but the expression was grim. "Maybe some people know how to spend it better than others."

"He didn't?"

"Some guys are sweet as puppies when they're drunk," he said. I wondered if he was one of them. If you listened closely, you could hear his words beginning to slur.

"He wasn't?"

"Maybe we could talk about you for a while," he suggested.

"I get weepy when I drink," I said.

"I pass out."

"Often?"

"Not as much as Manny," he said.

"He was an alcoholic?"

"I don't know what's wrong with me," he said. "I'm trying not to talk about him."

"Sometimes it's just best to get it out of your system."

"I thought women liked to talk about themselves."

I shrugged. "Maybe it's the cocktail girl in me. Tell me about him."

He examined his drink. "He really was an okay guy," he said. "Worked for Ironwear for a bunch of years. Always had a new joke. Some of them were even funny. Liked to talk politics. But usually didn't let it get sticky."

I felt my heart lurch. "Usually?"

"He could get pretty steamed up sometimes. Heard he used to campaign for some senator."

My gut cramped. I took a drink and tried to remember to breathe. "Some senator?"

"Yeah. The Latino one."

I felt a little sick to my stomach, but I felt excited, too. "I'm afraid I don't know—"

"The good-looking guy with the great voice," he said. "Roberto. Remono."

"Rivera?" I said.

"Yeah, that was it. Rivera."

14

Sex is all right, but a hot fudge sundae don't never ask if the baby's really his.

—*Shirley Templeton*

CHRISTINA." The senator *did* have a great voice. Even better in person than on television. It was Thursday afternoon. He was manning the mashed potatoes at Caring Hands again. "What a wonderful surprise."

"I was hoping to talk to you for a minute."

"Of course," he said, and glanced toward a young woman who stood a few yards to his left. "Thea, could you take over for a minute?"

"Certainly," she said, putting napkins near the flatware and hurrying over.

She was, in a word, sickeningly gorgeous. Okay, that might be more than one word. But you couldn't look at her and think in monosyllabic terms.

She was wearing nondescript blue jeans, a caramel-toned cami, and a simple Western shirt, but it wouldn't have mattered if she'd donned an apple barrel and frying pan. She still would have looked like royalty. Her hair was a long, wavy sweep of amber and her skin was creamy perfection, but it was her body that made me want to trade my genes in for a pair of sweatpants and a shotgun.

The senator met her gaze. She smiled shyly. He smiled back. I held my breath, wondering if they would fall into each other's arms, but he just murmured his thanks and stepped out from behind the table.

"Who's that?" I asked, voice innocent.

"Who? Thea?" he said, glancing down at me.

"Yes. She's . . ." A host of superlatives streamed through my head. "Rather pretty."

"Yes." He glanced back at her for a moment, but his face didn't light up like a tinseled tree. Instead, a shadow of worry flitted through his eyes. "Yes, I suppose she is."

Suppose! That was like saying you supposed L.A. had a gang problem. And why the worry? Did he think he had finally found a woman too young for him? Did he think he couldn't get her? Did he, perhaps, finally worry about the moral implications of seducing a woman younger than his last meal?

"Who is she?" I repeated.

"Thea?" he said again.

I stared at him. "Is there another woman here?" I asked.

He laughed and focused fully on me. "Well, there's you, Christina."

"Like I said . . ." I let the sentence fade.

"Thea Altore is rather an amazing young woman," he admitted. "She's been giving of her time here at Caring

Hands for more than a year now. She's very selfless. Bright." His attention wavered again, and he stared through me for an instant, as if seeing someone else. "Idealistic."

"And gorgeous," I added.

"Yes, that, too, I suppose," he said, seeming to shake off the mood as he closed the office door behind us. "Now, what can I do for you?"

"You can explain why you didn't tell me about Emanuel Casero."

I watched him blanch, but, honestly, I couldn't tell if his pallor was real or faked. Senator Rivera could make Anthony Hopkins look like a community-theater hack.

"I should have known you would find out," he said.

Because he had wanted me to? I wondered. Because he'd dropped hints? "He worked on your campaign," I said.

He didn't respond but stood with his hands deep in the pockets of his trousers, staring out the window. "A long time ago."

"As long ago as Kathy?" I asked, and sat down in the green plastic chair.

He closed his eyes for a minute. "Time rushes by so quickly. It all seems like a recent dream."

"How recent?"

He shook his head, sat. "Ten years or more."

"What did he do for you?"

"Manny helped coordinate volunteers."

"So you knew him well."

"Quite well, yes. I like to befriend my workers. The victory is really theirs, after all. One cannot forget those who help him—"

He seemed to be gearing up for a gusty speech. I felt the need to drag him off the soapbox before things got too slippery. "Did you forget *him*?"

"What?"

"I hear he was a staunch Republican but he had gotten out of politics. I was wondering if it was because of some rift between the two of you."

He sighed. "There are always some bumps during a campaign."

"Was this bump more like a mogul or a mountain?"

"Manny thought I should take a firmer stand against abortion. But I felt it was not necessarily my place to make that decision for a woman."

Sadness was in his eyes again. Which made me wonder rather uncharitably if there would be a whole host of little senators on the planet had abortion not been legalized.

"Is that when he quit?" I asked.

"No." He glanced out the window again. "It was some time later."

"Another conflict?"

"Not at all. I won the senatorial seat. He moved on."

"So there were no other problems."

"Mr. Casero was a good man, Christina. I would rather not besmirch his name."

"How do you feel about being dismembered with a band saw?"

He paled this time for real. I was sure of it. "So you think their deaths are somehow connected."

I didn't address that directly. "Do you know of anyone who might have had some grudge against them?"

"No. No campaign is without conflict, as I have said, but they were both fine, upstanding people."

"Did Kathy drink?"

"What?"

"Manny liked the booze. How about Kat?"

He shook his head, looking a little peeved that I was aware of Casero's bibulous nature. "Not that I remember."

"What *do* you remember?"

"She was a good person. Solid. Quite devoted to her family."

I caught his gaze. "In other words, she wouldn't sleep with you."

He drew a surprised breath, then gave me a wounded expression. "Christina, I cannot tell you how your low opinion saddens me." He put his hand to his chest. "It is like a dagger to my—"

"It must have been rather soothing when you learned the truth," I said, stepping carefully, wondering how much he knew of her.

"The truth?"

I rose to my feet. "Why ask me to investigate if you intend to lie to me at every turn?"

"I have not lied."

"There are those who believe the omission of truth to be a lie." I turned toward the door and didn't tell him I was not one of them. Does that make me a liar?

"Wait, Christina. I'm sorry." I glanced back. Hearing a Rivera apologize was something of an epiphany for me. He was on his feet. "I was quite attracted to Ms. Baltimore. That I will admit, but I am not the kind to—"

I put my hand on the doorknob.

"I have made mistakes," he added hastily. "I freely admit it."

I turned back.

His chin was held high, like a persecuted saint. "But she was unhappy. I could see it in her eyes."

"And you thought infidelity would make her ecstatic?"

"She was an amazing woman," he said. "Not just beautiful. But intelligent and kind and—" He shook his head. "It is hard to believe that she is dead."

"Did her husband know you thought her this paragon among women?"

"You make me sound quite despicable."

I didn't address that statement. "He worked on your campaign, too. Isn't that correct?"

"It is." His mouth pursed a little.

"You didn't like him." It seemed I was beginning to read the good senator.

"He did not deserve her. But then . . ." He sighed. "Perhaps none of us deserves the women who love us."

"She loved him?"

He shrugged. "I know you do not think highly of me, Christina. But there are those who believe I have a certain amount of charm."

"Therefore, she must have loved her husband to stay with him," I surmised.

Another shrug. "Stranger things have happened, perhaps."

"How so?"

He drew a heavy breath. "There were rumors that he struck her."

"Were they true?"

"In actuality, when it was clear that she did not . . . appreciate my attention, I distanced myself."

Translation: When he figured out she wasn't going to

sleep with him, he moved on to another, probably younger, possibility.

"Was there tension between you and her husband?"

His expression hardened. "Mr. Baltimore was a pea of a man, but he was still a volunteer for my campaign. I had no wish to cause trouble."

That much I believed. "So you let the abuse go."

There may have been guilt in his eyes. I wasn't sure. "Ms. Baltimore did not seem interested in my help."

"Did you confront the husband?"

"I thought it best to let them work out their differences."

I wondered how many times that had been said at funerals and visitations.

"Did she ever have bruises?"

"Not that I was aware of."

I watched him closely. If he was lying, I couldn't tell, but maybe he could have told me he was Aquaman with the same kind of conviction.

"How about the others? Did any of them complain about having her on your team?"

"How do you mean?"

"If I'm not mistaken, the Republican Party can be . . . less than tolerant of gays."

He stared at me blankly.

I stared back, waiting.

He scowled.

I cocked my head, still waiting.

And then his eyes widened. "She wasn't . . . She didn't . . ." I had never seen him flustered. I drank it in. But finally he shook his head. "I am sure you are mistaken."

"About?"

"Ms. Baltimore had a grace about her. A quiet, lovely femininity."

I raised one brow.

"And beautiful hair!" he added, sounding desperate. "I remember how it shone. An intern was brushing it. She wore it long and straight. It glittered like starlight beneath Mel's—"

He blinked and sat back down.

"I take it Mel was a woman?" I said.

"I just . . ." He shook his head. "I never . . ." He glanced up. "She was so pretty."

I kind of wanted to bitch-slap him with my purse, but I resisted. "How long have you lived in California, exactly?"

He didn't seem to hear me.

"It all makes sense now," he said.

"What makes sense?"

"Her disinterest," he said, tone awed, and for just a moment I reconsidered that slapping idea.

15

I fear that someday you will abandon the joys we
share and find another not worthy of your charms.

> —*François,*
> *who sometimes worries*
> *that Chrissy will leave him*
> *for a lover with a pulse*

*I*T WAS ALMOST DUSK when I returned home that
evening, but Harlequin gave me a droopy-eyed plea, so I
packed him into the Saturn and headed off to the dog
park. The temperature had dropped back into the three-
digit range, but I still felt self-pity creeping in, more
draining than the heat. My conversation with the senator
had made me kind of melancholy. Yes, he was vain and
self-centered and kind of a creep, but he was a powerful, attractive, intelligent creep. And he reminded me disturbingly of his son, whom, if I were idiotic enough to be
honest about, I had been lusting over for quite some time.
In fact, I'd been dreaming about him again, and although
my recent imaginings did not show him facedown on the

concrete, they were still disturbing. More than once I had awakened near the slippery peak of Mt. Satisfaction and found myself wishing dreams *were* omens of things to come.

The truth, however, was that I hadn't heard from Rivera since his departure five days earlier. And it was entirely possible that I was never going to hear from him again. My throat tightened at the thought, but I cleared it and moved on.

There was an irregular oblong path running uphill and down in the dog park. I circled the course with Harley approximately by my side. Now and then he would be waylaid by a good-natured Lab or a snooty borzoi. There was also a scrawny-tailed cur that looked disturbingly like the rodent of unusual size from *The Princess Bride*. But I refrained from screaming for my sweet Wesley and kept walking, trying rather desperately to bring my thoughts back to the senior Rivera and his impending problems instead of his conspicuously absent son.

Okay, maybe the two deaths were unconnected. Maybe Manny had intentionally offed himself or accidentally fallen like a drunken log into the river. Maybe Kathy had passed out. Or been killed by her ex. As far as I was concerned, Mr. Baltimore had entirely too many teeth, and I had seen enough prime-crime television to know that the husband (with or without a surplus of teeth) is generally the number-one suspect. In this case he was my *only* suspect. On the other hand, maybe Mr. Baltimore had known about the senator's attempt to seduce his wife and had harbored secret resentment all these years. Maybe—

I shook my head.

The idea was ludicrous. A lot of water had flowed under

the proverbial bridge since the Baltimores worked on the senator's campaign. Not to mention the fact that since that time Kathy had divorced Mr. Teeth and taken a female lover—maybe multiple female lovers. Surely Teeth had bigger offenses to worry about than an aborted seduction from decades before. Besides, subsequent research had yielded the fact that Teeth had remarried some three years ago. He seemed to have moved on. To have found another woman certifiably desperate enough to sleep with him. It never ceased to amaze me how—

"Hey, Miss Chris."

I stopped dead in my tracks. Harlequin stopped with me, having lost, or eaten, his scrawny-tailed companion.

A man stepped away from a leaning black walnut near the parking lot. He was wearing a straw cowboy hat and sunglasses.

My heart stayed, rather miraculously, within the confines of my chest. "D?" I said.

He smiled.

My gaze ricocheted right and left. Maybe I was looking for an escape route, or maybe I was looking for his entourage. Last time I'd seen this particular gangster, he was surrounded by a bevy of six-foot supermodels-turned-bodyguards. The scariest of whom, I was quite sure, had planned to cut my heart out with her laser vision.

"What are you doing here?" My voice sounded a little wobbly. Sometimes people who steal livers affect me that way.

This one looked really innocuous, though. He was sporting a blue plaid shirt made to look as if it had been worn mending fence. I wondered vaguely if it had cost more than my monthly mortgage.

"You wanted some information," he said. "So I thought I'd drop by."

I blinked. "I have a fax machine."

He grinned, glanced down. "This your pet?"

Harlequin was pressed up against my thigh, tail tucked between his legs. He wagged it carefully when D lifted a hand toward his moose-size head, then rolled out his tongue and lapped D's fingers.

D smiled and rubbed his ears. "Good to know he makes his own decisions."

I looked at him. The word "blankly" comes to mind.

"Doesn't prejudge just because of my profession. Not everyone's so open-minded," he said, and turned, lifting a hand to indicate we should continue on.

"Where's, ummm . . . Sandy?" I asked, expecting to see long-legged beauties popping up like mushrooms from behind every tree. D doesn't like men. Refuses to speak to them, I'm told. Perhaps I should be so inclined.

"Dare I hope you're jealous?" he asked.

"Scared, maybe," I said.

He faked a shudder. "I gotta admit, she terrifies me."

"How'd you know I was here?" I asked.

Harlequin sniffed his arm, then, either determining he was a good egg or possibly not giving a rat's ass, romped off to greet a lhasa apso. It cowered, peed, and considered dropping dead.

"You sure you want to be involved with the Riveras?" D asked.

I snapped my eyes back to his. "What'd you find out?" I asked, but he smiled and changed the subject.

"You look good," he said, and lowered his gaze a little. Despite the liver-stealing phenomenon, I was kind of glad I looked decent and hadn't taken time to change into my usual after-work rags. I was wearing a russet silk blouse with a shirred V-neck, buff capris, and wedge sandals, which, if I say so myself, show my legs off to their best advantage. "Nice shirt."

I cleared my throat and prepared to launch into some sensible conversation, but he continued.

"I've been worried about you."

I felt myself tense. What would it take to make a liver-stealer worry? "Why?"

"Miguel Rivera..." He shook his head. "I almost have to admire the man."

"Have you heard anything about him making a bid for the presidency?"

He glanced ahead, seeming to enjoy the evening. But maybe that made sense. According to the weather report, Chicago was currently being blown into Indiana by sub-zero, gale-force winds. "There's talk."

"Serious talk?"

He smiled again, enigmatic as hell and kind of cute.

"He make a bid for *you* yet?" he asked.

I glanced toward him and away. "No. Of course not."

He tilted his head a little. "The man's had more affairs than the foreign minister."

I think I scowled. "I don't know who—"

"It was a play on words," he said. "See, the foreign-affairs minister should have—Never mind. Point is, Rivera would screw a light socket."

"What about a lesbian?"

"What?"

"Did you hear anything about him and a woman named Kathy Baltimore?"

"Baltimore, like the city?" He seemed to be thinking behind his dark glasses. "Nope, she wasn't on the list."

"Nothing about her?"

"Why? Did he screw her?"

I didn't answer. "How about her husband?"

He raised a brow. "I didn't realize the good senator was so...omnivorous."

"I meant, did he have any problems with Mr. Baltimore?"

"Not according to my sources."

I didn't bother to ask who his sources were. I was afraid one might have been formerly known as Beelzebub.

"Who *has* he had trouble with?"

"Everyone else," he said.

"Can you be more specific?"

"He's screwed a lot of people."

"So you mentioned."

"I meant it more generically this time."

"What about an Emanuel Casero?"

"I think I've heard the name."

"Casero?"

"Emanuel, but maybe it was just in a biblical sense. God among us."

I looked at him, surprised, and he glanced back with a grin.

"Gangsters are allowed to read the Bible, you know. Those clever inquisitive Spaniards probably knew it by heart in the fifteenth century."

I opened my mouth to spout something genius, but thankfully he spoke again.

"I'm sorry I'm not being more helpful."

"No, you are," I said. "I just think...couldn't you have told me this over the phone?"

He glanced to the right. A man with a suit was walking a Doberman—sans suit.

"You can't trust phones," he said, sotto voce. "Who knows who might be listening."

I felt the hair on my arms prickle up, and I shifted my gaze to surreptitiously study the overdressed gentleman. He remained facing forward.

"Really?" I whispered.

D stared at me with serious intent, then said, "No," and laughed. "I just wanted to see you. Give you another chance."

It took me a moment to get my head back in the game. "At?" We had returned to the parking area near the languorously leaning walnut tree.

He took my arm and tugged me into the shadows.

"Sleeping with me," he said.

My mouth dropped open.

"This is a pretty spot," he said.

"Here?" My voice had zipped from wobbly to squeaky, missing all areas in between.

"Warm," he said, and stroked my arm. "Not too many onlookers."

"Not too many..." I glanced around, horrified and kind of turned on. "There are dozens."

"Want me to get rid of them?" he asked, and brushed a few strands of hair behind my ear.

"No." I felt a little breathless. A little overheated. A lot horny. I can't help it. It's not as if every wannabe cowboy makes me hot. Well, maybe it is, but...

"You deserve better, Chrissy," he said, and leaned in, but just then something wet touched my hand.

I glanced down. It was a nose. The nose was attached to a smiling blond canine.

"Rocky," someone called.

The voice rumbled across my quivering inner ear and straight to my nipples. I turned—*sure,* absolutely *certain,* Rivera couldn't have ended up in the same dog park at the same time. He didn't even have a dog, except for the retriever named Rockette he shared with his ex-wife, who was as cute as a . . .

I glanced up and there he was, standing just a few feet away, looking hard and intense in the dark-sex way only truly difficult men can achieve. I froze like dried linguine. Harlequin wasn't so inhibited. He romped giddily around Rivera's legs, then gamboled off with the retriever, apparently unconcerned about his beloved's canine infidelity.

Rivera lifted his midnight eyes. Our gazes clashed like thunderclaps. Silence echoed between us.

"This him?" D asked. The world came crashing back around my ears. "The infamous Jack Rivera?"

"Yes. Yes." It seems I had forgotten that Rivera affected me like a half-gallon jug of fermented moonshine, but it all came rushing back now. "D . . ." I didn't know the exact etiquette for introducing a crime boss to an officer of the law. "This is Rivera. Rivera—"

"He's shorter than I expected," D said.

"D," Rivera said, and took one taut step toward us. "That your first name or your last?"

D didn't answer.

My mind was jumping in concert with my nerves, but I tried to make nice. "I was just walking Harlequin. Lovely evening, isn't it?" Lovely evening! Holy crap! I sounded like a constipated librarian. "I mean, it was too nice out to—" I was yapping like a lapdog, but just then Rivera reached into his back pocket. I braced myself for an ensuing gun battle, but he only pulled out a badge. "I'm Lieutenant Rivera. LAPD." He flipped the badge shut and shoved it back out of sight. "And you are?"

A grin twisted D's mouth into what some brave souls might have considered a smile. "Your lieutenant seems a little insecure," he said.

"Who the hell are you?" Rivera asked, and took another step forward, but I shoved myself between them.

"D's a friend. From Chicago," I yammered. "Just in town for a couple of hours before his—"

"How good a friend?" he murmured, and lowered his hot-tamale eyes to mine.

I was breathing hard. There was a dark chemistry brewing between us. It may have been toxic and deadly, but it was also hopelessly alluring.

"We met years ago when—"

"How good a friend?" he asked again, and seared me with his eyes.

I felt the draw of him like a fist around my senses, squeezing me close, stopping my breath, but I fought the weakness. He had given up on me, walked out, quit the fight when I was just gearing up for battle.

"Who the hell are you to ask?" I gritted.

He jerked his head toward D but never dropped my gaze. "Who the hell is *he*?"

"You made it pretty clear you weren't interested."

"That doesn't mean you have to—"

"Are you or aren't you?" I snarled.

A muscle jumped in his jaw. He fisted his hands, controlled his breathing, then lifted his attention with slow deliberation from me to D. Their gazes struck like lightning. "If you hurt her, I'll carve my name on your fucking heart," he said, and, turning, stalked away, Rockette bounding along beside him.

The world returned to normal by slow increments. My heart was thudding heavily in my chest. Harlequin was still slobbery, and D was grinning like an ecstatic monkey.

"Well," he said, "that went better than expected."

16

I ain't taking no more rides on the stupid train.

—*Shirley Templeton,*
fed up with infidelity,
excuses, and men in
general

THE SEPTIC GUYS began digging up my yard the next day. It was Friday. I pretended my life wasn't a wasteland, woke early, showered, washed my hair, and artfully applied half a dump truck of makeup. After that I carefully dressed in a mulberry skirt and an ivory blouse with a little ruffle down the front.

I looked good. And why shouldn't I? There was no telling who I might see today. Maybe a mob boss. Maybe a senator with presidential ambitions. Maybe a rabid lieutenant who made me hot and angry and psychotic all in one fell swoop. Or maybe I'd meet someone normal. Stranger things have happened.

As far as I knew, D had returned to Chicago, but I didn't

know much. We'd parted at the dog park after our surreal meeting with Rivera, and I hadn't heard from him since.

I can't remember which clients I saw that day. I can only assume I spoke to a few and didn't screw up their lives any worse than they already were, but my mind was scrambling. Every spare second, I was on the Internet, researching recent California deaths.

There was a buttload of them.

By the time my final client left, I felt like my mind had been run through a Cuisinart.

"You okay?" Shirley asked as I staggered out of my office for the final time that day. The Magnificent Mandy had been kind enough to remain bedridden. "You look a little punch-drunk."

I took the chair not far from her. "Do you believe in coincidence, Shirley?"

"Coincidence?"

"Yes."

"Like, every time my ex had a poker game with the guys, it just happened to be the same time that tramp Malika was in town?"

I gave that a moment of judicious consideration. "Yes," I said finally. "Like that."

She sighed heavily. Her majestic bosom heaved. She crossed her arms over it and narrowed her eyes. "I maybe used to believe in coincidence. Sometimes bad things just up and happen. But more often than not, I think bad things happen 'cuz somebody somewhere's been taking them for a ride on the stupid express. Why do you ask?"

"I don't know." I leaned my head back against the chair. "Maybe I'm just searching for the meaning of life."

She made a *hmmmfff*ing noise deep in her chest.

"Do you think there is one?" I asked.

"Sure there is."

I perked up a little. Which means I managed to lift my head. "Do you want to share it with me?"

She nodded. "It's chocolate," she said.

I wasn't really all that surprised. I just hadn't heard it verbalized with such succinct eloquence before. "Chocolate?"

"Yeah. Chocolate and babies and the kind of dark jazz that makes your toes curl up in your shoes."

"Jazz."

She lifted her heft out of the chair and rounded her desk. "It's the good things in life, honey. The things that make you happy way down in your humming place."

I straightened a little. "I'm not sure I have a humming place."

"Oh, you got one. Maybe you just ain't heard from it for a while. I been around a long time, and I figured out this much: It ain't the big things that count. Not fame or bank accounts or who you know. It's those little moments when you smile to yourself and you don't really know why. You find a few moments like that for yourself or someone else and you got it all."

She shooed me out of the office a few minutes later. I draggled home like a lost puppy. There was a mound of dirt reminiscent of the Sierra Nevadas in my backyard, suggesting bad things for future showers and the contentment of my bladder, but I strapped on my running shoes and took Harlequin for a jog. It was getting dark by the time I got home, and I was dripping fluids from every pore.

"Miss Christina." I glanced up. Mrs. Al-Sadr stood on the opposite side of the fence. Below her long paisley skirt, her grass was as uniform and green as outdoor carpeting. "Your yard is ugly mess."

In all the time I had lived on Opus Street, I hadn't exchanged more than two sentences with Mrs. Al-Sadr, but I had to admit, five truer words had never been spoken.

"Yes, sorry about that," I said.

She shrugged. "A neat yard, it is the concern of husbands, yes?"

Having neither a neat yard nor a husband, I had no idea. I nodded and turned away, but she spoke again.

"Do you bath?" she asked.

"What's that?"

She was silent for a moment as if searching for the right words, then motioned, indicating me or the dirt mound or both. "You have need of bath."

Ten minutes later I was gathering up my toiletries. I didn't know the proper etiquette for using other people's water, so I packed my own bathroom condiments and trekked down the sidewalk. Mrs. Al-Sadr greeted me at the door with a shy smile. I schlepped past two solemn-faced, dark-eyed children and in moments found myself in heaven.

Their bathtub was one of those Jacuzzi types. I washed my hair, soaked, and found that I was smiling as I shaved my legs. Who would have suspected I would find my humming place in someone else's tub?

Finally, squeaky clean and as sweet-smelling as cookie dough, I pulled on sweatpants and T-shirt, then wandered, wet-headed, out into the living room.

Ramla, as she had introduced herself earlier, was reading a newspaper called *Al-Ayyam*. No one else was in sight.

"Thank you," I said, and hugged my damp towel to my chest. "That was unusually kind."

"I have the halvah," she said.

I raised a brow or two. "What?"

"Come." Folding her paper neatly, she stood up and traipsed past me into the kitchen. An oblong table boasted a pan of bars sprinkled with powdered sugar. "I have made the halvah. But I have no sisters with who to share."

In the end, we sat eating a foreign ambrosia that had apparently been created in her very own kitchen.

"Are you not lonely?" she asked finally.

I glanced up. The remainder of the bars were calling to me with buttery goodness, making me wonder a little obsessively if it would be rude to grab the pan and make a dash for my front door. "Lonely?" I asked.

She pursed her lips and studied her fingers, entwined upon the tabletop. Shame crossed her pleasant features. "I have the guilt," she said.

"It's going around," I admitted, still eyeing the bars.

"My husband says I should be in the song."

I tried to understand her meaning, but the bars had almonds and sugar, and did I mention butter? I love butter more than I love François.

"He say I am the lucky woman. My children are healthy. There is food." She motioned to the table.

It seemed like the perfect time to segue into a request for more heaven in a pan. In fact, I was choosing my next piece of ambrosia when I heard a strange, strangled noise coming from the far side of the table. Wrenching my gaze away from the dessert, I saw that Ramla was crying.

Now, I'll be the first to admit that if anyone is comfortable with tears, it should be a psychologist, but I'm from Chicago, where we only cry when the Bears lose and/or we run out of beer.

"Mrs. Al-Sadr?" I ventured, voice tentative.

"My sister, she is troubled," she said.

I nodded and listened.

*I*t was fully dark when I left her house and trekked up the crumpling walkway to my front door. Harlequin did a few prancing leaps to demonstrate his happiness, and I smiled. Loneliness is a funny thing. Sometimes abated by nothing more than a flop-eared dog the size of a small satellite. Sometimes not abated at all.

*S*aturday arrived right on schedule. Not wanting to over-use the peeing privileges at my neighbors', I walked down to the nearest Exxon to use their restroom, then had a bowl of cereal in lieu of nutrition and spent the remainder of the day at my computer.

I had promised Ramla I would do what I could. Her sister, it seemed, was in a bad marriage with a bad man in a bad part of Yemen, so I Googled immigration laws and settled in.

By five in the afternoon my bladder was making believ-able threats about implosion. Latching on Harley's leash, I popped into the Saturn, peed at Vons supermarket, then filled a cotton tote with groceries and headed back home.

Sunday went much the same, except that I had fresh milk and bagels in the fridge.

My Internet system is slower than an Ashtanga yoga

master, but I eventually learned that immigration possibilities were grimmer than I realized. By comparison, my little corner of the world seemed relatively placid, but hate crimes were hardly unheard of. A Muslim man had been shot in Detroit for no known reason other than his faith. A woman in Atlanta had her burka torn off while being chastised for wickedness.

The Moral Majority seemed to be having a field day with us imperfects lately: the gays, the . . .

My mind fumbled off on a tangent. Both Baltimore and Casero had, at least by some standards, wandered off the straight and narrow. One was a lesbian, the other an alcoholic. Did that suggest a trend, or was the majority of the population on a broader, curvier path?

Back to my investigation, I Googled odd deaths again. A rock climber had died while rappelling down a cliff in New Mexico. Authorities believed he died of an internal hemorrhage. A woman in Minnesota had been killed by a moose. The moose in question had declined comment. Chances were good, however, that he was disgruntled about human encroachment. But as far as I could discern, neither the victims nor the moose had any connection with Senator Rivera.

The rest of the reports were both revolting and mesmerizing. I stared at my computer screen, Google-eyed, and narrowed my search to *deaths and Rivera.* Salina Martinez popped up in a thousand formats. There were photos and accusations and long-winded stories concerning her job, her acquaintances, and her pulchritude. I moved on. I knew who had caused her death. In fact, the memory of an old man with a poker made me check the locks on my doors before settling back in my thumb-size office.

Sometime later I found the obituary for Francis Rivera. He was a shortstop for the Atlanta Braves. There was talk of steroids and batting averages, but no one suggested he had been either the senator's illegitimate son or his long-time lover.

Jimmy Rivera had died in Arizona, but he was ninety-two at the time of death, so murder seemed unlikely. I moved on.

Two months ago a woman named Carmella Ortez had perished in a house fire in her home in Baton Rouge. She'd been a Rivera before her marriage and subsequent divorce, but there must be thousands of Riveras on the Gulf Coast. I was scrolling dismissively downward when a photo snagged my attention.

A dark-haired woman was smiling at the photographer. Standing beside her, arm wrapped around her back, was a Latino demigod.

I glanced down at the caption, read the words, and felt my heart thump to a stop in my chest.

Miguel Geraldo Rivera, it read.

17

It's not what you know, it's who you sleep with.

—*The Magnificent Mandy*

ON THE FOLLOWING DAY I focused on my clients as best I could, but sometimes their problems seemed a little less pressing than my own.

Micky Goldenstone was one of the exceptions.

He sat on my couch, elbows on his knees, hands clasped. He had wide palms, shiny nails, and the lean, hungry look of a fighter.

"So, Micky," I said, and prepared for battle, "how was work this week?"

He brought his gaze to mine. Passion was running wild in his eyes. "The kid's seven."

I debated pretending ignorance, but why pretend when reality is so handy?

"Kaneasha's child," I said.

He jerked to his feet. "He's in the first grade. Or should be." He paced toward my lone window, body language growling.

"Have you spoken to her?"

I wasn't sure if he heard me.

"Name's Jamel. Lives in Lynwood with his aunt."

I said nothing. Micky would talk when he felt ready. "Don't know where his mama is. The sister—Lavonn—I remember her from the old neighborhood. Not pretty like Kaneasha." He stopped. Silence ticked off seconds.

"Does Lavonn know who the father is?"

He said nothing. Time echoed along.

"Do you think—"

"Didn't really seem like something I could ask," he said abruptly, and faced me. "Hey, this is Pitt from the hood. I raped your sister about the time she got knocked up. You think the kid's mine?"

"He may not be," I said, tone carefully steady.

He closed his eyes. I settled in for another silence, but he spoke in a moment. "Got ears like damn propellers."

Micky's were small and flat against his skull. I didn't make mention.

"Where did you see him?"

"Drove by Lavonn's house."

"Are you sure it was him?"

"He's got the ears."

I opened my mouth.

"My mother was a . . ." He paused, gritted his teeth, glanced toward the ceiling. "She taped my ears down when I was a baby. Taped 'em to my skull so they wouldn't stick out like a damn chinchilla's." He closed his eyes. Anger danced in his dark jaw. "Nobody even cared enough to tape his ears down," he said, and suddenly he was crying.

The remainder of the day went just about as well.

I discovered that I had gained another pound. I was still peeing in distant locales, and, if the truth be told, I still had no idea how or if Carmella Ortez fit into the big picture.

By the time I reached home, I was exhausted. There's nothing like a day of sitting on your ass, followed by a climate-controlled ride home, to really take it out of a girl, but a bowl of Häagen-Dazs revived me. Glucose disguised as a dairy product. Can't beat it.

Duly rejuvenated, I printed up photos of Carmella, Kathy, and Emanuel.

At one time or another they all had ties to Senator Rivera, and all died in some bizarre circumstances. Okay, maybe the deaths weren't all *that* bizarre, but none of the deceased lived a particularly high-risk life and all had died in unusual ways: Kathy Baltimore had been dismembered by a machine she was familiar with and usually kept shielded. Manny Casero—an excellent swimmer, according to Mac—had drowned. And Carmella Ortez had died in a house fire. Granted, fires could ignite anywhere, but according to the almighty Internet, Baton Rouge was the sixth wettest city in the United States, so it wasn't as if the region was plagued by prairie fires. That added her death to the *rather unlikely* category in my mind. On the other hand, why would anyone want to kill any of them? The question was burning a hole in my head.

I picked up the phone before I could stop myself. The senator himself answered on the second ring.

"Christina." His voice was like liquid sex. "It is good to hear your voice." I was never certain how to talk to liquid sex.

"Do you have a minute?"

"For you I have several."

I took a deep breath. "I'd like to ask you a few questions."

"Regarding?"

"Acquaintances from your past."

There was a long note of silence, then: "Christina, I want you to refrain from delving into this. Indeed, after some deliberation I realized that I was—"

"I cashed the check," I blurted. Despite my capitalistic bent and aspirations for larceny, I felt guilty as hell, but the SuperSeptic guys were demanding money if I wanted them to continue annihilating my yard.

"Good. I am glad," he said. "Consider it a gift. If one cannot give a small token of—"

"Do you remember a Carmella Ortez?"

The line went quiet, then: "She was a distant cousin. Why do you ask?"

"Do you know how she died?"

"What are you getting at, Christina?"

"Fatal house fires are pretty uncommon, especially on the Gulf Coast." And as far as I could tell, the cause of hers had been undetermined. "Less than fifty a year in Louisiana. I checked."

"Luck is a fickle mistress."

"And seems to be in short supply for your kith and kin. Did Carmella smoke?"

"I beg your pardon?"

"Cigarettes are the number-one cause of house fires in the United States."

"Christina—"

"Your son and I are no longer seeing each other, Senator," I blurted.

"I don't know what that has to do—"

"So there's no reason for me not to delve into this. Did she smoke?"

"I am certain he will come to his senses in time. He—"

"Did she smoke?" I repeated.

He sighed. "Carmella's mother's name was Inez. It means 'chaste' in my native tongue. A chaste woman did not go to church with her head uncovered. She did not take the Lord's name in vain, and she did not smoke. Violators were known to have their mouths cleansed with soap."

"It happens," I said, remembering my own sudsy childhood.

"Inez had her own recipe made from animal fat and lye."

I considered that fact but secretly doubted the use of Dove made the process a hell of a lot more pleasant. "So Carmella *didn't* smoke," I deduced.

"No."

"How do you account for the fire, then?"

He was silent for a moment, perhaps thinking. Perhaps wondering which hit man to hire to get rid of me. "Carmella had a fondness for candles," he said finally. "Perhaps one of them tipped."

Some half-forgotten thought niggled at my mind.

"Candles?" I said.

"Yes. During my first senatorial term she bought a little bungalow in Baton Rouge so as to be close to her Priscilla."

"Priscilla?"

"Her daughter. I visited once. The dining room was filled with light. I remember thinking it quite lovely. Sometimes the old ways—"

Something clicked in my head. "What color were the candles?"

There was a pause. "It was a long while ago, Christina."

"Uh-huh. What colors do you remember?"

"I believe they might have been purple."

"Purple?" My shoulders slumped as my slippery theories washed away.

"At least that is how they appeared to me with the flame shining through the melting wax. Carma had a flare for the dramatic."

"Carma?"

"That is what we called her when—"

"Could they have been black?"

"What?"

"The candles. Could they have been black?"

"Perhaps. And I believe there was a white one. They were in a circle with the light—"

"I'll talk to you later," I said, and hung up.

I scribbled *Wiccan, lesbian,* and *alcoholic* on a scrap of paper, then sat in silent thought. Was there a trend, or was I trying too hard? And if there was a trend, did anyone else know about it?

I went back to the computer and continued my search for bizarre deaths, then wrote down anything my convoluted little mind could possibly connect to the Riveras. After that I paced and stared at the phone like it was a viper, but finally I reached for it.

"Officer Tavis."

I tightened my grip on the receiver and wondered, not for the first time, if there was something congenitally wrong with me. "Yes, this is Christina McMullen."

There was a momentary pause, then: "Ms. McMullen." I

could hear him settling into his chair like a contented house cat. "How's life in the big city?"

"Fine," I said, voice cool enough to thrill a nun. "I was wondering if I could ask you a couple of questions."

"I'm not wearing any."

"What?"

"Underwear," he explained.

I scowled, partly at him and partly at my own rapidly deteriorating thoughts, but I frosted my voice and spoke clearly. "Are you and I living in the same century?"

"Not sure. What century are you in?"

"The one where police officers are routinely indicted for sexual harassment."

He laughed. "Call me old-fashioned," he said.

I rolled my eyes. "Who knew that Kathy Baltimore was gay?"

"Why do you want to know?"

"Curiosity."

"You know what I'm curious about?"

"Whether or not a cop can get the electric chair for inappropriate behavior?"

He chuckled. "Have dinner with me," he said.

"No."

"Please?"

"No."

"I'll give you my solemn vow not to perform oral sex."

I squirmed in my seat. "And I thought you were irrepressible."

"I'm a man of principle."

"Obviously. Who was aware of Baltimore's sexual orientation?"

"I'm free tomorrow night."

"I'm not."

"I won't even kiss your cheek."

"Seriously! What is wrong with you?"

"I haven't had a date in five months."

"That's probably because you're a pervert."

"It's because I have very strict rules."

"No oral sex with women you've never met?"

"I don't date women from Kern County."

"How big is Kern County?"

"Eight thousand one hundred and seventy-two square miles."

"What do you mean by date?"

"The usual definition."

"No copulating on the mayor's desk?"

"No sex. No necking. No movies. They can't even sit in my car unless they're in the backseat."

"You're lying."

"I wish I were. I'm horny as hell. I won't even shake your hand unless you shake first."

"Still lying."

"Won't even speak unless spoken to first."

"Officer—"

"I'll answer every question you have, unless prohibited by law."

I could feel myself weakening. "Just dinner?"

"Unless you fill out a legal affidavit requesting more."

I felt itchy and a little too warm, but I stayed firmly on my high horse. "If you're lying, I swear I'll sue Kern County for every hummingbird it owns."

"Tomorrow night. Seven o'clock. Your house," he said.

"I don't divulge my home address," I said.

He laughed and hung up.

18

Dating is like nightfall—there's got to be a mourning after.

—Chrissy McMullen,
clever to a fault

I'M GOING TO FAX OVER a list of names," I said. It was nine o'clock in the morning. My first client had yet to arrive. "I want you to give each of them due consideration, then tell me if anything rings a bell."

"I'm quite busy today," said the senator.

"Me, too," I said. I had a full client list, then I had to shoot myself in the head for agreeing to date another cop. "But people are dying, Senator, and it's not going to look good for your political future if the press attaches their deaths to you."

"I'll see what I can do," he said.

"Don't do me any favors," I quipped, sassy as hell, but he had already hung up.

Twelve seconds later Shirley rapped on my office door and stuck her head in. "There's someone here who wants to see you."

Unsavory images ran through my mind. Generally when people show up unannounced at my office, screaming commences. Sometimes there's blood. Once there was a dead guy with a hard-on. L.A., always exciting. "I'm sorry," I said, pushing the nightmares behind me. "I'm swamped right now. Ask them to make an appointment, please."

She stepped inside and closed the door behind her. "I'll get rid of her if you like, but my gut says you're gonna want to see her."

I scowled. My visitor was a woman. That meant she was 5.6 times less likely to kill me than a man. "What's her name?"

"She wouldn't say."

"Then—" I began, but at that moment the someone knocked on my door.

I snapped my gaze to the offending portal. Maybe there was fear in my eyes, because Shirley's jaw was set like a slandered pugilist's. She turned toward the door, took the knob in one meaty hand, and pulled it open a few scant inches. "I am sorry," she said. Her voice, I noticed, didn't sound sorry at all. More gritty. Kind of guttural. A little deadly. Have I mentioned my love for Shirley? "But Ms. McMullen is busy just now. If you'd like to—"

"You must be new here." The voice had a strange, halting accent and was dimly familiar. "Tell her royalty has arrived."

Shirley stepped outside, apparently crowding the

princess in front of her. "Listen, I don't care if you're the queen of Sheba. Ms. McMullen is—"

The visitor laughed. And then it hit me.

"Laney?" I said, and stood up.

"You must be Shirley," Elaine said, voice back to normal.

"And who—" Shirley began, but I burst onto the scene like a heat-seeking missile.

"Laney!" I said again, and she zoomed in for a rib-cracking hug. "What are you doing here?"

"I told you I was coming home."

"Not 'til tomorrow."

She laughed, ridiculously beautiful with her face unadorned and her strawberry-blond waves gone wild. "We got done shooting early," she said, and even though she was smiling, I knew she'd been worried about me. It made me feel kind of warm and sappy, but I squelched the unmanly emotions and made introductions.

"Laney, this is Shirley. Shirley—"

"You the Amazon Queen?" Shirley asked. There was suspicion in her eyes and dire consequences in her tone, but Laney ducked in and hugged her, too.

"I'm so glad you're here," she said, leaning back and gazing into the other's eyes.

"It's just temporary," Shirley said, but Laney smiled.

"We'll see. How's it going?" she asked.

"Business is good. A little—" I began, but Shirley interrupted.

"She nervous," she said.

"About?"

"Girl's got problems."

"The kind that'll get her killed?" Laney asked.

Shirley shrugged her massive shoulders. "She don't say much. Thinks she the rock of Gibraltar or something."

"Sometimes you can guilt her into—"

"I can hear you, you know," I said.

Laney laughed, then turned and hugged me again. She smelled like apple pie, kind of cinnamony and melty and perfect. "I don't have much time," she said. "I'm going to surprise Jeen."

I kept my fingernails from curling into my palms. J. D. Solberg is a hair-challenged little dweeb to whom I had introduced Laney some months ago. He's a certified genius, carries more money in his pocket than the whole McMullen clan has ever *made,* and is nowhere near good enough for Elaine Butterfield. But I managed to keep my opinions to myself.

"How long are you home for?"

"Just a couple of days."

We had only a few minutes together, but by the time she left I felt as if I'd been showered in lilac water. Like the world might not collapse around my shivering ears.

It was nearly five o'clock before I realized my so-called date with Officer Tavis was going to interfere with Laney's homecoming. She dropped back into the clinic just as I picked up the receiver to call her. Solberg—better known (to himself) as the Geek God—was at her side, grinning like a lower primate.

"Hey, we're going to Buddha's for dinner," Laney said. "Want to come?"

I refrained from clearing my throat. It wasn't that I didn't want to watch Solberg drool over Laney while I ruminated bean sprouts and lentils, but . . . "I'm afraid I'm busy."

"Do you have a date?" Laney asked.

"No."

"An undate?"

"Just a . . . meeting."

"With a man?"

"Ummm . . . kind of."

"Well . . ." Solberg was holding her hand and *still* grinning like a primate. "Rivera can come, too."

"I—" I began, but Laney interrupted.

"It's not Rivera."

"Not Rivera?" The grin disappeared from his monkey face. "You kidding me? You're stepping out on the lieutenant? Does he know? Have you done it before? Are you sure—"

Laney squeezed his hand. He fell into monkey silence.

"I'm sorry," she said.

I shrugged. I don't know how she knew about the falling out between Rivera and me, but she knew. I knew she knew, and she knew I knew she knew. It was freaky, but one can become accustomed to the freakiest of things if given enough time. Murder attempts generally being the exception.

"Well . . ." Solberg was temporarily stymied. "You could bring the other guy." He blinked. He'd traded in his glasses for a pair of contacts, at least while in Laney's presence, but he still managed to make it appear as if he were gazing through the bottom of Coke bottles. "It is a guy, right?"

I gave him a look. Laney was watching me like a falcon.

"You sure this is a good idea, Mac?"

No. "Sure," I said. "Rivera and I were never serious."

Except maybe the time he threatened to incarcerate me.

That was as serious as hemorrhoids. Or the time he accused me of murder. Or the time in the bathroom when he kissed my neck and I was within breathing distance of climbing him like a coconut tree.

"He could come, too," Solberg repeated, apparently reassured that I had remained on the hetero side of life, but Laney hugged me.

"Don't do anything stupid," she said.

"I'm insulted."

"I mean it," she warned, and after assuring me she'd see me on the following day, she left with Solberg trailing along like an inebriated puppy.

"That Laney, she's something else," Shirley said as I pulled my purse strap onto my shoulder and prepared to depart.

"Yeah," I sighed. "I know."

"And my Mandy . . ." She scowled as if confused by the complexities of the universe. "She took over Laney's job here?"

"Uh-huh."

"I'm sorry," she said, and left me to my misery.

I was all business when Officer Tavis arrived at my house. He was spot on time. Not a second early, not a second late. I was dressed all in black, barely an inch of skin visible below my clavicle. My slacks were creased down the front and classily cuffed. My jacket was stylish, my blouse buttoned up past respectable and well into the frigid zone.

"Hi," I said.

He stood on my stoop, looking clean-cut, wearing a pair of camel dress pants and a cinnamon button-down shirt with short sleeves. The hairs on his forearms sparkled like gold in the sunlight, matched to perfection by the hair on his head, which was parted just so and freshly shorn to a boyish but attractive cut.

"Hello," he said, and grinned just a little.

I didn't grin back. This was a business meeting and nothing else. "Did you have any trouble finding me?" I asked, ignoring the fact that I hadn't given him my address.

"Still a cop," he said, and ushered me down the stairs without touching my back, according to our agreement. I was hardly disappointed at all.

He drove a late-model Hyundai. It was a relatively modest car but still had my Saturn beat all to hell, unless you figure gas mileage. Which, at four bucks a gallon, I do. All the time.

We ate at a place called Fat Frankie's. I liked the sound of it. Not a bean sprout in sight. He ordered a rusty nail. I ordered a lemonade. If I was any more mature I'd have to reserve my plot at Whispering Pines.

I was perusing my artery-clogging options when I felt him staring at me over the top of the menu. His eyes were laughing.

"Out of sackcloth?" he asked. "Or just don't believe in pigment?"

I tugged down my jacket and gave him a prim glance. "I didn't want to give you the wrong impression."

"Then you're not in mourning?"

"I usually wait until *after* the date," I said.

He chuckled. The sound wasn't unpleasant. I had to remind myself that something wasn't quite as it should be. For instance, cops are supposed to be mean sons of bitches. What was wrong with him? "If you think a little black is going to discourage me, you've forgotten how long I've been celibate."

"You promised—" I began, and he laughed.

"Hands off," he said, and held them up as if to show that they were, indeed, not on my person.

I closed my menu, though I hadn't really decided between the heart-attack T-bone or the instant-stroke prime rib.

"About Ms. Baltimore—" I began, but he interrupted.

"What's your IQ?"

I paused. "I beg your pardon?"

"I was wondering if your IQ is equivalent to your looks."

"I don't even know what that means."

"There's a rating scale."

Our drinks arrived. I took a sip. "Please tell me there's not."

"If your IQ matches your looks, that'd put you in the forget-everything-you-learned-from-your-shoot-yourself-in-the-head-divorce-and-beg-her-to-bear-your-children range."

As compliments went, that wasn't bad, but I just straightened primly. *I* had learned not to trust cops. "Thank you, I think," I said, "but you agreed to answer my questions."

He lifted his hands again. They were still not on my person. "Fire away."

I didn't particularly like his phraseology. Sometimes folks really did "fire away." Have I told you about the dead guy with the hard-on?

"How much did you know about her?" I asked.

He shrugged. His shoulders were broad. If I cared about that sort of thing, my spine would have been melting just about then. I straightened with an effort and reminded myself that these days I was mostly impressed with men who didn't try to kill me. I had yet to determine whether Officer Tavis was among those revered few.

"It's a small town," he said.

"And?"

"And I'm pretty thorough. Not to mention intelligent. Ask me about *my* IQ."

"Just the facts," I said, and he smiled.

"Her name was Kathleen Kay Baltimore. Born March twenty-seventh, 1958. Maiden name Schultz. One child, a daughter named Jessica, age twenty-four. She was divorced from Mr. Kevin Myron Baltimore on May 7, 2000. Bought her home on Parsley Street five years ago and died November twenty-seventh. Cause of death determined to be loss of blood, but the autopsy showed there may have been an undetected heart condition."

That was a lot of facts to remember without crib notes. What *was* his IQ?

The waitress appeared. After an elongated moment of agony, I ordered the prime rib with a salad instead of soup. I was pretty sure that would bring my caloric intake out of the spontaneous-obesity range.

Officer Tavis ordered the salmon, lightly crusted, accompanied by a lean Caesar salad.

He smiled when we were left alone. "I'm intelligent *and* health conscious."

"If you weren't a sex addict, that would almost be impressive," I said, a little miffed that he had out-matured me.

He laughed. "If I were a sex addict, I'd have died of withdrawal four months ago."

I couldn't help but smile, so I took another sip of lemonade to cover for it. "What did you know about Ms. Baltimore on a more personal level?"

He sighed. There was something in his eyes. A little sadness certainly. But was there guilt, too? I scoured his face.

"Pretty. Ambitious. Tough. Kindhearted."

Wow. "Sounds like you were infatuated."

"I think everyone was a little bit smitten."

"Smitten?"

He grinned. "My mother read gothic romance novels."

"Out loud?"

"She was a big influence on me."

"How so?"

He smiled again. "I thought we were talking about Kathy."

I was appalled at myself. I wasn't interested in this guy! Yes, he was good-looking and intelligent and funny, but he was liable to wind up in jail soon for sexual misconduct, and I wanted no part of that. "Of course. Thank you." I smoothed my jacket. "Why was everyone smitten?"

He glanced toward the bar. The stools had long wooden legs and brown fringed cushions. None was un-occupied.

"Seven months ago Arty Netz thought it'd be a good idea to run his crotch rocket into Mrs. Parker's retaining wall. Town had a spaghetti dinner and silent auction to help pay hospital bills. Kathy donated a dining-room set. Solid oak with matching chairs. All handmade."

"Furniture? That's what it takes to smite a whole town?"

"We're easy in Edmond Park."

"Something I noticed upon our first meeting."

He grinned and raised his drink. "Every school bake sale, she'd donate one of those tier cakes. She used to decorate for some fancy restaurant in L.A."

"Do you know which one?"

"I didn't think that was going to be part of the foreplay."

I gave him a look. "We agreed there wouldn't be any foreplay."

"I thought you'd change your mind when you saw my manly arms."

He *did* have manly arms, but I didn't say as much. "What else do you know about her?"

"She made regular donations to the church."

"Which church?"

"All of them."

"A good Christian woman, then."

He tilted his head and said nothing.

"No?"

"If she was affiliated with any religion, I didn't know about it."

I thought about that for a minute. "Did she ever say anything about the time she spent campaigning for Senator Rivera?"

"Not to me."

"To whom, then?"

He shrugged. "Sometimes folks would visit her from out of town."

"Any names that you can remember?"

"Did I mention my IQ?"

I made a face. "Names."

"There was a guy named Cal Bentley who came a couple times a year."

"Anyone else?"

"Believe it or not, I have a few other things to do than to catalog the comings and goings of Edmond Park's citizenry."

"Yeah?" Our meals arrived. I refrained from inhaling mine like a hippo on an alligator and instead made a decisive yet ladylike incision into the meat. "Like what?"

He tasted a bite of his saffron rice. "Sometimes Miss Mable's cat gets caught in her cottonwood tree."

"I thought that was a job for the fire department."

"We draw straws."

Okay, so he was good-looking, tall, and self-effacing, but I didn't care about that sort of thing. I tasted the prime rib and felt my salivary glands light up like Roman candles. "Why'd you choose the police force?" I asked.

He smiled. "Mom said women liked men in uniform. Why psychology?"

I considered lying. "There are a lot of nut-jobs. I thought it would be a lucrative field."

He laughed. "Not enough crazies in Schaumburg?"

I stopped eating long enough to really look at him. He had laughing eyes, but there was something solid and hard behind them. "You must be short of cats," I said.

He gave me a look.

"You've got an awful lot of time to check up on innocent people."

"Like you?"

"That *is* who I was referring to."

"I never considered that your previous place of residence might be a secret."

I let it go with some difficulty. "How did your mother influence you, besides the penchant for using antiquated words and flashing badges?"

He shrugged. "I got her eyes."

"What'd you get from your dad?"

"Not much," he said, but something sparked in his aforementioned eyes. "How about you?"

"How about me what?" I wanted to follow up about his dad but reminded myself I wasn't there to learn about him.

"You left your family two thousand miles behind. What's that all about?"

I tasted my salad. It needed more dressing, but I refrained from dumping the remainder of the little pitcher onto the lettuce. Go, me. "I couldn't help them."

He stared at me a moment, then laughed. The sound was soothing somehow. "Too crazy?" he asked.

"The prognosis was grim."

"Well..." He glanced toward the hostess. She was rather attractive, if you like the tall, blond, so-pretty-it-makes-your-eyes-water type, but he didn't quite seem to notice. "It's not uncommon."

"Anyone specific in your family?" I asked.

He brought his gaze back to mine, smiled a little. "How do you feel about multiple partners?" he asked.

I gave him a look that should have withered any possibility of future offspring. "I believe we had an agreement."

"Temporary insanity. How's the beef?"

I dabbed my mouth primly with the napkin. "Very nice."

He'd eaten all his salad but was neglecting his salmon. "Are you gay?" he asked.

"What?"

He watched me, but if he was mocking me I couldn't feel it. In fact, it almost seemed that there was admiration in his eyes. "You're either uninterested or damn unlucky."

"What are you talking about?"

"You would have been married years ago if you wanted to be," he said. "Not all men are assholes, Chrissy."

I blinked at him, considered disagreeing, and decided against it. "Anyone you know?"

He glanced away for a second. Maybe there was a moment of tension on his face. "You'd probably do well to avoid police officers."

"Meaning you?"

"Actually, I was talking about Lieutenant Rivera, but now that I say it, I see how you could have misunderstood my meaning."

The waitress had delivered the check in its little plastic notebook. He stuck a credit card in it and handed it back.

"It was a reach," I said.

"I'm pretty straightforward," he said. "I like sex—if I remember correctly I like it quite a bit. I mean . . . I like women in general, but . . . I'm not looking for a relationship."

"Why not?"

He paused for a second before answering. "My ex liked sex, too. Only not so much with me as with others."

"Oh." I watched him. Something flittered through his eyes. "I'm sorry."

His lips twitched up. "Sorry enough to sleep with me?"

I ignored the question. "How long were you married?"

"Five years. I thought they were pretty good years. I mean, we weren't dancing on rooftops or anything but . . ."

He shrugged. "We weren't crying in the cellar, either. At least not enough for her to cheat on me."

"With whom?"

He thought about that for a second, face solemn. "I don't think there were any goats involved."

"Always a relief."

He looked at me and laughed. "This Rivera—is he blind or just damn stupid?" he asked, and there was something in his voice that made me feel a little soupy.

"Could be a little of both." I stood up. He stood up beside me. I'm tall. He was taller. Despite everything I've learned about men and women and life in general, I can't help but think that taller's better.

"There's a lot of stupid going around," he said, and looked down into my eyes.

He was standing pretty close. Not touching, but close enough so I could feel the heat of his arm. We had enough celibacy between us to commit a felony.

"I brought that affidavit if you've changed your mind," he said.

"Affidavit?" I sounded a little breathless, a little disoriented, a whole lot crazy.

"The one that says you'd like to have sex with me."

I was staring at him. His arms were handsomely muscled and lightly tanned. His chest was broad and his chin dimpled. He was a Ken doll with audio.

"Say you want to have sex with me," he urged.

"I—" I began, but then I felt something. A spark so fierce it jerked at something deep inside me. I turned like a broken puppet, only to find that Lieutenant Jack Rivera was standing not five feet away.

19

When blondes have more fun, do they know it?

—*Brainy Laney Butterfield,*
who happens to be blond

SILENCE THRUMMED AROUND US, and suddenly it felt as if everyone else in the world had been sucked into oblivion. Rivera took a step toward me, and I, like a fly drawn to sticky paper, took a step toward him.

Feelings bubbled like boiling tar through me. Memories buzzed along my tittering nerve endings. And each of them featured Rivera. In some of them he was wearing clothes. In all of them he was touching me, burning me with his hands, branding me with his eyes.

"Jack," someone said, but the voice seemed to come from a long way away. "Jack," she said again, louder now and whinier. He halted on a teetering step.

I stopped.

"Jack honey." We turned our heads in unison. The woman who tugged at his sleeve was blond, petite, and cute enough to be in a pet-store window.

"Our table's ready." She had a voice vaguely reminiscent of a certain cartoon mouse. "We have to go."

The world stood frozen, waiting, and then Officer Tavis spoke. "You must be Lieutenant Rivera."

We stared at my undate in unbreathing tandem.

He was smiling tentatively and extending his broad hand. Rivera did neither. Instead, he turned back toward me, eyes as sharp as a cobra's. But the searing passion was gone, replaced by a thousand watts of frustration and contempt and another dozen emotions I could neither read nor catalog. "Making up for lost time, McMullen?" he rumbled.

My heart was pounding like a runaway broomtail. "Rivera," I breathed. My voice sounded funny, like something from a crackly old movie, too melodramatic to be taken seriously.

Still, he almost moved toward me. I could sense it in the tightness of his jaw, in the snap of his eyes, but finally he fisted a hand and exhaled.

"Feeding him first to keep up his strength?" he asked. His eyes were flat now, his tone the same.

Minnie Mouse had linked her arm through his. She looked proprietary and cocky and bleached to the bone. Inexplicable anger coursed through me like lava in a lamp. "Rent A Blonde still open?" I asked.

He scoured Tavis's long form. "Least I didn't have to pay by the inch."

"Officer Tavis happens to be a respected—"

"Officer!" he snorted, and threw back his head and laughed.

I'm not sure what happened next. One moment I was standing there like a relatively sane human being and then I was torpedoing forward without any kind of lucid plan in my head. But in that instant Tavis grabbed me around the waist and snagged me back to his side.

I think I heard him swear.

"Let me go." My voice sounded a little rabid.

Tavis's sounded like he was speaking to something that slavered. "Not 'til you calm down." His lips were very close to my ear.

Rivera stared at me for another heart-pounding second, then turned and walked away, Minnie on his arm.

"Chrissy?"

"I'm calm," I rasped.

"And I'm the king of Albania. Come on," Tavis ordered, and prodded me toward the door. For a couple of seconds I'm afraid I might have actually tried to break away—kind of like a pit bull on a short leash. But eventually we were outside. Past the ogling diners. Past the stunned hostess. The air felt cool against my hot cheeks. Tavis tucked me into his car, touching the top of my head like they do on *Cops* when the perp is safely handcuffed and subsequently packed into the backseat for safekeeping. At least I was up front like one of the big kids who can be trusted with a radio and sharp objects.

We sat in silence for a long time. I could feel him staring at me. In fact, I was pretty sure I could hear him thinking, *What the hell* . . .

"What the hell?" he said finally, tone amazed and, maybe, if he had a sick-ass sense of humor, a little amused.

I closed my eyes and tried to block out the hideously fresh memories. They were like a broken reel, running circles in my head. "Tell me, Officer Tavis," I said, voice blessedly calm, "do you happen to own a handgun?"

"I *am* a cop," he said.

I nodded, seeing the logic. "Would you mind shooting me?"

He chuckled, sat for a while longer, and finally started up the car.

We pulled smoothly out of the parking lot onto the cross street. Traffic buzzed past. I watched the cars, maybe fascinated by their progress, maybe too embarrassed to face another human being for as long as I lived.

"Sorry about touching you," he said.

I didn't respond.

"But I was afraid you were going to kill him." He paused, reflecting on that. "Or . . . something."

I wished a little dimly that *I* had a gun, although, if the truth be told, I wasn't really sure what I would do with it. I have a pretty strong sense of self-preservation. If I owned a handgun I was more likely to shoot Rivera than myself, and, if I remember correctly, there's a fairly stiff penalty for killing an officer of the law.

"Want to tell me about it?" he asked, and glanced across the plush seat covering toward me.

"I'd rather shove a hot fork up my—" I took a careful breath, found a little bit of sanity. "I'd rather not. Thank you."

I could sense him grinning but didn't feel quite prepared to look at him. Anger and I don't get on well, and I was pretty sure that my rage could, fairly easily, be transferred from one cop to another.

"Shall I assume it's not over between you two?" he asked.

"Oh . . ." I felt extremely tired suddenly. "It's over."

"So you don't care about him anymore?"

I think I shook my head.

"I see. Do you always make that sound when you see someone you don't care about?"

I still didn't bother to look at him. "I didn't make a sound."

"Uh-huh . . . It was kind of like a wild animal in pain." He thought for a minute. "Or maybe a dog in—"

I snapped my gaze to his.

He cleared his throat and faced forward. "Well, you're not a dull date, Christina McMullen. I'll give you that."

I let my eyes fall closed and took a fortifying breath. "I'm sorry," I said, and he laughed.

"It's all right. Things were getting a little slow at the station."

I sighed. "Glad to lend you grist for the gossip mill."

He pulled up to my curb, turned the car off, and faced me. "I don't not kiss and tell, Chrissy."

I stared at him. He was really good-looking, and he seemed like a nice guy. Though, truth to tell, I generally don't have the capacity to differentiate a nice guy from a serial killer. It's something of a character flaw in a licensed psychologist. And in a woman who hopes for continued survival.

"So what's going on with you two?" he asked.

I tried to stay silent, but he had the kind of eyes you talk to. "We just . . . We're like hairspray and a pack of Camels. Everything's going along fine. You're feeling good, made-up, coiffed, having yourself a smoke, then suddenly—poof, your beehive's gone up in flame."

"You ever . . ." He paused, perhaps searching for terms that wouldn't make me rip out his throat. "Have you been intimate with him?"

"Intimate!" I think I guffawed. I might have chortled. And I may have hacked up a hairball. "No one's *intimate* with Rivera."

He nodded. "Okay. You screw him?"

I took a deep breath. Glanced out my window and shook my head. "Never quite got around to that, either."

"Maybe you should."

I snapped my attention back to his. He shrugged.

"Get it out of your system," he said.

I shook my head slowly.

"Or . . ." he suggested. "For the right incentive I might be willing to sacrifice myself and play replacement. You know, for the well-being of your obviously deranged psyche."

This didn't seem like a likely time to laugh, and yet I did. The tension went out of my body. My shoulders slumped. I dropped my head back on the rest behind me. "What the hell is wrong with me?"

"Well . . ." He let out a breath, sounding as if he'd been holding it for a while. "I've got two guesses. Want to hear them?"

I didn't look at him. "No."

"You're either horny . . ."

I rolled my face toward him, eyes deadly flat.

He grinned. "Or you're in love."

I blinked. "I was planning to be insulted by the horny comment, but now I'm torn."

"You still saying you have no feelings for him?"

"Would you believe it if I really threw myself into selling it?"

"Well . . ." He glanced forward, tapping rhythmically on the steering wheel. "You two looked kind of *Animal Planet*. The lion and the wildebeest."

"Am I the lion or the wildebeest?"

"Could go either way."

I closed my eyes. "Have I apologized yet?"

"Yeah, but if you're really sorry, you could make it up to me by—"

"I'm not going to sleep with you."

He chuckled, then sighed. "Is that why you're doing this?"

"Doing what?"

"Scratching at the Baltimore case. Is it to impress him?"

I thought about that for a second. "Actually, that's why he's not speaking to me."

He thought for a moment, then nodded. "He wants you to stay out of it. Police business and all that."

"We have history."

"Any of it good?"

"Not much."

"But he's under your skin."

"Did you guess that intuitively?"

He laughed, tapped the steering wheel again, then went sober. "I got a call from the governor."

I turned toward him, mind shifting gears. "About Baltimore?"

He held my gaze. "About meth houses."

I shook my head.

"He said we've got to concentrate all our efforts on

cracking down on the meth labs. That he made a promise to his constituents."

My mind was churning. "Do you think he wants to make sure you don't look into Baltimore's death?"

He didn't respond, but his expression said that I'd guessed right for once. "Meth's a big problem in the rural areas."

"You don't think her death was an accident."

"Two kids died just last summer." He looked through the windshield. "We shut down the operation. But they keep springing up. Ammonia's easy to come by on the farm. They're just kids. Bored. Confused. Things happen. Even if it's not in L.A."

So he'd been warned off the case and he was going to comply. "Was it her husband? Do you think he was involved?"

He sighed, shook his head. "Truth is, I don't think he has the balls for it."

"Someone else, then."

"There was no forced entry. No sign of a struggle."

"So it was someone she knew. You said she had a lot of friends in Edmond Park."

"Look elsewhere."

I watched him. "Because you don't want a black mark on your little piece of paradise?"

"I'm good at my job, Christina."

"And you don't want to lose it."

"I can do some good here. If you get the kids early enough, you can sometimes save them."

"And Kathy Baltimore doesn't matter."

For a moment I thought he'd defend himself, but he didn't. "Set up a timeline," he said.

"What?"

"Lay out the facts. Give yourself lots of space. Use everything you know. How, when, where. Look for a pattern."

"You're not going to try to stop me?"

He chuckled. "Shit, if Rivera can't stop you, I don't have a chance in hell."

"You could try."

"If I did, would you—"

"No sex," I said, then: "Maybe you're covering for Baltimore's husband."

He didn't respond.

"Are you?" I asked. "Is that—"

"I know a monster when I see one."

I narrowed my eyes. "What are you talking about?"

"My old man . . ." He paused. "Mom was lucky to survive."

"He beat her."

"Whenever he was drunk. Which was usually." His throat constricted. He took a deep breath, seemed to clear his head. "And I . . . I kind of fell through the cracks. That's not going to happen to the kids in Edmond Park."

I nodded. I believed him. Maybe I was naïve, but it seemed unlikely after all this time. "Well . . . it's been—"

"Damn entertaining," he said, and chuckled, mood seemingly restored by the time I exited the car.

20

I believe my father may have been born during low
tide of the gene pool.

—D, a self-made gangster

I BOUGHT POSTER BOARD at an office-supply store
larger than most third-world countries, removed the
seascapes from the wall of my office at home, and pinned
up the overgrown paper instead. After that I taped up the
pictures of the three victims and wrote their stats beneath
their photos, per Tavis's suggestions. I wrote *lesbian* under
Kathy's pic, *alcoholic* under Manny's, and *Wiccan* under
Carmella's. Next I dragged my checkbook out of my
purse, squinted at the microcalendar on the back, and
noted the dates of their deaths.

They meant nothing to me. But I was in too far to quit
now. I didn't even try to pretend otherwise. Instead, I
picked up the phone.

"Senator." I was gripping the receiver like an undersize linebacker on his first catch.

"Christina." He sounded surprised to hear from me. "It is late. Nothing is wrong, I hope."

Yes, a shitload of things were wrong. I had recently acted like a hormonally charged nut-job, I was obsessed by a case that no one seemed to take seriously, and a man who hadn't had sex for nearly half a year had looked at me with pity in his eyes. Pity!

"Did you get a chance to look over the list of names I sent you?"

"Christina . . ." He sounded exasperated and a little tired. People have been sounding like that since the day I learned to say "candy." "As I have told you, there is no need for you to go to this trouble. The deaths are a terrible tragedy. But I have discussed them with several experts in the field. They all agree that this is nothing but a coincidence."

Then why had he originally asked me to look into it? And why would he later insist that I stay out of it? The sneaky part of me that understood men like the senator suggested that he wanted me on the case while he officially stated that he wanted no such thing. Maybe to cover his ass if his son became irate. Maybe for reasons even the sneaky part of me couldn't understand.

"Was the governor one of them?"

"What?"

"Did you ask the governor to make sure Kathy's death wasn't investigated further?"

There was a pause. "I would have little reason to do so."

"Is that a no?"

"Yes." His tone was a little frosty.

I mulled that over for a second. "And what about—"

"I've told you all I know," he said. Someone murmured something in the background. It sounded like a woman. "One minute," he murmured back at her. I imagined him carrying the phone into his office as his footsteps echoed on the hardwood. Salina Martinez had died on that hardwood, her face still as perfect as a porcelain doll's.

"I'm sorry. I didn't know you had company," I said.

"An old friend."

For reasons unknown, an image of Thea Altove's stunning baby-doll face popped into my head. I wondered momentarily if I should try to be diplomatic. But I was uncomfortable breaking with tradition. "How old?" I asked.

He paused for a moment. "I have known Teddy for a long while."

I thought about that for a second. "Did he have some sort of unfortunate accident in his formative years?"

"I am not certain I understand what you—"

"His voice sounded pretty high," I explained.

If he found me amusing, he hid it admirably. "He brought his lovely daughter with him. Thea. I believe you may have met her at Caring Hands."

I scowled. I'm a lot of things, but I'm not psychic. So why had I envisioned Thea's shining face?

"Haven't daughters of old friends gotten you in enough trouble already, Senator?" I asked. He had known Salina's father also.

"They wished to see my rancho." His voice was a little cool when he responded. "She is an excellent equestrienne."

I could imagine them together, perfectly dressed in their

Western finery. Despite their age difference, they looked inexplicably right together. I shook the image out of my head. "About the names—"

"I shall be at home tomorrow evening if you feel the need to discuss matters further."

"I'd rather discuss matters now." Patience may be a virtue, but it's not mine. I'm still looking for mine.

"My apologies," he said. "But I will not be rude to my guests."

I squelched the question about whether he would *screw* his guests, and we hung up a moment later.

I felt grubby and tired and in need of a bath. But I had no bath. My current bath was in the next house, which reminded me of Ramla's tears.

I spent the rest of the evening looking into immigration policies but didn't learn much.

The next day sped by like a unicyclist on crack.

My first two appointments were newcomers to my clinic. Always nice to know there were fresh crazies hatching every day. Mr. Lepinski came next, though he didn't have an appointment and he didn't come alone.

"Ms. McMullen." He stepped through my door with his usual temerity, but there was happiness in his eyes. "I'd like you to meet someone."

Coming fully into the room, he motioned a woman in behind him. She was in her mid-thirties, plump, with hair reminiscent of an earlier decade. Her pants were a nondescript beige, as was her blouse. In fact, she was almost invisible. Until she smiled.

"This is Penny," said Mr. Lepinski, and his lips crept into a grin big enough to make his mustache twitch.

She reached out her hand. We shook. "Ms. McMullen . . ."

She cleared her throat. Her eyes were as pale and blue as distant mountains. "I'm sorry to barge in like this."

"No problem," I said. All grown up. "It's nice to meet you."

They sat down side by side, not holding hands but looking like they kind of wanted to. Try as I might, I couldn't really remember feeling like that. Although I had a vague recollection of wanting to rip off men's clothes. And an even clearer recollection of wanting to rip out their hearts.

"I've been wanting to..." She glanced at Lepinski. He was smiling full bore now. It looked strangely natural on his peaked face. "Well, I've been wanting to thank you."

"Thank me?" I settled back in my chair, trying to look intelligent, but it had been another long day.

"Well, yes. The truth is...if you hadn't...if it weren't for you, Howard would have never left his wife. I mean..." She looked appalled by her own words. "Not that I'm a home wrecker or anything."

I had to admit, she didn't look like a home wrecker or anything. She looked kind of like wallpaper.

"But Sheila, she's..." Her brow furrowed. I had an idea it might have been as angry as she could look. "It's not that she's a bad person..." She paused. Her mouth twitched. She switched her gaze to Lepinski. "Well...you know what...she kind of is," she murmured.

And I liked her immediately.

By the time they left, I was a little in love, but I refrained from giving Lepinski a high five. Instead, I told Penny, "I'm so glad you stopped by." I planned to say something equally acceptable to Lepinski, but instead I just waggled my eyebrows at him. He looked momentarily shocked, then grinned deliriously, ducked his head, and followed her outside.

It was the highlight of my day.

Knowing I would be seeing the senator that evening, I called Laney and asked to have lunch, but Solberg, forever selfish with her time, had already snagged that meal. So we determined to meet on the following day.

I arrived at the senator's domicile at 7:04 p.m. He lives in Pacific Palisades, an upscale community on the Santa Monica Bay and a couple of castes above mine. I'm just below maggot. He might not be a cow, but his status as a mammal is pretty well locked in.

"Welcome, and please . . . come in," he said, and raised a gracious hand, apparently having forgiven me for implying he was out to sloop another friend's daughter. Perhaps because he was out to sloop another friend's daughter.

I was a little surprised he hadn't moved out of his posh digs after Salina's death, but who am I to question the way of the mammal? The house looked much as I remembered it. The vestibule was large, paved with marble, and open.

"Can I get you anything to drink?" he asked, and led me through an arched doorway into the living room. It was vaulted. Persian rugs covered the pale hardwood. Half a football field from the stone fireplace, an ornate, antler-pronged rack held headgear. A low-crowned cowboy hat for playing caballero. A Lakers cap, great for cheering Kobe at the free-throw line. And a captain's cap; yachting was just one of the senator's passions.

I was out of my depth and sinking fast.

"There is a splendid red," he said. "A little ostentatious perhaps, but quite piquant."

I was incapable of deciphering wine gibberish, but I was pretty sure it involved alcohol, and even a maggot is smart enough to know that I had done enough drinking around the Riveras. In fact, I believe I had once imbibed enough to admit to *Mrs.* Rivera that I did indeed want to see her only son sweaty and naked.

"Maybe just a glass of water," I said, and hoped that wouldn't be a little strong for my constitution.

He canted his head. "You must indeed have something rather serious to discuss."

"Three people have died," I reminded him. Maybe my tone was a little dramatic.

He nodded, looking both intelligent and sincere before turning toward the kitchen. If his constituency had seen that expression, I was pretty sure they would have voted him king high commander. But maybe that was his hope.

In a minute he was back, bearing a glass of ruby wine for himself and sparkling water for me. He indicated a grandiose leather couch that stood near the fireplace. I took it while he settled into its smaller comrade on the opposite side.

While I daintily sipped my water, he placed one ankle over his opposite knee. His pant leg draped perfectly, revealing a scant inch of dark, high-quality sock and polished leather shoes with a sassy tassel. His shirt was as wrinkle free as a cheerleader's chipper brow.

I felt a little crunchy.

"So despite everything, you continue to believe the two deaths were somehow connected," he said.

"The three deaths," I said.

He shook his head. "Carma died months ago."

"Two," I said. "Two months."

He scowled, nodded, took a sip of his wine, and swirled it gently, seeming lost in his thoughts.

"Can you think of anything that might have changed around that time?" I asked.

He shook his head, swirled some more. "I am an old man, Christina," he said, and smiled, intelligent, serene, and gently self-reproachful. "Little changes in my life."

I refrained from snorting. "What of Salina?" I considered adding *"the gorgeous Latino woman who was half your age,"* but I thought it might sound a little uncharitable.

"My fiancée was killed by a madman whom I once counted as a friend," he said, and paused. "The world will never be the same without her."

I watched him. His eyes were mournful, his expression solemn, but he turned his lips up in a grim smile. "Perhaps I am not as coldhearted as you think."

Perhaps. But what did I know of him, really? His own son seemed to think him capable of murder.

"I loved her," he said. "Maybe it was an unusual love, a love that you neither understand nor condone—"

I opened my mouth to object, but he lifted an elegant hand to stop me. Which was just as well, because I *didn't* condone his multigenerational philandering and I had no desire to admit it.

"But it was love just the same," he said.

"She was half your age." Okay, now I said it.

"Is age what determines affection?"

I considered debating the issue, but I was pretty sure I had come for a reason. I shifted, restless. He reminded me of his son in too many ways for comfort.

"Tell me about Manny Casero," I said.

He drank again. "What do you wish to know?"

"Everything."

"I have not seen him for some years."

"Then tell me a little."

He sighed, settled back. "His name was Emanuel. But he liked to be called 'My Lord.' "

I started in surprise. "What?"

He smiled at my shocked expression. "He was christened Emanuel. Someone mentioned the true meaning of the name—God with us." He shrugged, a casual lift of impressive shoulders. "Manny had a position of some power amongst my staff. He suggested his...*underlings,* if you will, could simply call him Lord and Master."

I mulled over the thought, trying to see the scenario in my mind. As a general rule, people don't like to be subjugated. Americans are particularly touchy. "Perhaps that would have been reason enough to make someone want to kill him," I suggested.

But the senator smiled. "Manny was not a man with whom one could be angry. No. He was amusing. He was charismatic. I believe, in fact, that women found him quite attractive."

"Women often find alcoholics attractive," I said, voicing an opinion that had mystified me for some time.

"He was fond of drink. That I will admit. But it was not a problem. At least not at that time."

"Maybe it was his God complex that caused the trouble, then."

He smiled as if I understood so little—about men, about women, about life in general. I could hardly disagree. Even François baffled me sometimes. "It is not as you think. He was excellent for morale. Enthusiastic. Optimistic. There was not a person on my staff who did not like him."

"How refreshing," I said. "A utopia." Maybe I'm becoming jaded.

"It was a well-run campaign."

"Uh-huh."

He sighed. "There were, of course, conflicts from time to time. Some of which . . ." He glanced sorrowfully into his wineglass. "Some of which were my fault."

I remembered the scandals about interns and secretaries. And anyone else with the appropriate sex organs. "Such as?"

"It is not easy being the leader of the Moral Majority."

I almost spewed water through my nose, but I hadn't done that since my brother Pete had blasted my brother James in the face with a blob of applesauce, and I didn't want to ruin my record. Maturity is a slippery thing for a McMullen.

"And a senatorial campaign incurs a great deal of costs," he added.

I nodded, trying to look naïve and a little blond. It wasn't very difficult.

"Some of my supporters . . ." He paused, searching for the perfect word. ". . . disagreed with my fund-raising methods."

My blond little ears perked up. "Such as?"

"Perhaps you have heard of a Mr. Craig R. LaCrosse."

The name rang a vague bell that seemed to be attached somehow to the entertainment industry. I thought back through a half dozen actors' events I had attended with Laney before she'd become an Amazon Queen. "Isn't he a director?" I thought I remembered some slasher flicks.

"A producer." The senator sighed. "A patriotic man. And quite passionate about his beliefs. He gave rather generously to my early campaign, but there were those who did not want to become involved with Hollywood. The surrounding immorality would not sit well with my constituency, or so they thought."

"And you think this guy could somehow be involved with the deaths of—"

"Mr. LaCrosse died some years ago," he said. "I simply wished to dispel your misconception that I believed my campaign was trouble free."

I ran that information around in my head for a minute while I sipped at my water. It was still fizzy. I don't like fizzy. "What other problems existed amongst your people?" I was vaguely aware that my terminology made him sound a little like Moses.

He placed a hand on the horizontal length of his lower leg and watched me. "There were those who did not think we should campaign on Sunday."

"Seriously?"

"You were raised Catholic, were you not, Christina?"

I was raised stupid. "Even for a Catholic the idea's a little outdated, isn't it?" I asked.

"This was some time ago, Christina. Before the prevalence of laptops and Blueberries and iPods."

I didn't have any of those things. I wanted them, but not as much as I wanted a working commode.

"It was a slower time." He smiled. "There were different sensibilities, and much of my staff was quite devout."

"But you *did* campaign on Sundays?"

"A man must take a stand, and I have found it impossible to please everyone. I felt it more important to spread the wisdom of our policies than to worry about offending a few constituents."

Translation: He wanted to win.

"Who was against the Sunday idea?"

He shook his head. "I no longer remember the details. It was a small ripple in a large pond."

"Who was *for* it?"

He stared at me for a moment, and then his brows lowered. "Kathy Baltimore."

I felt my heart rate bump up.

"She was a very ambitious woman. When she threw herself into a project, she threw with all her heart. Perhaps that is why she stayed with her husband so long, even though..." He shook his head, looking surprised and a little disturbed.

My mind skittered on.

"You said Emanuel was attractive."

He smiled. "I said women found him attractive. There is a distinct difference, to my mind."

"Do you have a photo of him?"

"Of Emanuel? Yes, I believe I might," he said, and left the room. He returned shortly, carrying a stack of leather-bound photo albums. Me, I keep my pictures in a shoe box from Wal-Mart. Sometimes I cut myself out of the image if things have gone awry with my hair or my face or my body weight. There aren't a whole lot of unscathed pictures in the ol' Wal-Mart box.

Sitting down beside me, the senator opened a book and flipped through a few pages.

"What about Kathy?" I asked. "Did *she* find Emanuel attractive?"

He glanced over at me. Up close, one was more aware

of his age, but it did little to make him less appealing. I truly resent that about men. Maybe even more so than the fact that chocolate makes my ass as wide as a dump truck. "I do not believe they knew each other.

"And as I have said, Christina, my staff was extremely moral."

"Who was not?" I asked.

He shook his head like a quiet sage, then tapped a photo imprisoned in plastic.

"This is Emanuel."

I glanced down. The man in the picture was dark. He wore a heavy mustache and no beard. I wouldn't have said he was handsome, but I could see that he had a smile that could make things happen. He was framing a *Vote for change, vote for Rivera* sign.

"How about him?" I touched the picture. It was fading a little. "Was he moral?" I asked. "Except for the drinking?"

He shrugged. "Perhaps he felt himself a bit overly important."

"Were those his worst sins?"

"So far as I know."

"There must have been someone with worse."

He caught my gaze with grave sincerity. "Then I would have to choose myself as the greatest sinner, for I cannot throw stones."

Save me from martyrs and vegans. "What did *you* do?" I asked.

He raised his free hand. "Life in politics hides few secrets."

"What few did yours hide?" Good God, I'm clever.

He paused, then turned a few pages and gazed nostalgically at a faded 4×6.

I glanced down, recognizing his ex-wife. Rosita Rivera was small, curvaceous, and impishly lovely. Smiling, she had wrapped her arms around a young couple, one on her right and one on her left.

The senator's expression was solemn. "I see now, through wiser eyes, that she deserved better."

I didn't bother to agree. To say the senator was a philanderer would have been something of an insult to philanderers. "Who's she with?"

"Volunteer coordinators."

I took a closer look. The woman was plump and cute, with big eyes and a bigger smile. The man was lean and wiry, with brown hair that curled like a fresh perm.

"What's *her* name?" I asked.

"Yvonne." He said the name with a pensive dreaminess.

I glanced up at the tone, but it took him a moment to meet my high-browed gaze.

"And, no," he said finally, "I did not sleep with her."

"Did you try?"

He looked peeved. "She and Steve were something of an item at the time."

"Steve who?"

He pointed to the picture of the sandy-haired fellow. "Steve Bunting."

"Did they marry?"

"I don't believe Steve *ever* married, which is rather a shame." He smiled a little. "His parents were a lovely couple. Old, but extremely devoted to each other. I think, perhaps, Steve could have—"

"Was it because he found you and Yvonne together?"

"What?"

"Is that why they never married?"

"As I said, I did *not*—"

"You didn't sleep with her." I gave him the stink eye. "But what *did* you do?"

"Christina—"

"A bunch of people have died, Senator."

He sighed. "Perhaps I lusted in my heart."

I stared at him blankly and managed to refrain from guffawing like a hyena. "Where else did you lust?" I asked finally.

"Perhaps it would surprise you to know that I have known several women with whom I did not have relations."

"Were any of them attractive?"

He opened his mouth to object, but I raised a hand. "All three of the victims were connected with you in one way or another. The police have no leads." The room went silent. "They're not even *looking* for leads." Why was that? Was the governor *really* that concerned about the meth problem in a city the size of my eye tooth, or had someone asked him to make sure Kathy Baltimore's death went undisturbed? And if so, why? Might someone be worried about *my* investigation? "We need to figure out who you might have offended."

He scowled as if quite put upon. Death—ever inconvenient. "There was a young woman from Austin."

God help me. "What was her name?"

He paused, and when he spoke again, his voice was imbued with a surreal kind of wistfulness. "Cynthia Larson."

"How young?"

He pursed his lips. "I don't believe age—"

I was getting tired. Perhaps it's epidemic around politicians. "How young?"

"She was well over the legal limitations."

"How well?"

"Age—" he began again. He sounded as if he were warming up for a lecture, so I shoved the album into his lap and rose to my feet.

"It's been a long day," I said. I was a little worried the ploy might be aging, but he sighed, then motioned toward my just-unoccupied seat. I sat back down with some misgivings.

"I believe she was twenty-three," he said solemnly.

In my defense, I'd like to say that I did not throw the remainder of my fizzy water in his face and stomp on his head, so let's hear it for me. On the other hand, I did call him a couple of rather uncomplimentary names in the solitude of my brain. "Who knew about her?" I asked. My voice might have sounded a little schoolmarmish.

He set his jaw, perhaps taking umbrage at my tone.

"Your wife?" I asked.

"Lord, no!" Said with some feeling, I noted. It was good to know Rosita could still put the fear of God into him.

I scowled. "Who, then?"

He drew a sad breath through his nose and looked regretful. "The young man with whom she was involved may have become aware."

I refrained from spitting at him. "What was *his* name?"

"It was many years ago." He shook his head. "In truth, I do not remember."

I wondered vaguely if he had ruined so many lives that he no longer recalled all the debris scattered in his wake. "Was Cynthia involved in your senatorial campaign?"

"No. Long ago. When my aspirations were simpler."

I waited, knowing him well enough to realize he'd expound given time and an unattended ear.

"In 1984 I became mayor of San Andres, a humble village in Texas. It was not so very far from where I was born."

I started, surprised. "I thought you were born in Mexico."

He stared at me for a second, then smiled. "I could hardly hope to be president of this great country if that were the case, could I, Christina? No." He sobered, a little like a scholar tutoring his unschooled pupil. "Mama gave birth to me in a dusty little town just south of Laredo. My parents were very poor. Migrant workers." He paused, nodded, looking back. "But jobs were scarce. When I was not yet a year of age, they returned to the bosom of their families."

My mind scrambled around a bit. "And later you reentered the United States, took up politics, and lived the American dream."

He laughed. "Perhaps that is an oversimplification, but, yes, I suppose that is the case."

"And Cynthia . . ." I shook my head, misplacing her last name.

"Larson," he supplied.

"Cynthia Larson helped you, but you no longer remember the name of the only other person who knew of your involvement with her."

He frowned.

"Did I leave something out?"

"Teddy."

"Teddy . . ."

Another sigh. "Theodore Altove also knew."

I scowled.

"I believe you met his daughter some days past at Caring Hands. Thea," he added. "Named after her adoring father."

I lifted my brows. "Thea? The supermodel with hair?"

My choice of words didn't seem to make him any happier. I vaguely wondered why. I mean, what man wouldn't want to be associated with a supermodel with hair?

"Her father and I were very close," he said.

"What happened?"

"Between him and me?" He shook his head. "Nothing unfavorable. I have known him since the early days. He was a brilliant strategist, quite instrumental in my mayoral campaign and later in my first race for senator. But Thea was growing up and Teddy was a man of great devotion. He did not think Los Angeles offered the proper environment for raising a child."

"So he disapproved of your affair with Ms.──"

"It was not an affair."

"What was it, then?"

He flipped his hand at me. "A slip. Nothing more."

"Did she think so?"

"I am not certain." He raised his chin. "But I could not, in good conscience, see her again."

"So you dumped her."

"She was young. Beautiful. Full of possibilities. I doubt she gave it a second thought."

"How many thoughts do you think her nameless boyfriend gave it?"

"I do not deny that I have made mistakes, Christina."

I kind of wanted to continue my line of questioning, but I've made a few mistakes myself. Seventy-seven and counting, in fact. And that's just in the dating department. "Do you know where she is now?"

"I have not thought of her in more than a decade."

Probably because of all those other twenty-three-year-olds he'd . . . Damn, I was running out of words for sex. "Is that a no?"

"Yes."

I nodded, thinking back.

"How did Teddy find out about it?"

He sighed, deep and heavy. "I told him."

Gotta tell you, I was surprised. "Seriously?"

"He . . ." He shook his head. "I believe he had his suspicions beforehand. He said he was worried for my soul."

"And your campaign," I supposed.

"He was a fine consultant," he said, and stared silently at the album. A sandy-haired man in his early thirties stared up at him from a grainy photograph. Fair-skinned and somber, he had his arm wrapped around a solidly built woman with horn-rimmed glasses and a high-cheekboned, no-nonsense face.

"Who's that?" I asked, but the senator was deep in his own thoughts.

"I was not without blame," he said softly, as if this were some little-known secret he was sharing with me alone.

I resisted mocking. "Are these the Altoves?"

"Teddy," he said, and nodded.

I took the album. The photo looked as if it might have been a Polaroid. Humankind's most useful invention next to, say, Jiffy Pop. The picture had been taken in the desert. Altove's hair was thinning, pushing back past the curve of his scalp, and it looked as if he might have been hiding under a desk somewhere when the great Whodunnit had handed out smiles, but he was not an unattractive man. I couldn't be quite so charitable with his wife. She had a face that reminded me somehow of a cement mixer. And Thea had come from this union. I wasn't really surprised. My brothers, to a man, thought there was something inherently funny about dead vermin showing up in unlikely places. Genetics. Go figure.

"Who did *he* tell?" I asked.

"What's that?" The senator seemed to draw himself back from an uncertain past.

"Mr. Altove," I said, and tapped the picture. "With whom did he share your secret?"

"No one."

I tilted my head.

"He is my friend," he said. "My true friend."

"Did he work for you during your last campaign?"

"I called him now and again for advice, but he had other politicians with whom to concern himself. Teller of Nebraska would not be a congressman today without him." He nodded to himself. "Teddy enjoys the Midwest." He gazed into the distance again, then saw me watching him. "I feel blessed indeed to have a chance to work with his lovely daughter after all this time."

I stared at him, remembering the graceful figure, the luminous hair, how her eyes shone when she looked at him. "I bet."

His expression went dark. He drew himself up, pulling the photo album from my lap and setting it carefully beside him on the couch before rising to his full height. "I would never, under threat of death, lay a hand on her," he said.

"Yes, well . . ." I stood up beside him. "Excuse my skepticism, Senator, but—"

"Not so much as a finger," he said. "If you do not believe that, then I would prefer that you leave my house this instant."

I stood there, speechless and flabbergasted for a moment, then: "I'm sorry," I said. "I didn't mean to offend you."

For a moment I thought he might toss me out on my ear, but finally he shook his head. "No, it is I who should be sorry. Of course I deserve your disdain."

"I don't disdain you." Not exactly. "You're a well-respected man. Intelligent, educated . . ." He was still staring at me. I swept my hand sideways, encompassing the three hats that waited on the antlers. "Well dressed . . ."

He sighed wearily and closed his eyes for a moment. "I have had my successes, I suppose, but where family is concerned . . ." He looked older suddenly, worn. "My wife cannot hear my name without cursing. Gerald will barely speak to me."

I shrugged. I had the same problem. "Your son can be difficult," I said. "He has his own demons to fight."

He smiled slowly and took my hand between his. "And you are caught in the battle."

I raised a brow.

"Between Gerald and his demons. Between me and mine." He stroked my knuckles and gazed deeply into my eyes. A little shiver skittered along my veins. It traveled up my arm, zipped past my elbow, and shimmied across my nipples like a cool bolt of lightning.

I stood in frozen horror. "Well . . ." The word was breathless, stupid, stunned. I couldn't be attracted to this man. Absolutely could not, but the shiver was scattering downward. "I should be going."

"So soon?" he asked, and stroked my fingers.

"Yes," I croaked, and, snatching my hand from his, sprinted out of the house, slamming the door behind me.

It's entirely possible that I have demons of my own. I rushed home to discuss the continuing confrontation between intellect and instinct with François.

21

Don't worry. It's scientifically unlikely that the universe will explode into a million particles at any given moment.

—J. D. Solberg,
who has, oddly enough,
studied these things

THE DRIVE HOME was uneventful—except for what was going on in my head. It was racing like a rabbit-happy greyhound.

So there had been problems among Rivera's staff. That was hardly surprising. Especially since the problems seemed fairly insignificant. A spat regarding the Sabbath, a minor affair that no one knew about.

But maybe Rivera was understating everything. It would be interesting to get another perspective. But whose? His acquaintances seemed to be mostly dead.

I would look into Cynthia Larson's whereabouts, but I had little hope of actually finding her. She had probably been married four times and undergone two sex changes by now.

But perhaps Mr. Altove was a possibility.

I parked my Saturn in its usual spot by the curb but didn't exit immediately. Instead, I took the Mace out of my purse, laced my fingers between my keys, and said a prayer to good old Dymphna, patron saint of hapless morons. I then glanced up and down the street. Sometimes I'm not notably bright, but given enough attempts on my life, I can learn. Unlocking the car doors finally, I stepped out and hurried toward my house.

The single bulb was burning dutifully above my front door. After scanning the darkened yard like an osprey, I shoved my key into my lock. It turned easily. I stepped inside, and that's when I knew...

Someone was inside my house. I could feel it tingling in the soles of my feet, rasping in the very air I breathed, lifting the hairs at the back of my neck. Nothing was out of place. The door had been locked, my security light was blinking properly from its place on the hall wall, but there was something wrong.

The memory of a man's dead, staring eyes burned into my mind. He'd died in my front yard, blood seeping into the dirt. Maniacal laughter whispered through my mind. My joints felt wooden. My scalp prickled. I backed toward the door, heart thumping, lungs laboring.

A shadow loomed suddenly from the kitchen.

I jerked my Mace shoulder high and shrieked. "Stay back. I've got a gun."

The silence reverberated, then: "Mac?" Laney said.

It took a couple of lumbering attempts for my mind to register that it was really her, but she was shaking her head and looking concerned about my sanity, so it probably was. Harlequin loped in. He looked loopy and ecstatic. Next to Lucky Duck and Rivera, Laney was his favorite plaything.

"Are you taking your lion's mane like you promised?"

All the blood had rushed to my toes. I dropped the Mace to my side.

"Lion's mane?" My voice sounded pale and watery.

"Mushrooms," she said. "To ward off dementia."

"Mushrooms?" My arms felt limp. "Holy crap, Laney, I could have killed you."

She flipped the foyer light on, set her glass of whatever juice on the little table by my door, and examined the Mace. "You don't even have the trigger on."

I felt wobbly and a little nauseous. "What are you doing here?"

"You didn't get my message?"

I shook my head, weak and disoriented. "Did the message say anything about you scaring the crap out of me?"

"I may have neglected that part."

I wobbled into the kitchen and plopped into the nearest chair. "At least you could have turned on a light."

"Environmental responsibility. You don't even have fluorescent bulbs," she said, and, arming my security system, took the chair beside mine. "I'm sorry, Mac. They say a good fright's good for your system, though. Like low-voltage electrical shock."

"I thought you weren't coming 'til tomorrow."

She shrugged. "I wanted to make sure I made good on my vow."

I managed to tilt my head.

"To arrive before the next attempt on your life."

Feeling was beginning to return to my fingertips. "Everything okay between you and . . ." Sometimes if I say Solberg's name out loud, I get a little sick to my stomach. If I think of him with Brainy Laney Butterfield, I have to take a Dramamine.

"Jeen," she supplied.

"Yeah, him." I rubbed Harley's ears. He grinned like a drunken freshman. I've never particularly liked drunken freshmen, even when I was one.

"Everything's fine." Picking up her tie-dyed, organic, llama-friendly bag made by Bolivian indigents, she pulled out a lemon. A heart had been carved into the rind. "He gave me this."

I blinked. "Because he's a certified nut-job?"

"Because I'm three hundred sixty-five times sweeter than sugar and can balance the acidity."

I nodded. "I feel a little like I'm going to hurl. Do you happen to have an antacid or possibly the root of a something-berry in there?"

She laughed and dropped the lemon back into her bag. "How did it go with the senator?"

I shook my head and found my feet, or perhaps the other way around. Going to the fridge, I opened it up and peered inside. A tumbleweed blew by. I closed it.

"His water is fizzy," I said.

There was a moment of silence, then, "Have you been drinking?"

"The most enlightening part of the evening," I said, "is that water can fizz."

"I take it you didn't learn much."

"Well . . ." I sat down again, stretched out my legs. Harlequin had abandoned me for Laney. I couldn't blame him. If I could do the same, I would. "I mean, it's not as if I'm taking this very seriously or anything. Just looking into a few things as a favor."

"So you didn't cash his check."

I hesitated, searching for a likely lie, but the truth burst on me like the crack of dawn. I glanced up, suspicious. "You know I cashed his check, don't you?"

She didn't answer directly. "I saw the tagboard on your office wall."

"I was bored," I said.

She shook her head. "Why can't you just play Scrabble like other sexually frustrated geniuses with Ph.D.s?"

"I beat Harley three out of four games," I said. "He didn't want to play anymore."

"I was thinking you might try it with someone from genus *Homo sapiens*."

"I don't know anybody."

"Is the good lieutenant giving you that much trouble?"

"The good lieutenant, as you very well know, is trouble."

She smiled. "Otherwise you would have been bored a long time ago."

I shrugged.

She watched me, eyes narrowed a little. "How's the other guy?"

"I know a lot of other guys. Most of them are certifiable."

"You want normal, try Iowa. What's his name?"

"There is no one," I said.

"Strange name. What does he do?"

I gave her a look. "He's a cop."

"The guy who asked about casual sex?"

I cleared my throat. "Maybe."

She sighed. "You seemed so intelligent in fifth grade," she said.

I refrained from sticking out my tongue.

"Why policemen?" she asked.

"There are only so many geek gods." I remained mute on the *thank heaven* part, but she laughed and the world seemed brighter.

"You all right, Mac? Really?"

"I'm fine. How about you?"

"The schedule's crazy and I miss you something terrible," she said, and suddenly I felt a little weepy. "Are you *sure* you're okay?"

"Just tired."

"You're going to cry, aren't you?"

"Oh, please," I said, and she laughed again.

"Put on your jammies. I'm staying the night."

"I'm not that easy."

"Yes, you are," she said, and the world felt right.

We slept in the same bed, like little kids hiding from their parents, and talked about everything under the moon. I told her that Rivera wasn't speaking to me, that Officer Tavis's smile was too pretty for words, and that Mrs. Al-Sadr had cried about her sister with whom she wanted to share a mouthwatering ambrosia called halvah. I told her about my conversation in a bar called Happy Daze. That I'd missed the fact that Kathy Baltimore was a lesbian even though I have a Ph.D. And that there had been nothing but a few seemingly insignificant problems within the senator's campaign.

She told me that her props master was a lovely, soft-spoken gentleman from Saudi Arabia. That she worked fourteen-hour days and had received thirty-two letters from a single fan in one week.

I lay in the darkness listening to her talk and wondered with dusky surprise if I would trade places with her.

"If I ever get out of the entertainment business, I think I'd like to buy a farm," she said.

"A farm?"

"Keep a few chickens."

Harlequin was lying between us. "Are we speaking in metaphors?"

"Do you know how the big coops treat chickens? It's despicable. I'd let mine roam."

"Uh-huh."

"And I'd have a goat."

"Because..."

"The milk is homogenized naturally. Better for your digestive system."

"Of course." I felt sleepy and as content as a cuddled kitten.

"If I got a couple of horses, would you ride with me?"

"If I could wrestle Solberg out of the way."

"Can you imagine Jeen on a horse?" she asked, and we giggled like schoolgirls, or like idiots.

The room went quiet, soft with camaraderie and contentment.

"How much danger are you in?" Harlequin was snoring like a drunken sailor and took up a tremendous amount of room. Laney was playing with his paw. I rubbed an ear. The moonlight slanted across the bed, shining on Laney's hair and Harley's ribby thorax.

"I don't even know if the deaths are connected."

"Coincidences are just spiritual puns," she said.

"I don't know what that means."

"What a coincidence."

I rolled my eyes. "The police have determined them accidental," I said.

"All three of them?"

I nodded. Maybe she couldn't see me, but it didn't matter. She could read my mind. Sometimes it's spooky. Just then it was almost soothing.

"What does Rivera think?"

"It's out of his jurisdiction."

"That hasn't necessarily stopped him in the past."

"I think he's given up on me."

She didn't say anything for a second, then reached across Harley's boxy head and pushed some hair back from my face. "Maybe he's trying to."

"I think he's succeeded."

"Would it help if I told you about the extremely well-accepted fish-in-the-sea theory?"

"It's worth a try."

I could sense her smile. "Apparently there are a lot of them."

"Do they try to kill you?"

"The mercury levels are disturbingly high."

I smiled and rolled onto my back. "Are you going to marry Solberg?"

"Ask some other time," she said. "When you're not so despondent."

"I'm not despondent."

"Please don't get yourself killed, Mac," she said. Her voice felt soft and foggy in the darkness. It was no secret why every living being adored her.

"Okay."

"Who do you think killed them?"

"I take it you don't believe in that accident gibberish."

"If I said yes, that I feel it in every organ of my body, including my appendix, that all three of them died of unsuspicious if rather unlucky circumstances, would you drop it?"

"How *does* your appendix feel?"

"A little queasy," she said, and sighed. "I have to tell you something, but I don't want you to read more into this than necessary."

"Into what?"

"Promise me you'll think things through before you react."

I tilted my head toward her. She was no less beautiful in the moonlight. "You're really a man?"

"Try not to be an idiot."

"If only."

"They died on three consecutive days of the week," she said. "Starting on Monday."

The world went quiet. "What?" I said, but my voice barely made a ripple in the darkness.

"I checked your timeline," she said. "It's mathematically improbable."

22

Dating—the socially acceptable alternative to the rack.

—*Mr. Donald Archer*

I FELT A LITTLE EDGY on Friday. I'd stayed up until two in the morning staring at my office wall with Laney. She was right. They *had* died on consecutive days. But then, of course, she could do algebraic equations on her pinky finger. Days of the week were fairly elementary.

Between clients, I sat in silence, letting my mind wander. Not that it had much of a choice. It was something of a nomad these days.

My intercom rang. I pushed the appropriate button. "What's up?"

"Ms. McMullen?"

I was still amazed that I had a secretary who could use something as complicated as the phone system. After

Laney had left my office to become the Amazon Queen, I had begun to despair.

"Yes?"

"I made an appointment for a new client."

"I thought my schedule was packed."

"Your four o'clock, a Mr. Hassler—probably not the author—needed to cancel. I found a spot for him tomorrow. Then I slipped Mr. Donald Archer into his slot."

"Shirley?"

"Yeah, honey?"

"What happened to the Magnificent Mandy?"

"Truth to tell, I'm not exactly sure."

"I didn't really want you to kill her, you know."

She chuckled a little and hung up. I did the same, minus the chuckle. Clients came and went.

My four o'clock arrived. Shirley buzzed to announce my newbie. I stood up to greet him. The man who stepped through the doorway had a familiar face. He also had curly hair, green eyes, and twenty pounds more than recommended by the healthy-heart people. It took me a while to place him, but finally the memories congealed. I had spoken to him in Sespe over a vodka cranberry. I'd introduced myself as Mac. He'd introduced himself as the same.

"Ms. McMullen, this is Donald Archer," Shirley said.

I blinked, mind ticking, and took the carefully printed record she offered. "Thank you, Shirley," I said. She nodded and left, closing the door behind her.

I waited in silence for an instant, not sure where to go from here. Was this another coincidence? A spiritual pun? A...

"I'm sorry," he said.

"I beg your pardon?" I was buying time as if I had the cash.

"I didn't lie to you in the bar. At least, I didn't mean to."

Pieces of the puzzle were floating around my brain like dollar bills in one of those money phone booths you see on game shows. "Donald Archer," I said. "You own Ironwear Incorporated."

He smiled. The expression was a little sheepish. "My father," he said. "My father owns Ironwear."

I motioned vaguely toward the furniture and took a seat in my chair. "Why'd you want me to believe you were an employee there?"

"It wasn't intentional. I mean, I *am* an employee, sort of." He wobbled his head. "It just happened. Things were said. Then I didn't know how to get out of it."

In my world, things don't just happen. For example, when someone tries to kill me, it's intentional. "Listen, Mr. Archer—"

"I didn't want to be Mr. Archer."

I gave him the cock-headed expression Harlequin had taught me. "What?"

"Not to you."

"What are you talking about? How did you find me?"

He winced, looking apologetic. "I'm really rich."

I cleared my throat and tugged on my blouse. Ongoing problems with the Super Septic guys and my lack of a convenient washing machine had caused me to take casual Friday to a new low. I was wearing too-short slacks and an ivory shell. The wrinkles in the slacks and the boxy demeanor of the shirt might have pushed it a little past casual and into the vague borders of "ick." "This is very unorthodox, Mr. Archer. I don't believe—"

"See. That's why I just wanted to be Mac."

I gave him a look.

"People treat you different when you're just Mac."

Another look.

"You know, you weren't exactly the Gandhi of honesty, either," he said.

I felt a little uncomfortable with that idea, but I kept my voice steady. "A woman would have to either be dangerously optimistic or ridiculously stupid to give her name out at every two-bit bar in California."

"Well, you're not stupid," he said, then hurried to add, "but I'm not, either. I mean, I'm no Einstein, but I'm all right."

"Why are you here?"

He actually blushed—actually, literally, physically blushed. It was kind of endearing. I mean, Officer Tavis hadn't colored while talking about multiple partners, and I was quite sure Rivera had no blood vessels in his face whatsoever. "I just . . . I found you interesting."

"Interesting."

"I was hoping you'd go out with me." It was blunt and quick and a little painful.

"Are you serious?"

He winced, face twitching a little. "Ouch?"

"I didn't mean it like that," I said, but maybe I did a little; the man had tracked me down like a Pinkerton. "I mean . . . you're rich. You said so yourself. Why me?"

"You're beautiful," he countered, blinking.

I refrained from saying anything stupid. What are the chances? "I can't date clients."

"Then I won't pay you. Let me buy you dinner."

I shook my head.

"Lunch?"

"I don't think this is a good idea." Translation: I didn't want to be killed by a crazy guy with kinky hair even if he was capable of blushing.

"How do you feel about condominiums?"

I glanced at him askance, like someone might look at an unknown variety of spider. "Living in them or—"

"I thought I could buy you one."

"Perhaps you should leave."

"No, listen, really." He fidgeted. If he had had a hat, I'm pretty sure it would have been in his hand. "Ms. McMullen, I'm not crazy, I swear. It's just . . . my last relationship was a doozy."

I felt deflated. That was usually *my* line. "Dating sucks," I admitted.

"It was three years ago."

"Listen, I'm sorry, but I haven't been incredibly lucky myself."

"I'm a nice guy," he said. "Really. Ask anyone. Ask my mom."

I stared at him. "What's her phone number?"

He didn't laugh, didn't smile. Just rattled off the number.

I stared at him like a blank-faced mannequin for a second, then searched my desk and scribbled down the digits.

"Are you really going to call her?"

"Would she lie for you?"

"I hope so," he said. "But I kind of doubt it."

"Listen, Mr.—"

"Mac," he said.

"Mr. Mac. You seem like a nice guy, but I—"

"I am."

"Okay, but—"

"And did I mention how rich I am?" He said it like a hopeful urchin, and I couldn't quite help but laugh.

"I think you made mention."

He smiled. "And pathetic," he added.

"I'm kind of working that out for myself," I said. "But, listen, the truth is, it's been kind of a hard year for me."

"I promise not to try to kill you."

My brows shot into my hairline.

He cleared his throat. "I . . . umm . . . I kind of checked into you."

"Checked into—"

"Okay." He glanced away, swallowed. "I hired a private investigator."

"What?"

He looked worried, wounded. "Did I tell you my last girlfriend was crazy?"

"Literally, or . . ."

"She said the baby was mine."

I stumbled through the land mines of unspoken possibilities for a minute. "But it wasn't?"

"It wasn't even *hers*."

I shook my head, confused but admittedly fascinated. Someone crazier than my dates. How disgustingly refreshing.

"She had 'borrowed' it." He made air quotation marks with his fingers. "From a friend."

I thought about that for a second. "I once dated a guy who thought he was Jesse James."

"The outlaw or the car aficionado?"

"The outlaw."

"That's weird."

"Otherwise it wouldn't be?"

"Sandra Bullock's hot." And supposedly that explained things. "I once dated a girl who kept ducks."

"Farming is a venerable occupation."

"In her bedroom. Twelve of them. It smelled like the penguin exhibit at the zoo."

"Someone tried to kill me there once."

He blinked. "I think I overpaid the investigator."

I raised a brow.

"That seems like a pretty significant fact to leave out."

I sighed. "Don't bother getting your money back. I lied. He didn't really try to kill me *there*. He was just thinking about it at the time. I know, because he admitted it later. While he was trying to kill me. With a poker."

He nodded thoughtfully. "I fell in love with a girl who swore she used to be a llama."

I made an impressed expression, but came back with a zinger. "I once dated a guy who had a crush on my hot-water bottle."

He opened his mouth, then shook his head, defeat written all over his face. "Go out with me," he said.

"I don't think—"

"I'll be a gentleman. I'll pay. I'll even double-date."

I was prepared to refuse again, but then I shrugged.

"Less likelihood of getting murdered in crowds," I said, and he laughed.

23

In my opinion, kissing a lady's hand is a fine tradition. After all, a man must start somewhere.

—Senator Miguel Rivera,
at his most flirtatious

FRIDAYS CAN BE UNPREDICTABLE. Sometimes clients feel the need to store up extra therapy for the oncoming weekend, but this close to the holidays they seemed to be heading straight for a likely alternative—eggnog.

My last client left at 4:55 in the afternoon. I would be celebrating Christmas at Laney's apartment, so there was hardly a reason to clean, but I still hadn't finished shopping, so I closed the office early to brave the holiday crowds. Wheeling through Target, I found frilly pink pajamas with pom-pom footsies and a matching lace headband for Christianna. At six months of age, my niece was still as bald as a cabbage, and I was pretty sure her feminine ego might be flagging. But after setting the ensemble lovingly in the cart, I was overcome by a possibly irrational fear that I was trivializing her intellect and bought her a singing alphabet toy to balance her psyche.

By the time I reached home, there were two messages on my answering machine. One was from Mom, reminding me that *good* daughters call their mothers with the same regularity that they change their underwear. The other was from Senator Rivera's secretary, who asked that I stop by Caring Hands on the following day at noon. There was little to no explanation. I tried to call the senator to ask what this was regarding, but I only got his voice mail, which was neither informative nor particularly conversational.

After sharing a lightly burned dinner of sautéed chicken and brown rice with Harley, I called directory assistance for Austin, Texas, and asked for Cynthia Larson. Not surprisingly, no such person was listed, but there was a Cindy Larson. I got the number and called her. She was ninety-three years old and told me in no uncertain terms that she was as fit as a fiddle and attributed her well-being to the fact that she didn't eat cinnamon. I congratulated her on both her health and her wise gastronomic decisions, then asked if she knew, or had known, any other Cynthia Larsons, but that's where the communications broke down. She was only interested in opining about spices.

After that, I Googled the Larsons in Austin and found a host of options on a handy little site I'd never heard of before. It even listed relatives, but none of them matched the senator's short-lived flame. Still, I printed up the list and vowed to start calling them immediately. Immediately being right after a dose of flirty fudge ice cream.

Ten minutes and three pounds later, I began at the top of the list, perfecting my pitch as I worked my way down. The first three didn't know any Cynthias. The next one hung up before I had explained how I owed money to an old friend who had helped me out in a pinch, and the fifth swore at me in fairly colorful terms.

As interesting as the experience was, I needed a break, so I tried directory assistance again, this time for Baton Rouge, and asked for a Priscilla Ortez. I knew that Kathy Baltimore had been a lesbian and, according to Donald Archer, Emanuel had been a lush, but I didn't really know if my Wiccan theory would hold water.

There was only one Priscilla Ortez in the Baton Rouge area. She answered on the third ring.

"*Hola.*" The woman's tone was upbeat and energetic.

"Yes, hi . . . is Carmella there?"

"Carmella?"

"Yes. I'm calling from Our Lady of Guadalupe."

"The church?"

My hands were sweaty. Lying might be second nature to me, but it's still hard work. "I'm the treasurer here, and the task has fallen on me to call any members who might be able to boost our coffers. I'm afraid our monthly donations aren't quite up to par, and the Lord's work must go on."

"Mama wasn't a member of your parish."

I sniffed. "It's true that she hasn't attended services for some time, but Catholicism has changed. Even though she's been absent, we still consider her one of the flock."

"That's very open-minded of you, but—"

"Ergo, she can still make a charitable donation before the end of the tax year. A thousand dollars would go a long way toward new vestments for Father Pat."

"A thousand dollars?" Her voice was becoming a little shrill.

I wiped my right palm on the leg of my ugly pants. "Donations can't absolve sins, of course, but sometimes they can help the sinner feel—"

"My mother was a practicing witch."

Bingo! "Oh, well...perhaps *you*—" I began, but she had already hung up.

*T*raffic was atypically well mannered on the 2 that Saturday morning. I had slept in, then gone running. Because I had gotten mostly nowhere regarding immigration and couldn't bear to face Ramla's basset-hound eyes, I showered at a truck stop. Unfortunately, I hadn't had enough time to find a Laundromat and was dressed marginally worse than I had been on the previous day. My sweatpants were frayed, and my T-shirt, while in decent shape, had suffered some kind of mystery breakfast stain en route. But maybe the folks at Caring Hands weren't the kind to pass judgment, many of them being homeless and all.

I arrived there shortly after noon. The parking lot was cracked like a desert floor and nearly empty, but inside, the multicolored crowd was milling. I skimmed the faces, searching for the senator, and stopped, frozen.

Lieutenant Jack Rivera was standing not thirty feet away. My heart hiccuped in my chest. He looked good. Tired and worn, but still darkly alluring. He wore blue jeans, faded at the knee and riding a little low on his leaner-than-a-bush-warrior's hips. A ribbed T-shirt showcased the ropy muscles of his arms and just brushed the ends of his too-long, midnight hair.

And he was laughing.

For a moment I actually thought I was mistaken. The dark lieutenant, laughing? But then I recognized his companion. I'm not sure how I had managed to temporarily ignore a woman like Thea Altove, but such is the power of insanity.

They were facing each other, conversing like old friends—or worse. But suddenly there was a breathless stillness to the place. I wasn't sure what it was, couldn't identify it immediately, but then I turned and saw Senator Rivera. He, too, had spotted his son and was striding purposefully through the crowd toward him.

The lieutenant turned slowly toward his father, dark eyes shifting, hard body flexing. As for me, I skittered behind a refrigerator-sized Jamaican man, but I needn't have worried about being noticed. The Riveras only had eyes for each other. In fact, if I wasn't mistaken, flames were momentarily shooting from those eyes, even though the conversation seemed to be relatively congenial, at least on the senator's part.

As for the younger Rivera, his body language was shouting some words not acceptable in polite society. The senator raised a hand, indicating the back of the building, and, finally, after an abbreviated delay, they excused themselves from the supermodel with the hair and moved together through the crowd toward the senator's office.

I darted my gaze there and back. There and back. The senator obviously had his hands full. Therefore I should leave, but that went against everything I stood for as a snoop and a lunatic. So I shifted carefully away from my human shield and through the crowd. Barely breathing, I stepped into the corridor where they had disappeared. The senator's door was just closing. Glancing down the hall, surreptitious as a wild ferret, I tiptoed to the portal and laid my ear against the grainy oak.

"You wanted to talk to me?" Rivera's voice was a low, angry growl.

"What are you doing here, Gerald?" the senator asked.

"You tell—" began the other, but suddenly I heard footsteps coming my way.

Panicked, I jerked to the right as if heading toward the back of the building. But I would rather have cut off my ear than miss the conversation, so my hand—completely disconnected from my conscious self and common sense—reached out and turned the knob of the next door. It opened silently beneath my fingers. My heart stuttered in my chest. I was ready to spout apologies and as-yet-undetermined explanations, but the room was empty. Pushing the door closed behind me, I shut my eyes and told myself not to be stupid. Too late.

Footsteps tapped harmlessly past the door, and in a moment I had scooted between a folding chair and a stack of cardboard boxes. I pressed my ear to the wall. It was as thin as papier-mâché.

"We do very important work here," the senator was saying.

"So your philanthropic nature insists that you help," Rivera said. "Is that what you're trying to tell me?"

The senator sighed heavily. "This injured-son routine is getting a bit weary, is it not, Gerald?"

"You don't really expect me to believe that your

esteemed presence here has nothing to do with Gallup polls?"

"I admit that I have made mistakes," said the senator. He sounded weary and put upon. "But we cannot all be perfect like—"

"Made mistakes!" Rivera began, then laughed. "Is that why you wanted me to come? So that you could somehow convince me that you are not as perfect as I have always believed you to—"

"I have no wish to have Thea turned against me."

There was a moment of silent surprise, then: "Thea?"

"Don't bother pretending ignorance."

"Thea?" Rivera spat out the name like old chaw. "I hauled my ass halfway across town so you could warn me off a girl I've never met?"

"It wasn't—" the senator began, but Rivera stopped him with a mocking laugh.

"Jesus! This is rich. You—"

"Don't you take the name of the Lord in vain if you wish—" The senator's voice had dropped to a hiss. I strained my ears, but there were footfalls in the hall again, distracting me.

I froze, not breathing, but the noise tapped past and away. I pressed my ear more firmly to the wall.

"Tell me, Senator, have you fucked her already or are you still just hoping?"

The tension was palpable, even on my side of the wall. "You were always a foul-mouthed boy who never—"

"And you were always a foul-minded lecher."

"You ungrateful—" the senator began, then took a long, challenged breath. "Theodore Altove is a very dear friend of mine."

I could imagine Rivera's disdainful stare. He was aces at it. "I'm afraid you've lost your gift for pontification, Senator. Because I have no idea what you're talking about."

"Thea is Teddy's daughter."

There was a momentary delay, then, "No shit."

"Keep your voice down."

"This is almost too good to be true. My *father*." He stressed the word. "The man who was engaged to marry my fiancée. The man who caused her death—"

"I had nothing to do with her death."

"That same man is trying to keep me away from his . . ." He paused. "What is she to you exactly, Senator?"

"You wouldn't understand."

"Really? What is it I can't comprehend? That there's a deep spiritual bond between you? That she has an old soul that only you in your infinite wisdom can understand while you screw—"

"Shut your mouth!" hissed the senator, and suddenly I realized that I had become too absorbed in the familial volleys and had missed someone's arrival in the hall. I turned, breath held, waiting for them to pass by. But the footsteps stopped. I leapt away from the wall, but as I did so, my foot caught the trash can. It bumped against the desk, rattling like kettle drums.

When I glanced up, there was a woman standing in the doorway. She was middle aged, short, and stunned. "Can I help you?" She was looking at me with a mixture of shock and reprimand. Rather like one might look upon finding a cow in the silverware drawer.

I thrashed around wildly in my head, but for the life of me I couldn't come up with a single plausible reason for my current whereabouts. What was I to do but say "Sweet potatoes," in a voice that rasped and lisped and sputtered all at once.

Her brows shot up like helium balloons. "I beg your pardon."

Maybe part of my mind was desperately searching for sanity, but the crazies had a good firm hold on my larynx. "I like sweet potatoes," I said, slurring my words. "And giblets."

She opened her mouth, closed it, tried again. "Are you looking for the meal line?"

"Meal," I repeated, dumber than french fries.

"It's down the hall and to your right."

I nodded and shuffled out.

"And if you need new clothes, we offer those as well."

I scurried away, face burning, still muttering about yams and chicken innards. When next I glanced back, she had disappeared into her office. I blasted out of there like a rocket ship on speed.

I was still embarrassed hours later when I arrived at Best of Vegas. The rambling art deco restaurant was located on Harvard Drive, where the rich and spoiled like to loiter. I had heard mouth-lubricating reviews from the senator and others who dined there regularly but had never had the pleasure myself. Just that week, however, I had received an all-inclusive, one-day-only coupon and, wanting to be beholden to no man, thought it a clever idea to use it or use it.

"Christina." Archer was waiting in the brightly colored lobby, dressed in a suit and tie. He motioned vaguely to his ensemble. "I never know what to wear."

"You look fine," I said.

He smiled. "Well, you look spectacular."

I did look pretty good. Knowing Laney and Geek Boy were going to join us, I had pulled out the stops. Not that I'd intentionally put in any stops, but the lack of clean laundry had definitely given me pause. Earlier in the afternoon, however, I had remembered my unclaimed dry cleaning. Hence, I had hustled over to Zippy Cleaners. My plum-colored silk blouse was neat as a pin, my black knee-length skirt well pressed and pencil thin. Well, on Laney it would have been pencil thin. On me it was more the width of a . . . well, of my hips. But I still looked damn good.

We were escorted through stained-glass doors to a semicircular booth near the back, where we were seated.

"You hungry?" Mac asked.

I considered asking him if hippos had big asses but refrained. A little class wouldn't hurt anything, especially when ordering a meal slightly more expensive than my house payment.

" 'Cuz I'm starved," he added, and immediately began perusing the menu. "Would it seem criminal if we ordered without them?"

"Laney's not easily offended," I told him, "and Solberg . . . well, I don't care if you offend Solberg." I'd given Archer a thumbnail summary on the phone of Elaine, her career, and her improbable pet/boyfriend. He'd still shown up. Scanning the appetizers now, he asked me several salient questions regarding my affinity for portobello mushrooms and shrimp scampi. In a minute he had placed an order for both.

After a short segue of relatively painless conversation,

the appetizers arrived. One was flaming, one simply resting on its lovely laurels, but I fear we might not have given them their due respect, because ten minutes later they were no more. Amidst scattered talk of family and polo shirts, the platters had somehow become empty. Donald winced.

"Please tell me I didn't eat all of that," he said.

I refrained from belching. I'm a classy mushroom's worst nightmare. "I think I had a little."

"Are you sure? 'Cuz I eat too much when I'm nervous." He unbuttoned his jacket and fidgeted a little. "I'm nervous a lot."

I had to admit I was starting to kind of like this guy. Just then Laney arrived. She was wearing a pair of blue jeans that had had some hard knocks and a multicolored belted tunic. Nothing special. I waited for my date to pass out at the sight of her in all her unvarnished glory, but he managed to remain vertical. Another point for Rich Boy.

Soon we were all settled in.

"So . . ." Solberg grinned at me. "This your new squeeze, Chrissy?"

"Donald Archer," I said, not taking my best raptor gaze off Solberg, "this is J. D. Solberg." They reached across the table to shake hands. "He likes to call himself the Geek God."

To Solberg's credit, he looked a little chagrined as he glanced at Elaine. I was hoping he was embarrassed by his own ridiculous past, but, truth to tell, he wasn't nearly the ass he had once been. Laney's been known to reform cannibals and ax murderers, too.

"And this is Elaine Butterfield," I added.

Archer nodded. "Royalty," he said.

She shook his hand. "It's nice to meet you."

He settled back in the booth, smoothing his tie away from the detritus of our hors d'oeuvres. "Where are you from?"

"The Amazon," she said, and smiled.

He glanced at me and back. "You're an Amazon queen?"

Her smile broadened just a little.

"And here I didn't even know those Amazon ladies were real."

The three of us blinked at him in startled unison.

"Oh, shit." He looked stunned enough to flee. "I just said something stupid, and we haven't even gotten our entrées yet."

By the time the meal was finished, I'd laughed more than I had since my brother Pete mistook my science project for pudding. Both Laney and Solberg had stuck to mineral water, but Archer and I each had a single drink. Maybe they made the evening go by a little more smoothly, but I had a sneaking suspicion it would have been all right without it. Donald was intelligent enough, down to earth, and ridiculously comfortable to be with.

"Seriously," I said. Elaine had gone to the restroom. Solberg was probably pacing like a rabid dog in front of the bathroom door, afraid she'd shimmied out the window and hightailed it back to her filming location in Idaho or wherever geek gods with hair implants were in scarce supply. We remained by the table, which was covered with a full dozen emptied platters. "You really didn't recognize Elaine Butterfield?"

He glanced at me through thick lashes. "I don't watch much television. You said she was royalty or something. I..." He shrugged.

"I meant she's an actress—and gorgeous."

"Is she?"

I canted my head at him. "If we don't keep armed guards close at hand, men tend to throw themselves at her feet."

"Why?"

I blinked. "Because she's *gorgeous*."

"Is she?"

Ahh, so there was the problem: He was nuts.

"I'm sorry," he said, fiddling with a half-empty glass. "It's just that I . . . I don't . . ." He paused and took a deep breath. "I can't tell."

"You can't tell . . ." I waited for him to fill in the blank.

"I can't tell if women are attractive or not. I don't know why. I think there might be something fundamentally wrong with me."

I opened my mouth to remind him that he had dubbed me "spectacular," but he spoke before I embarrassed myself.

"You make me laugh," he said. "I like to laugh. And when I'm around you my heart feels kind of . . . soggy."

I reached for the tab, just delivered by a slick-haired server dressed in black. I was eager to see how much I wasn't paying. "Soggy?" I said.

"I'm no better with words than with clothes," he said, and, smoothing his tie again, took the bill from me.

"I have a coupon," I said, but just then he removed a wad of bills from his wallet and shoved them into the folder. Not counting, not looking at the charges. Nothing. I wasn't positive, but I was pretty sure I saw a half dozen hundreds in there.

The server bowed reverently and strode off, possibly to retire.

I rose to my feet. I think I may have also reached wistfully after him as if to draw back the cash. "I think . . . Did you just give him a million-dollar tip?" I asked.

Donald rose beside me. "I'm not very good with math, either. Listen, Christina . . ." He shuffled from foot to foot. "I think I really like you."

Okay, so he was overweight and not terribly self-confident, but he was kind of sweet and apparently ungodly rich. I glanced around.

"Christina?" he said.

"Usually at this point someone tries to kill me," I said.

He grinned a little. "See any likely suspects?"

"Not—" I began, but suddenly Rivera appeared in my peripheral vision. I think I actually did a double take. I mean, what were the chances? I'd seen him just a few hours before, but now, unlike earlier, he was dressed in dark dress pants and a smooth, body-hugging jersey that highlighted the shift of every sensuous muscle. His midnight hair was combed back, and his eyes were as intense as a hunting falcon's. It wasn't until he leaned toward his companion that I realized he was with anyone at all.

"Thea," I breathed, barely able to force out the name.

"What's that?" Archer asked.

They looked like an L.A. version of Ken and Barbie. Him dark. Her fair. Both so beautiful it made my insides hurt. I turned to Archer, breath held.

"You like me?" I asked, voice barely audible to my own ringing ears.

He didn't bolt for the hills, but he did step back half a stride. "I think so. But—"

"You find me attractive?"

"Like I said, I can't—" he began.

"Is there someone you'd give your kidneys to make jealous?"

One thing about Archer: He wasn't stupid. He didn't look away, didn't so much as glance to the side. "Does he have a good view of us?"

"If he were any closer we'd be standing on him."

"How do you feel about French kissing?"

"Right about now—" I began, but he was already pulling me into a full-body hug and locking his lips to mine like a starving man at an all-night banquet.

24

Some people say the way to a man's heart is through his stomach. In actuality, you have to make an incision through his skin, both dermis and epidermis, then carefully sever and separate the sternum. Only upon viewing the exposed thoracic cavity can you reach the heart—if indeed the male of the species actually possesses such an organ.

—Dr. Sarah Kaminsky, Chrissy's psych
professor, who displayed a strong
interest in medicine and perhaps a
little bitterness toward men

*M*AC. MAC!"

I came to slowly. Archer might be overweight and underassured, but he could kiss like a drunken sailor.

"What?" My voice was mumbly. I turned toward Laney like a woman in need of smelling salts, but she only tilted her head toward the front door. I careened my attention in that direction and discovered that Senator Rivera had also arrived.

Neither Rivera was looking at me—they had their gazes locked on each other. The elder was smiling, but it was the kind of carnivorous expression that belied his perfectly tailored suit, his urbane manner.

I couldn't hear the words, but I could imagine them. *"May I have a word with you, Gerald?"*

Gerald's answer would not be so congenial, but the supermodel with the hair was standing right there, watching with the wide eyes of an ingenue. What could he do but ease away from her? The two men stood together now, looking like fuming *GQ* models. We watched the way one would focus on a train wreck, but it didn't come to blows. The conversation was short, terse, and packed with enough animosity to blow the roof right off the restaurant. At the finale, the lieutenant leaned in and growled something in his father's face. Then he stalked off, glanced down at the poor supermodel with the hair, and led her off to their table.

He never once glanced toward me but kept his gaze glued straight ahead, his jaw set like a recalcitrant pugilist's.

"Holy shit." Archer's voice was close to my ear. "Is that Lieutenant Rivera?"

I nodded. His private investigator must have been pretty thorough when ferreting out information.

"Is that his old man?"

I'm not sure I even managed a nod that time. Rivera and the supermodel were just being seated.

"Do you think he saw us kiss?"

I swallowed, and at that second, like the devil himself, Rivera lifted his gaze to mine. I could swear fire shot from his eyes, devouring me, consuming me. I felt my knees buckle, but Archer caught one arm. Laney caught the other. In a moment they were shuffling me toward the front door.

Outside, the air felt heavy.

"You okay?" Laney asked.

I wobbled a nod.

"Holy crap!" Solberg was jittering like a June bug. "What do you suppose that was about?"

"Do you want to sit down?" Archer asked. There was a garden only a few yards away. He herded me in that direction and eased me onto a park bench. Then he sat beside me as Laney and Solberg took seats opposite us.

"What just happened?" asked Solberg, still jumping even though he was seated.

"Who's the girl?" Laney asked.

I swallowed a lump of unidentified emotion and glanced back at the restaurant. "The supermodel with the hair?"

"I guess."

"Her name's Thea Altove."

"Why was the senator so pissed?" Solberg asked, then apologized for his scalding language.

I closed my eyes for a second and blew out a breath. Such unsteadiness was ridiculous, of course. "He doesn't want Rivera to date her."

"How do you know that?" Laney asked.

I tried to refrain from telling the truth, but resistance was futile.

"Maybe I eavesdropped."

"Where?"

"Caring Hands."

She was still staring at me, so I continued. No one can resist Laney and her lie-seeking gaze.

"In the office next to the senator's."

"And?"

I shook my head. "I didn't hear much, only the senator warning Rivera not to date the supermodel."

"So he brought her here, to the senator's favorite spot?"

"This is the senator's favorite spot?" Solberg asked.

Laney ignored him. "Why?"

"Did you see her?" I asked.

"You think the senator wants her for himself," Laney said.

"No shi—No kidding?" Solberg's tone was raspy. "She's . . . like . . . twelve."

"Time-honored tradition," Archer said.

We turned toward him. Some of us may have forgotten he was there. I'm not proud to admit I might have been one of them.

He shrugged. "Wealthy men. Young women," he explained. All eyes were on him now. "My current stepmother is the same age as my shoelaces."

I made a face.

"Has the senator been wooing her?" Laney asked.

"Wooing?" I said, still a little disoriented.

"Don't think too hard," she warned.

I nodded dimly, recognizing good advice when I heard it. "Not that I know of."

She was scowling. "Then why not let Rivera have her?"

"She's a hottie," Solberg said. "The old man's probably working up his nerve."

We turned on him as if he'd lost a few brain cells.

"The senator once called the Speaker of the House a yellow-bellied turncoat," Archer said.

We turned on *him*.

He cleared his throat, a little uncomfortable under fire. "I'm just saying, I don't think he lacks nerve."

"What, then?" Laney asked, but I had a sneaking suspicion she might already have forged her own theories.

Archer shrugged. "If he wants her, he's sure as hell not going to want his son to have her, even if he doesn't claim her for himself."

"But would that be worth making a public scene?" Laney asked.

"Sometimes men don't make a lot of sense when their egos get involved," Archer said.

We stared at him.

He grinned a little. "Just an observation."

"It seems like the old man would have more important things to worry about," Solberg said.

"Like what?" Archer asked.

It was silent for a second, but after the kiss it seemed like my unfortunate date deserved to know the truth. I gave him the abbreviated version about the deaths and how they involved the good senator.

"So there have been three bizarre deaths related to Rivera," Archer said.

"*Loosely* related," Laney reminded him. Of the present company, she was probably the person least wanting to get me killed.

"How do we know that?" Solberg asked.

I turned toward him with a scowl.

"I mean," he said, "how do we know there haven't been more?"

"I checked into it," I said.

"How?"

"On the Internet."

"No offense, babekins, but if technology and you were

in the sack together, you wouldn't need no prophylac-
tics."

Laney was looking at him with her ever-clear eyes.

"I'll look into it, angel," he said, and she gave him the
whisper of a smile.

His subsequent dowder-headed expression creeped me
out a little. "Well," I said, having recovered enough to be
cruel, "looks like it's time for me to go home, since I don't
like to hurl in public."

We said our good-byes. Archer walked me to my car. I
turned when I got to my humble little Saturn.

"I'm sorry," I said, and fiddled with my car keys.

"For?"

I glanced up. There was humor and uncertainty in his
voice.

"Well . . ." I cleared my throat. "For being an idiot, for
one thing."

"I don't think you're an idiot." He tilted his head. "In
love with another man . . ." He let the sentence hang there.

God save me from recurring themes. "It's not love," I
said.

"What is it?"

"I don't think there's a name for it that can be voiced in
polite society." More key-fiddling. "The kiss . . ." I said.

"What about it?"

"I'm sorry about it."

He glanced over my head. He was just tall enough to do
so. "Wish I could be."

"What?"

"Kinda seems if I had a pebble's worth of pride I'd be
pissed, huh?"

"Aren't you?"

"It's not every day I get to kiss a woman like you, Christina."

The sentence was said with sincerity and feeling. If compliments were meals, it would have been prime rib. "It was a good kiss," I said.

"I put everything I had into it. Another couple seconds I would have needed a defibrillator."

Despite everything—world hunger, the bubonic plague . . . Rivera—I couldn't help but laugh. "You're okay, Archer."

He didn't say anything. Doubts shouldered in.

"Aren't you?"

"Nicer than him," he said, and nodded toward the interior of the restaurant, where Rivera sat with a girl younger than his dog.

"That's not saying much," I said, and sighed.

"Then why are you—" he began, but I knew the question.

"Because I'm demented."

He paused a second, then nodded. "It's an interesting family. I've always thought so."

I glanced up, curious, heart starting to pound a little. "What do you mean, you've always thought so?"

"Dad was a big supporter."

"Of the senator's?" Paranoia bellied up to the doubt, shoving it rudely aside.

"Yeah."

I felt tense and stupid to be so. "Is that why you're here?"

"What?"

"To protect the senator?"

"I—"

"Did you have Manny killed?"

"What?" He actually stumbled back a step.

"Was he going to cause trouble for the senator?"

"What are you talking about? Manny was a drunk. As far as I know, he passed out cold and fell headfirst into the river."

"Do you think *I'm* planning to cause trouble for him?" I was rambling. I know I was rambling. Maybe I even knew then, but I couldn't stop myself. " 'Cuz I'm not. I didn't want anything to do with another Rivera. He came to me. Asked me to look into the deaths. Ask him yourself."

"Listen, honey, you should forget about all this."

I narrowed my eyes at him, thinking. Manny had started a lawsuit against Ironwear. Essentially, Archer *was* Ironwear. Maybe that's why Emanuel was now in the morgue. Or maybe it was even more twisted than that. Maybe Archer was behind all of it. All the deaths. Maybe he had an unrevealed past with the senator. Maybe the old man had slighted him, or run over his cat, or, more likely, slept with his girlfriend. "What was your last girlfriend's name?" I asked.

"Debra. Why?"

"How long did you date Cynthia?"

He stared at me. "I don't know what you're thinking," he said. "But I swear I've never dated a Cynthia."

"How about a Cyndy?"

"No."

"Cyndra?"

"Hey," he stopped me, expression concerned. "I don't even vote."

"What?"

"I wouldn't know a Republican from a Hoosier."

"You're not planning to kill me to protect his reputation?"

"Geez, Chrissy!" he said, and, despite the fact that I insisted on speaking, took my hand in his. "What has the world been doing to you?"

I swallowed. The feel of his skin against mine was kind of soothing. "It hasn't all been great," I admitted.

He sighed. "You're not going to drop it, are you?"

"I need the money," I said.

He canted his head.

"The senator paid me," I said. "To figure out if the deaths were accidents."

"That seems like a pretty strong case for his innocence."

I shrugged. "People are . . . complex." I was going to say something less positive, but Archer was a nice guy. Maybe.

"I could check things out," he said. "See what the senator's been up to. My dad's . . ." He shrugged. "He's smart, but he's not . . . well, he's not real nice, still I could ask what he knows about the Riveras."

"What do you mean, not nice?"

"I'm the prince of understatement."

"You think your father might have some dirt on the senator?"

He nodded, and then, leaning close, he kissed me. It was nice, gentle but evocative. "You're as crazy as an avocado, but I kind of like you," he said, and left.

I was halfway home before I remembered the prince-of-understatement statement.

25

I don't need no PMS. I can be a bitch under my own steam.

—*Shirley Templeton,*
God love her

SUNDAY PASSED IN A HAZE. I spent three hours with Laney, shopping, laughing, and catching up on the minutiae of our lives.

Monday attacked me before I was ready. "I talked to the sister." Micky Goldenstone was back, but he wasn't crying. Neither was he sitting. He was pacing, prowling around my office like a sleek black panther.

"Lavonn."

He nodded, but I wasn't convinced he'd heard me. He may have simply been agreeing with some unheard dialogue that tolled in his head alone. He continued to pace.

"What did she say?"

He closed his eyes, and I wasn't sure he would answer, but then he did. "Said she remembers me."

I braced myself. Micky's sessions were more like a high-speed roller coaster than therapy.

"She smiled," he said, and stared out the window. "Like I was her best friend in the world." He nodded. "Invited me in. Asked if I wanted a Coke or something. Said she'd had a crush on me. That all the girls did."

I took a careful breath, not wanting to disturb him. Trying to wait. But it was no good. He was lost in the turmoil of his past. "So Kaneasha didn't tell her about the incident."

I knew the instant the question left my mouth that I had chosen the wrong phrase. Micky wasn't one to mince words. He was more apt to serve them whole and let you choke them down or puke them up. Didn't matter to him.

"Incident?" he said.

I caught his gaze and squeezed it tight. Despite what I knew of this man, I liked him. I couldn't help myself, and I didn't want to lose any gram of respect I may have gained during the last few months of therapy. "The rape," I corrected.

He stared at me, then dropped onto the couch and closed his eyes. "She never told nobody. Kept it to herself. Kept it..." He turned toward me. Eyes burning with emotions I didn't even really want to understand. "She's dead."

It took a moment for his words to sink in. Longer still to figure out how to respond. "Oh, Micky. I'm so sorry."

"Died of an overdose."

"Did you speak to Jamel?"

A muscle jumped in his jaw. "For a minute."

I nodded, urging him on.

"He's . . ." He drew a deep breath, searching for words or thoughts or strength. I wasn't sure which. "He's been with Lavonn off and on for four years."

I wanted to apologize again, but he cut me off.

"She got two kids of her own. Still in diapers."

I wanted to tell him everything was all right. Jamel would be fine. Children were resilient. They made do. They soldiered on. But maybe he wouldn't be, sometimes people weren't, and quite often they didn't. I had to remind myself that I had no idea how his son would turn out, and even if I did, it wasn't necessarily my job to appease his guilt. Sometimes pain's a catalyst. Sometimes it's just pain. On a good day, with a nice waxing moon and a dynamite scrying glass, I might be able to divine the difference.

"Did he seem healthy?" I asked to fill time. "Well adjusted? Was he—"

"She got a boyfriend," he said, and wiped his palms down the lean length of his thighs.

I braced myself. I knew enough of his childhood to guess where this was going. "And . . ."

"He's an ass," he said, and jerked back to his feet.

I drew a careful breath, watched him pace, and realized I missed Mr. Pearl. Mr. Pearl's most pressing problem was that he got fidgety when his potatoes breached the boundaries of his brussels sprouts. I suggested in our first session together that he buy some of those clever, picnic-type plates that are divided into sections. He'd dubbed me a genius among therapists and has come back every Tuesday since.

Micky's problems were a little trickier. So far there had

been no talk of my astounding cleverness, but I nodded like a ruminating shaman, still hoping we'd get around to that conversation. "Perhaps you should consider that your past might be coloring your perception. Sometimes it is difficult for a person with your history to—" I began, but he turned on me, eyes afire, lips snarling.

"The boyfriend's an ass!" he said.

"Okay." I nodded, dropped the certified shrink talk, and settled back. "What makes him an ass?"

"How the fuck would I know? Some people are just—" He stopped himself, expression appalled, and sat, covering his face with his hands. "Shit! *I'm* an ass."

"Sometimes," I said, and didn't let myself smile.

But his mercurial moods weren't so stern. Dropping his hands, he sat up straight. His lighthouse grin peeked at me and was gone. "You're gonna be a hell of a mom, Doc."

I considered that in shuddering silence for a moment and moved on. "What are you going to do now?"

He rested his head back against the top of my couch and drew a noisy breath. "The kid's my responsibility."

"Partly, anyway."

"Partly!" He was angry again, quick as lightning. "You're thinking she had a choice in the matter?"

"Didn't she?" My voice was the epitome of the calm before the storm. Him being the storm. Me being... I don't know. Maybe stupid?

"You better check your notes, Doc. Could be you forgot that I raped her?"

"Sometimes absorbing all the blame is as detrimental as accepting too little," I said.

"What the hell is that supposed to mean?"

I felt like shrinking under my seat cushion at his tone.

But being intimidated has never done me a hell of a lot of good. Spitting into the glaring eye of authority hasn't been so hunky-dory, either, but that's another story. "If you take all the blame, others won't get their fair share."

He stared at me a second, then, "Fuck that," he said.

I nodded, reminding myself to save the crappy shrink talk for lawyers, the board of psychology, and ugly dogs that peed on my shoes. "Okay, maybe she didn't have options about getting pregnant. But—"

"Maybe!"

"The child might not be yours. And even if he is, what then? She made her own choices after that. The drugs. The abandonment."

"You think it's easy?" he asked. His tone was deadly calm. "You think we don't have enough problems without our damn kids raising kids?"

"Is this the part where you tell me how hard it is to be black?"

It took him a moment, but finally I caught a glimpse of chagrin in his expression. "I think I pay you enough to bitch a little."

"If that's how you want to spend your time."

He sighed, pragmatism overcoming dramatics. "You think she should have gotten rid of it?"

Holy crap, I couldn't even decide what to do with my plant cuttings. God forbid I be put in charge of procreation of the species. "That's not for me to decide. You know that. And even if it were, it's a moot point now."

"She was just a kid."

"And now *he* is," I said. "Move on, Micky."

He glared at me, eyes angry, but I stopped him before he could blast me with his burning ghetto logic.

"Or . . . you can wallow in self-pity. That's a constructive option, too."

He paused for a moment, watching me. "Are you being facetious?" he asked finally. He sounded truly affronted. "Am I paying you a shitload of money for your sarcasm?"

"Sorry," I said, and meant it. I needed his shitload of money to pay my shitty bills.

He glanced toward the window and swore. His posture softened a little. "What should I do?"

I tried to force myself to relax. Turns out I'm incapable. "What are your choices?"

He shook his head. "I could pay child support."

"Without legally claiming him as your son?"

"Why not?"

I shrugged, knowing he'd realize the answer in a minute. "It might assuage your guilt," I said.

He lowered his brows, thinking things over, then: "You think the boy wouldn't get it."

I said nothing. Generally it's my most effective method of psychoanalyzing.

"That fucking boyfriend," he said, and suddenly he was pacing again, striding across the room in frustration. "Fuckin' corn-fed fat-ass. Cocky as hell." He stopped, turned toward me. "Maybe I could start a savings account."

I watched him. "Micky, you don't even know if you're his father."

Seconds ticked away. "Does it matter?"

"Maybe not. If you don't think it does."

"If I'm not, it ain't through no fault of mine."

"So you're going to make yourself pay, even if he's someone else's child."

Tension cranked up tight, then: "You're right," he said. "Throwing money at him would be a stupid-ass thing to do."

I hadn't meant that exactly, but I let him talk things through.

"Stupid, shortsighted, self-centered." He nodded in concert to his thoughts.

I gave him encouraging silence.

"Thing to do is get custody," he said, and I managed to refrain from gasping.

The phone beside my bed rang at one of those small hours of the morning ear-tagged by God Himself for sleeping. I picked up the receiver on something like the eighty-second ring.

"Babekins!"

I winced at the nasally voice. Brainy Laney had returned to the hinterlands of Idaho for filming yesterday and wouldn't be back until Christmas Eve. I resented the fact that she was gone even more than I hated the idea that the Geekster remained. The fact that she'd left a message on my answering machine saying her Saudi friend was going to check up on Ramla's sister only made the situation slightly more palatable.

"What time is it?" I asked.

"You know I can't sleep when Angel's gone." He sounded as chirpy as a midnight cricket, and slightly more irritating.

"I can," I said, and blinked blurrily at the alarm. "Is it three o'clock?"

"Could be."

"Three o'clock in the *morning*?"

"Probably. Say, listen. Remember how I said I'd look into weird deaths?"

I narrowed my eyes, mind kicking miserably into a slow semblance of life. "Yeah?"

"Turns out there are a buttload of 'em. You know a gal was killed by an elephant in Tennessee last year? Course, you can't really blame the pachyderm. I mean, they'd named her Winkie. And who the hell...sorry...*heck* would—"

"I'm not too tired to drive over and kick your ass," I said. Sometimes I'm a little crabby when people wake me at three in the morning. Sometimes I'm equally crabby at four in the afternoon, but I don't have such a convenient excuse.

Solberg chuckled as if I were joking. Since the advent of Elaine in his life, there wasn't much that could get him down. Maybe I resented that most of all.

"Okay. Okay. Anyway, there's a ton of freaky shit... sorry...*stuff* happening. Someone should write a book. Hey, you want to—"

"Solberg..." I warned.

"All right. Keep your pants on. Here it is: Guy died while scuba diving off the shore of Kauai."

"What was his name?"

"Amos Bunting."

I yawned. "I've never heard of—"

"But he went by the name of Steve."

"Steve...Steve Bunting!" My mind kicked out of neutral with a painful lurch. "Holy crap!" I was suddenly wide awake. "He was a coordinator for one of the senator's campaigns. I saw a picture of him."

"Yeah, well, he's dead now. Ran out of oxygen—"

"When?"

"What?"

I was scrambling out of bed toward my office. "When did it happen?"

"Just last month. I guess Hawaii's good for diving even—"

I hauled him up short. "What day of the week?"

"What?"

"Just tell me, damn it!"

"Thursday," he said, and I wrote it in bloodred permanent marker on my tagboard.

26

Maybe money can't buy happiness. But it can get you a nice little villa in Tuscany, and that's close enough for me.

—Dagwood Dean Daly,
professional gangster

I WOKE EARLY on Tuesday morning. Someone would die on Friday! I knew it! Well, I knew that someone would die on *a* Friday. Or had already died. Somewhere in the world. On the other hand, maybe it wouldn't take a Ph.D. for most folks to figure that out.

After discovering Bunting's demise, Solberg had scoured the Internet for other deaths related to the senator and had come up with bupkis. Knowing the Geekster's world-renowned techno abilities, I had to believe there was, then, bupkis to be found.

Shelving that information, I ran up Vine Avenue with my trusty canine at my side. Or, more precisely, I chugged along like a panting orangutan with Harlequin dragging me all the way. Running sometimes clears my head. This time it only lubricated it. The temperature had climbed to eighty-three degrees by eight a.m. Maybe somewhere near Santa's workshop, global warming is welcomed like the second coming, but L.A. is one of those cities destined to be set adrift by the melting (and therefore pissed-off) glaciers, and I gotta tell you, most of us on the West Coast aren't all that thrilled with the idea. Sweat was dripping into my eyes like Chinese water torture by the time I reached my front gate.

"The bath, it is empty."

I wiped the sweat off my face with a wilty sleeve and focused on Ramla Al-Sadr. She was standing in the middle of the sidewalk, dressed in enough clothes to ensure modesty and heat exhaustion.

"Would you like to use?"

"I'm sorry," I said, "I'm afraid I haven't learned anything useful about your sister yet."

"That is to be expected," she said, expression troubled yet stoic. "These things they take the time." She wrinkled her nose. "But you cannot forgo the bath until she is here."

By the time I was drying my hair, Ramla was nowhere to be seen. I slunk across my yard and into my own house before I had to face her and my failure again.

Finally, late and despondent, I headed off to work.

My life felt disjointed. I saw five clients, then swilled down a burger at an In-N-Out on the way home and ended the day in my home office. After scribbling down all the information I could find regarding the four victims, I stared dismally at my wall, but there wasn't much there. I had the least amount of info on Bunting. According to what the senator had told me, he had never married. In fact, he'd lived with his parents off and on for most of his life. But Solberg had learned that since their deaths eighteen months earlier, he'd resided in Europe.

The next couple of days were filled with quiet frustration and overt craziness. Still, there was no good explanation for the ensuing phone call, other than the fact that my wall was covered with the flotsam of unresolved deaths. Well, maybe my dark mood had some effect, too. True, I'd been on more dates in the past week than even my rich fantasy life usually offered, but I felt a sort of off-center loneliness. Ramla's stoic sorrow gnawed at me, while my sense of not belonging seemed magnified by the looming holidays. I'd sent off gifts to Christianna and the others, but the gesture felt empty. All the same, there was no supportable reason for my current lapse in sanity.

"Rivera." I clutched the receiver in white-knuckled fingers. I was trying for convivial and coolheaded. Instead, I may have sounded breathy and a little high. I'd experimented with a half dozen other salutations in my mirror earlier in the day, but "Hello, darling" seemed a little Zsa Zsa and "Yo" sounded kind of ghetto coming from a woman whose skin tone was a shade lighter than skim milk. "Do you have a minute?" I asked.

There was a brief delay, during which I imagined the lieutenant narrowing his eyes, bitter-sharp mind churning. "Slow night for you, McMullen?" he asked.

It was after eleven o'clock. I'd spent the past seven hours trying to talk myself out of calling him. If I'd had my druthers I would have been asleep for a gerbil's lifetime by then, but the previous night had been a doozy. Usually the dead and the nocturnal me have a good deal in common. But it was the dead who had kept me awake.

In fact, it was Kathy Baltimore herself who consistently reappeared in my dreams. She asked me what day it was. I told her it was Friday. At which time she began singing hymns, but she had no mouth, and only one arm.

Creepy as hell. It's times like those that make a girl kind of wish she had someone to talk to in the wee hours of the morning. Someone sans tail and collar.

"No sleepovers?" Rivera asked. His voice rumbled through my sleep-hungry system like dark rum, but I fought the effects. There were other fish in the sea. Who cared that none of them resonated in my humming place? They didn't try to bait me with every spoken word, either. Which was exactly what he was trying to do. Still, I kept my tone as sunny as a kindergartner's. "Just me and Harley and a carton of yogurt," I said.

"Didn't like the way Curly Top looked when he got down to his skivvies?"

I could only assume that Curly Top was Donald Archer, but I smiled at his poor attempt to rile me. "Not everyone can be a fifteen-year-old supermodel," I said.

"Isn't that the shits." I could hear him easing into a chair and imagined him leaning back, probably smugly post-coital. The idea made my guts knot up like pretzels. Still, I shouldn't have mentioned his latest conquest. I chided myself silently, remembering belatedly that I didn't need him. Didn't care who he coitaled. Nevertheless, I spoke again.

"Is she there now?" I asked. "Or is it past her bedtime?"

He chuckled. I gritted my teeth, closed my eyes to my own snowballing stupidity, and tried a more mature tack.

"Listen, Rivera, I didn't call to start a pissing contest."

"Wouldn't do you any good, anyway." He sighed, proud. "I have a bigger dick."

"You *are* a bigger——" I began, then yanked myself up short, took a deep breath, tried again. "I was hoping to speak to you." I closed my eyes. My hands were shaking. Stupid. So stupid. "Possibly without spewing acrimony?"

"About?"

I had been considering how best to phrase this for hours and had come up with some elegant phraseology. I took a deep, quiet breath and tried my knockout punch. "I've given the situation due deliberation." I paused, maybe for effect, maybe to round up any remaining brain cells that might still have a flicker of life. Rivera tends to scramble my mind like an eggbeater. "And I believe someone intends to kill your father."

There was a moment of absolute silence.

And then he laughed.

I gripped the receiver with Amazonian bonhomie and waited for his fun-loving jocularity to subside. "Tell me the truth," he said finally. "Is it me?"

My hands had quit shaking and the ghoulish images of the past few nights receded. Anger, it seems, is something of a panacea for me. "I'm certainly thrilled to entertain you," I said. "But this is not amusing."

"Lots of things aren't." His chair creaked. I heard him stand, listened to his footfalls bluster across the floor, and wondered if he wasn't, perhaps, quite as postcoitally content as he had first seemed.

I drew a deep breath and took the plunge. "I need you to take a look at something."

The pacing stopped with abrupt finality. "It's been a hell of a day, McMullen." His tone had gone from dark rum to fermented grog. "If it's not you in a black negligee, I'm not interested."

My lungs considered exploding. My heart surged a little and my scalp tingled dangerously. From his drawer beside my bed, François growled an affronted-Frenchman challenge, but I kept my tone watermelon cool. "I don't own a black negligee."

Floorboards creaked restlessly. A couple of still-flittering brain cells suggested that he was pacing again. "White'll do," he said.

I gave his words sage consideration for a fraction of a second. In fact, I would have considered longer, would have taken hours, *days* to come up with a scathing response, but my lips spoke up without permission.

"All right," they said.

"What's that?" Nothing squeaked or moaned or moved. In fact, the world seemed absolutely incapable of doing anything but waiting in breathless anticipation.

I gripped the receiver tighter. "I said all right."

There was a pause for five and a half seconds, then: "I'll be there in half an hour."

I didn't bother to remind him that in L.A. it takes longer than that to cross the street, but, as it turned out, it was lucky I didn't waste the time, because he arrived in just over twenty minutes.

I had spent the first five telling myself he was just yanking my chain and wasn't really coming at all. The next . . . oh, twenty-seven seconds I was busy blathering on about how it didn't matter what I wore; this was just my ingenious ploy to get him to listen to me. The next quarter of an hour I hustled around like a panting virgin with the pre-honeymoon hives.

By the time I opened the door I was wearing a silk nightgown with matching robe.

He stood on my stoop, looking like a world-weary warrior, hair tousled, eyes burning, muscles tight with tension and man juice. He stepped inside without an invitation.

I swallowed any good sense that might still be hanging around and shut the door. Harlequin did a wiggly-worm dance around his legs.

"Can I get you something?" I asked. Smooth. Dark-jazz smooth.

He stared at me, thunderstorm eyes blazing. "You back on the menu, McMullen?"

I lifted my chin and refrained from jumping him like a hound on a rump roast. I didn't need him. I had Officer What's-His-Name and the guy with the curly hair. And François! I mustn't forget François. But, good God, his eyes burned me like a blowtorch. He circled me a little, as if I were prey.

"My old man worth whoring for?" he asked.

A couple dozen nasty zingers whizzed through my mind like flaming arrows, but I kept them firmly locked between my teeth and turned away, sauntering hip-crazy to my office. I stood there, not looking back, waiting. It took a moment, but finally he came up behind me. I could feel him gazing over my shoulder, staring at the board.

I didn't say anything, just stood waiting, tense and breathless.

"All you need is a deerstalker and a pipe and you're ready for supersleuthing," he said finally.

I turned from the tagboard. I was dead on my feet and bubbling with frustration, but I had my temper in a stranglehold. "The first murder took place on a Monday," I said.

He scowled, as if thinking against his will, and nodded at the names on the board as if familiar with them. "Ortez?"

"Yes."

"How was she killed?"

I fudged a little. "Arson."

He nailed me with his eyes. "Proven?"

I hurried to the wall, robe flaring behind me. I was pretty sure I looked like Wonder Woman, cape flying, hair flowing in the mysterious breeze possibly caused by her wonder plane. "Kathy died on a Tuesday. Manny on a Wednesday. And . . ." I tapped the tagboard and turned.

He lifted his hot gaze from me and nailed it to the board. A muscle jumped in his jaw.

"Bunting on a Thursday," he said.

I felt taut, breathless. "Yes."

He stared at the carefully garnered information for a dozen heartbeats, then shifted his attention back to me with slow deliberation. "Just one problem."

I waited.

"Baltimore's death was determined an accident."

"So were the others." It was meant as a challenge but sounded more like a weak-assed apology.

He focused on me fully, narrowing the world down to my face. "You could have just told me you were horny, McMullen." The air was motionless between us. "No need for excuses. I could have probably made it here three minutes faster."

Our gazes fused. I wanted to tell him to go screw himself, but if anyone was going to do the job I kind of desperately wanted it to be me. "How about you think with your head instead of your dick," I said instead.

We glared at each other, tension brewing like a toxic potion, but finally he chuckled and turned away. Drawing a deep breath, he shoved his hands into the front pockets of his frayed jeans. "Okay. I'll play along. Why do you suppose these people were killed?"

"Because they worked for your father." I was suddenly excited. The fact that he was even considering my theory felt hopelessly exhilarating. The fact that he hadn't shot me yet was kind of a bonus. "That much is certain. But the rest is unclear. Is it because they were imperfect? Or maybe they slighted the killer. But look—every one of them was closely connected to your dad at one point, and none of them fits the Moral Majority's conservative ideal."

He looked unconvinced. And ornery as hell. I hurried on.

I tapped the board again. "Wiccan, lesbian, alcoholic—"

"What about Bunting?"

I opened my mouth and shut it. "I haven't quite figured that out yet."

He glanced at me.

"I just learned about his death."

"Any living relatives?"

"Not that I've found. He never married. His parents died a year and a half ago."

He was reading the information as I spoke it, but his brows were low. "At the same time?"

I opened my mouth to respond, but I didn't have the answer and I couldn't afford to look weak. "The point is," I said, "people are dying. And more quickly now. Carmella was killed two months ago. Steve, in November. Five weeks apart. Then just three weeks between him and Kay, and only a day between her and Manny."

"Only problem is . . ." He turned toward me. "The deaths were accidental."

"Oh, don't be naïve!" I snapped.

He stared at me, surprised. I stared back, angry.

"I've been called a liar, an ass, and a murderer," he said, and, snorting, ran splayed fingers through his hair. "Been a while since anyone accused me of being naïve."

"How about stupid?"

The shadow of a grin flirted across his devil-may-kiss lips. "More recent."

I drew a hard breath. "Listen." I was hoping for cool. Struggling for sane. "I know it sounds far-fetched, but you know as well as anyone that the senator has enemies."

He didn't agree, but he certainly didn't argue. "Why now?"

"I don't know. Maybe to keep him from becoming the leader of the free world."

For a moment I thought he'd scoff, swear, and possibly self-implode, but he surprised me again. "That doesn't give us much to go on. Half the country would rather take a poker up the ass than see the senator in the Oval Office."

"But the other half would cheer."

"Probably because the left half has been pokered."

I shook my head, trying to clear it of the image. "How many people know he's considering throwing his hat in the ring?"

"Maybe a better question is who would think it worth risking life inside to have him dead."

"I don't believe the killer thinks he's at risk," I said.

"What?"

"Think about it." I was excited again. "No one's looking into the deaths. Everyone believes they're accidents. Even you," I added.

"Well . . ." He raised a practical hand. "I'm naïve."

"Don't be an ass, Rivera."

His lips twitched. "So it's finally come down to sweet talk."

"Listen," I said, "your father wants me to believe his campaigns were one big happy family, but I know there were problems."

"You think?"

I ignored him. "Ortez was Wiccan. Manny drank like a fish. Kathy was gay. I'm not sure what Bunting's deal was, but I'm certain there was something. All flawed, but all allowed into the senator's inner circle. What if they knew something they shouldn't . . . the sins of another . . ."

"Who?"

The senator himself? The idea flashed through my mind. But that would make him culpable, and I wasn't ready to believe that. "What about Salina?" I asked.

"What about her?" His voice was rumbly, his body tense.

"What if someone thinks the senator was responsible for Salina's death? What if someone wants him to pay? Wants him to worry? Wants him to see the circle narrowing down to him?"

"Someone besides me?"

I opened my mouth, then closed it slowly. We stared at each other.

"If you're accusing me of murder, you can come out and say it," he said.

"What?"

"You're usually more straightforward than this." He stood very still, predator eyes steady.

"I never even considered—"

"Was this *his* idea?" he asked. "Or did you come up with this brainstorm all by yourself?"

"I didn't—"

" 'Cuz it's not as if I don't want him dead. I just—"

"Oh, for God's sake! Shut the hell up!" I rasped. "You're not half clever enough to think of something this complex."

He raised his brows at me. Seconds ticked tensely away. "Let me get this straight. You think I'm too stupid to commit murder?"

"And too damn impatient. Can I explain now?"

He motioned expansively with one hand.

"What if someone thinks your dad killed Salina? Someone who cared about her." My mind was spinning like a cyclone. "Someone who's known him for a long while."

He didn't interrupt.

"They know he sees himself as the leader of the Moral Majority. His political team was his band of archangels."

Rivera snorted, but I gave him an impatient palms-out gesture and hurried on.

"They see the hypocrisy and want to make them suffer. All of them." I indicated the board. "But mostly him."

"The senator."

"Yes."

He studied the board. "You really think someone plans to kill him."

The entire idea suddenly seemed ridiculous, but I could hardly back down now. It would seem as if I'd just wanted to lure him over so he'd see me in my Wonder Woman ensemble. "I think it's a distinct possibility."

"Tomorrow."

I chewed on my lip, and he turned back to the board.

"Why is the time span narrowing?" he asked.

"Because of his bid for the presidency?"

"He hasn't announced his intent," he said. "At least not to the general public." A muscle jumped in his jaw. "Or me."

I ignored his tone and skimmed the board. He didn't seem surprised by the news and I didn't particularly care if he was injured by his father taking me into his confidence. "Who?" I mused.

He stared at me. "Are you asking who else my father has killed?"

"No. Before—" I began.

"I was being sarcastic, McMullen."

I turned toward him with a scowl.

"This is asinine," he said.

"Because he couldn't have been somehow involved in a murder?"

"Because if he had I would have known."

I gave that a moment of thought and decided I believed him. "And?"

He shook his head.

"Then who's going to die on Friday?"

"On *a* Friday," he corrected.

I gave a conceding shrug but held my ground. We stared at each other for a minute, but finally he blew out a breath and half-turned away.

"Ever heard of coincidence?"

"Yeah, I heard there's no such thing."

"Where'd you hear that?"

"From you."

"I've said a lot of other shit, too."

"Are you seriously telling me you think this is all just a strange twist of fate?"

He paused, stared at me, focusing intently, whittling

the world down to me. "I wouldn't have thought white would be your color."

"Don't change the subject."

"You're the one in the nightie."

I cleared my throat, feeling hot and vulnerable. "It's a gown."

"Yeah? I can't tell with the robe."

I lifted my chin a notch. "Your loss."

"Take it off."

"You're crazy," I said, but I suddenly felt itchy and... well, kind of horny.

He took a step toward me. "Why'd you call?" he asked. "Really?"

"Isn't your dad's life reason enough?"

His grin was twisted, dark, and cocky as hell. "Whatever it takes to get you in the mood."

"Drop the act," I said, but he was close now, close enough that I could feel the heat of his body blast me.

"What act is that, McMullen?"

"I know you care about him."

He laughed, but his gaze never left mine. "You being a shrink again, McMullen?"

It was hard to breathe, harder to think. Despite everything that had happened between us, he did things to me that no one else did—heightened my senses, jangled my nerves. "No one needs a shrink more than you."

He reached out, touched my cheek. Feelings sparked through me like a live electrical wire. "That what you think I need?"

I swallowed and tried to be smart. "Listen, Rivera..." I kept my tone cool. Kept my hands to myself. "I won't deny that I've been attracted to you in the past, but—" He skimmed his fingers along my jaw. My eyes flittered closed.

"But what?" he asked, voice tickling deep inside me. "Officer Milquetoast drove everyone else from your mind?"

It took me a moment to curl my fingers into my fists, lest they do something stupid, longer still to realize who he was referring to, but when I did I forced a nod. It was jerky and unsatisfying, but at least I hadn't yet mounted him like a jockey on the track favorite. "He's a nice guy," I said.

Rivera grinned. The expression did nasty things to my equilibrium. "If I remember correctly, the last nice guy you met turned out to be a hit man."

"This one's a cop."

His mouth twisted up even further. Dropping his hand slowly, he tugged the tie of my robe loose. It fell away, simply slipped to the floor as if on command. He put his hand on my waist.

I couldn't remember the last time I'd inhaled.

Warm, slow, and strong, his hand glided up my belly, over my ribs. He leaned in. His breath felt heavy against my face. His hand cupped my breast with light possessiveness. And then he kissed me, lips slanting across mine, drinking me in, inhaling me.

My innards felt cold, my brain overheated. His thumb tripped over my marble-hard nipple. A shriek jerked at my lips but never escaped. It might have been a protest. It might have been a plea.

He drew back half an inch, eyes burning into mine. "Never trust a cop," he said, and left.

27

Marriage: Just say no.

—Shirley Templeton

CHRISSY?"

"Yes." The phone had jarred me out of that lovely space between coherency and full-drool sleep. It was late Friday night. As far as I knew no one else had died. I had no idea what that meant.

"This is Donny."

My mind was spinning, but I wasn't gaining much ground.

"Donny Archer."

I shuffled upright, remembering he had promised to check out the senator. Shoving my pillow against the headboard, I glanced at Harlequin. He gave me a one-eyed squint, then twitched back to dreamland.

"Are you okay?"

"Me?" I realized suddenly that I was crumpling the bed-sheets in nervous fingers. I loosened my grip and smoothed the faux linens. "I'm fine." A second ticked by. My fingers squeezed again, frozen. "Why wouldn't I be?"

"No reason. I just...I've been thinking about you. I had a really good time the other—"

"Did you learn something?" My voice sounded croaky, but I couldn't wait any longer.

It took him a moment to catch up. "Not much. I'm sorry."

"So the senator didn't kill anyone?"

He drew a breath. "Sounds like it might be the opposite."

"What?" I froze. "What are you talking about?"

"I don't know. I mean—"

"Did something happen to him?"

"No. No. Sorry. I just meant...well, like I said, Dad's a big fan of the senator, so he didn't want to besmirch his name, and—"

"What did he say?"

"You were right. The senator's kind of a womanizer."

I exhaled carefully. That was like saying dirt was dirty. "Anyone specific?"

"No, he just said...well, he said that despite the senator's...appetites, he knew how to keep his money for himself."

"What does that mean?"

He cleared his throat. "Dad pays the approximate equivalent of the national debt in alimony."

I remained quiet, thinking.

"Apparently the senator doesn't marry the women

he . . . admires." There was a pause. "Or pay child support."

The world was silent.

"There's a child?"

"No. I mean, I don't know. Dad just said Rivera knew how to stay clear of . . . costly entanglements."

"Costly—Do you think there are children he's not claiming?"

"I can't say. I—"

"Why?" I sounded a little manic even to my own ears.

"What?"

"Why can't you say?"

"Because I don't know."

"Oh." I tried to breathe normally. But it was difficult. Harley, on the other hand, didn't seem to be having any trouble. He was beginning to snore.

"Are you sure you're okay?"

I can't tell you how many people ask me that after they get to know me a little. I closed my eyes. "I might be losing my mind."

"Yeah?" He paused for a second. "You crazy enough to go out with me again?"

In the end I told Archer that if I was still alive after the new year I'd give him a call. We hung up a short while later.

That weekend I finished up my shopping and mailed off the last of my out-of-town gifts. I emerged from the post office relatively unscathed. Hostilities hadn't escalated past a couple of minor skirmishes.

Evenings were spent poring over my scanty clues. After

Rivera's visit—and a lengthy discussion with François regarding the lieutenant's shortcomings (no pun intended)—I had checked into the deaths of Steve Bunting's parents. As it turned out, they *had* both died on the same day. And both in their sleep. Excitedly suspicious, I delved further, only to learn that the elder Mr. Bunting had been suffering from congestive heart failure for some time. The hospice nurse remembered him well.

"Such a gentle man," she said. "And very devoted to his wife, despite his discomfort. The morphine often made them a little . . . distant. But he was always so concerned about her. I think it was a blessing that they both passed on the same day."

A blessing? I wondered. Or murder? Despite my psychotic sleuthing, I couldn't determine whether their son had been with them that night. Nevertheless, it seemed odd to me that a man who had lived with his parents suddenly found the wherewithal to spend a year and a half on the Continent following their deaths.

After some internal debate, under Bunting's name I scribbled down the statistics I'd garnered, then wrote *Murder?* below that in bold red letters.

*M*icky Goldenstone arrived in my office a little early on Monday. It was Christmas Eve. He looked relaxed but tired as he settled onto my couch.

"Holidays wearing you out?" I asked.

He watched me in silence for a moment, then: "I told them," he said.

I sat very still. "You told them . . ."

He drew a deep breath, settled back against the cushions. "Kaneasha's sister. Her mama."

"You told them about the rape."

He smiled a little, but the expression was grim. "I was too much of a chicken shit for that." He glanced out the window. "I told them we was..." A muscle jerked in his jaw. "Together."

I let that sit for a moment.

"Turns out Lavonn..." He looked back at me. "Lavonn's got some financial problems. It's been hard...you know... taking care of all three kids."

"So—"

"They agreed to a paternity test."

My office went quiet.

"Merry Christmas to me," he said, and flickered a small smile filled with terror and guilt and the shy beginnings of hope.

Elaine returned that evening. She'd asked me to pick her up at the airport. Apparently Solberg had been called out of town at the last minute on business and wouldn't return until late that night. I didn't allow myself the luxury of considering the possibility that their ungodly union was cooling—or that he'd died in his sleep.

The hubbub at LAX surpassed insane. But when Laney appeared, slipping through the crowd in blue jeans and a sweatshirt, the world seemed to quiet. After she'd signed three autographs and turned aside a couple of marriage proposals as gently as possible, she ducked into my little Saturn and sighed.

We talked nonstop on the way to my house. She'd decided to stay with me for the night, but when we passed Roscoe Boulevard, a little chapel caught our attention. It was filled with light and music, and when we turned into the parking lot, "Silent Night" pulled us into the sanctuary.

In the end we were only there for half the service, but there were hymns and candlelight and not a single priest to glare at me with all-knowing eyes.

We returned home happy. The fact that the SuperSeptic guys had delivered a Porta-Potty made me ecstatic. Laney made lentil soup with all-natural ingredients she'd smuggled in her carry-on. I made popcorn balls with all things unnatural. We laughed and exchanged gifts and laughed some more as Harlequin systematically destroyed his new squeaky toys.

Christmas dawned, warm and smoggy, pretty much like every other day of the year. Because Laney hadn't had much time to prepare, Solberg sprang for the Christmas meal. To my surprise, we didn't end up at a fourteen-star restaurant in Beverly Hills. Instead, he'd ordered a catered meal consisting of every conceivable delicacy, and his house—expensive as hell but weirdly futuristic—seemed almost cozy when filled with the holiday smells of high-calorie goodies.

I ate myself into a near-catatonic state, but Harlequin was gazing at me like a sex-drunk lover, head level with the top of the chrome dining-room table. I slipped him a piece of honey-glazed ham. He slurped it down and gazed some more.

"Time for gifts," Solberg said, and the exchange commenced.

I gave him a rug. A literal rug, explaining it was meant

to pick up the slack when he ran out of body hair to transplant onto his head. He gave me a blow-up boyfriend. I was still reading the instructions when he cleared his throat.

"I got something for Angel, too," he said.

I didn't like the sound of his voice. When I looked up he was already on one knee facing Laney. I froze, mesmerized, horrified. The ring he pulled from his shirt pocket had a stone the approximate size of the moon.

"Elaine . . ." His tone was choked, his face as pale as the rock he held in his shaky right hand. He cleared his throat. "Elaine . . ." he began again, but he couldn't go on.

"Yes," she said, and I started to cry.

28

Solberg: nature's greatest argument against cloning.

—*Chrissy, still a little bitter*

*I*T WAS SOMETHING of a relief to go back to work, proof positive that I wasn't the only one who was crazy. I saw two clients before noon. Officer Tavis called me at two.

"How you doing?" he asked.

I glanced out my window and thought about Brainy Laney Butterfield, a virtual goddess, about to marry a man who harvested his hair from south of his beltline. What did that mean for mortal women?

"I'm doing well."

"Yeah? Who's the lucky man? The good lieutenant?"

I scowled, trying not to remember my behavior on the night I'd seen Rivera with the blonde. "I'm sorry, Officer," I said. "I'm a little too busy to be sexually harassed right now. If you'll—" I began, but he was already laughing.

"Don't hang up. Listen . . ." His voice sobered smoothly. "Kathleen Baltimore got an offer to work in politics again."

"What?" I sat up straight, mind pumping.

"Queenie said Kathy got a call a month or so ago from somebody who wanted her to help out with a campaign."

"Who? What campaign?"

"I don't know. But she was considering it. Said it was a generous offer, but she couldn't discuss the details yet."

"What else do you know?"

"We closed down another meth operation."

"About Kathy."

"Nothing," he said. "Sorry."

What did it mean? Had the senator called her? Had he gone there himself? She would have trusted him, and he certainly had the funds, but I couldn't imagine him as a killer. Maybe a lady killer, but not an *actual* . . .

"Hey," Tavis said, "don't get yourself killed, okay? I'm still hoping to see you naked."

I rolled my eyes and hung up. Five minutes later I called Rivera.

He answered on the third ring. "What are you wearing now?" he asked.

"Holy crap, what is wrong with you guys?"

There was a dark pause. "What guys is that, McMullen?"

I couldn't help myself; I liked the harsh rasp of jealousy in his tone. Liked the way his voice lapped rough and titillating against my senses. But I stifled my girly foolishness and ignored the question.

"Have you spoken to your father yet?"

"About what?"

I resisted grinding my teeth. "About the fact that his life is in danger."

I heard him sigh as he settled into a chair. "I'll give you an A for imagination."

"Imagination starts with an I."

"Amateur starts with an A."

"Don't be a—"

"If I promise to dig into it a little, will you drop it?"

I hesitated. I shouldn't have hesitated.

He swore. "I know *CSI* makes crime look sexy as hell, but real life doesn't work that way. Murderers aren't rocket scientists, McMullen. They don't take a damn millennium to plan out intricate accidental deaths. They're just pricks who've had too much to drink and were turned down by girls in—"

"You think he's a scientist?" I asked.

"I think he doesn't exist!" he rasped. "The deaths are coincidental. Accidental. Unconnect—"

"You're right!" I said. "I should have seen this before."

"What the hell are you talking about?"

"Whoever he is, he must be highly intelligent."

"Christ! Are you listening at all? I want you to drop this. Leave it alone. Do—"

"I have to go," I said, and hung up.

I called the senator immediately, but he wasn't in and I was forced to leave a message. The rest of the afternoon flew by, blowing me along with it. By the time I got home I felt like I'd been flagellated by a half dozen overzealous monks. I dropped my purse on the counter and got the Skippy out of the cupboard. I had left my blow-up boyfriend in the kitchen where François couldn't see him and stared at the box while I ate peanut butter out of the jar. Chunky. I'm not a barbarian.

The phone rang while my mouth was gummed up, but when I saw it was a call from the senator I swallowed as best I could and picked up the receiver.

" 'Ello?"

"Christina?"

" 'Es."

"Christina, are you well?"

I swallowed, took a swig of milk from the carton, and wiped my mouth on the back of my hand. I'm not sure, but I thought I could feel Blow-up Boy cringe even from inside his box.

"I need to talk to you," I said.

"Is something wrong?"

"Yes. I—"

"Shall I send the police? Are you in danger?"

"No," I said. "You are."

There was a moment of silence, then, "Chrissy, please—"

"Who's the smartest person you know?"

"I beg your pardon?"

"The brightest person in your acquaintance. Who do you think it is?"

He thought for a moment. "Bill was a Rhodes scholar."

"Bill . . ."

"I prefer the present administration, of course, but Bill had an appreciation for the finer things in life."

My mind felt a little murky. I was eating peanut butter out of the jar while conversing with a man who talked about presidents on a first-name basis. "Do you think he might have killed Kathy?" I asked.

There was a pause. "Have you been drinking, Christina?"

I shook my head and tried to clear my mind. "When was the last time you spoke to Kathleen Baltimore?"

"I beg your pardon?"

"Someone called her recently. Offered her a job in a campaign."

"Who was it?" His voice had lost some of its smooth self-assurance. In fact, for the first time, he almost sounded shaken.

"I think it was the same person who killed her."

"I believe it was an accident, Christina. The police agree. She fell into her saw."

"Steve Bunting is dead. Did you know that?"

There was a short, soft pause. "I hadn't heard. How did it happen?"

"He died while scuba diving."

He said nothing.

"Off Kauai."

"Ahh, well . . ." I could all but hear him shrug. As if that explained everything. "It is a man's way to die at least and has nothing to do with—"

"He died on a Thursday."

"I don't know—"

"Manny drowned on a Wednesday. Kathy bled to death on a Tuesday, and your cousin's house burned to the ground on a Monday."

"What are you suggesting?"

"I'm suggesting you lock your doors and hire a body-guard," I said, and hung up.

29

He's an undersize pissant with delusions of adequacy.

—Lily Schultz, Chrissy's
first employer (and
personal hero) regarding
all of her husbands and
most of her subordinates

I WAS AS JITTERY as a virgin in a sorority house all day Thursday. By Friday I was certifiable.

My phone rang at 5:34 in the afternoon. I had twenty-six minutes before my next client. It was Solberg.

"Rebecca Harris died this morning in Fresno." Despite the news, his tone was ungodly happy. I didn't want to know why.

I tightened my grip on the receiver and tried to breathe normally. "How was she involved with the senator?"

"His secretary when he was a mayor in some flyspeck in Texas."

"What else do you know?" Solberg may have been a

myopic little dweeb, not good enough to wipe my best friend's nose, but he was a first-rate snoop.

"Cause of death was a fall."

"A fall?"

"From a cliff. She was kinda an exercise fanatic. Some of them medical types are."

"Medical—"

"She went to the Denver School of Nursing. Married a carpenter type in '87. Moved to California in '91 and propagated five years later."

"They waited all that time to have kids?"

I could hear his shrug over the phone. "Some folks ain't so excited about motherhood as you, babekins."

"How old was she?"

"When she died? Forty-seven."

"When she worked for Rivera."

"Twenty-four."

My heart ticked away. The perfect age for a philandering senator. "Was she pretty?"

"Compared to what?"

I had forgotten that he now judged women by Brainy Laney standards. Ergo, everyone was as bland as rice cakes. "Compared to . . . say, mortal women."

"I dunno. Brown hair, kinda plain maybe."

Not the kind to set the senator's world on fire, then. Although, as I've indicated, Solberg was hardly qualified to judge women's looks. "And this from a man who used to date amphibians," I said.

"Amphibians," he repeated, and chuckled.

Since he had begun seeing Laney, nothing much bothered him. Now that he was engaged, he was probably bulletproof. I scowled out the window toward the coffee shop next door. A chocolate chip scone would make the world a better place. "Was there anything odd about her?"

"What's that?"

"Anything the Moral Majority might disapprove of?"

"She was a registered Democrat."

"Always?"

"Probably not when she was an infant," he said, and snorted a laugh.

I closed my eyes and reminded myself I had missed my opportunity to kill him. Regardless of how insane it might seem, Laney was in love, and nothing short of an exorcism was likely to change that.

"What else?" I asked.

"Looks squeaky clean to me. Worked full time at Larker Medical Center. Was den mother for her kid's Cub Scout troop, volunteered at the Children's Hospital twice a week, and was leader for her circle at Shepherd of the Hills Lutheran."

I spent Saturday nervous and fatigued and breathless, waiting for the other shoe to drop. It didn't.

Sunday was slightly more productive. By evening I knew as much about Rebecca Harris as I could without sharing a dorm room. By two I had done everything I could think of to investigate the senator's affairs. By three I was passed out in bed and Kathy Baltimore was whispering questions in my head again.

I awoke in full darkness, feeling spooked and breathless, listening to Harley's heavy breaths. Apparently Kathy wasn't bothering *his* dreams. Pattering to the bathroom, I stared at my reflection in the mirror and told myself it would be ridiculous to drive all the way to Fresno for Rebecca's visitation on Wednesday. But even as I fell back to sleep, I knew I would.

On New Year's Eve morning, I asked Shirley to cancel my appointments for January 2. I saw three clients, went home early, and fell asleep on the couch long before the first glimpse of the famous dropping ball in Times Square.

I had no idea what time it was when my doorbell rang. I woke up with a start, scared and disoriented. The TV was on mute. Outside, it was as dark as my dreams. Someone knocked. Impatient and loud. Rivera's face flashed through my mind, stopping my breath, freezing my thoughts. Harlequin barked, one deep, resonating note. I found my feet with some difficulty and wobbled to the bathroom. The woman in the mirror above the sink looked tired and pale. A crease ran the length of her right cheek. It was possible she was a ghost, but I wasn't holding out much hope.

My visitor knocked again, louder still. Harley was galloping between the door and the living room, nails clicking like castanets.

I smoothed down my skirt, ignored my hair, and headed toward the door. "Who is it?" Even my voice sounded pale.

"Dick Clark."

My mind spun lazily, then: "D?"

He stepped sideways so that I could see him through the gauzy fabric of the side window. "I've got enough champagne for us *and* the dog."

I opened the door. He came inside. I glanced down the walkway, although I'm not sure why, and when I looked up he was staring at me.

"You expecting him?" he said.

"Who?"

He smiled. "It wouldn't hurt to make him jealous, you know," he said, and lifted both hands. There was a bottle in each.

"I'm afraid . . ." I blinked, still feeling disoriented. "I'm not much of a drinker."

He shrugged. "Practice makes perfect. You got flutes?"

I did. In a couple of minutes we were settled on the couch. He poured the wine.

"Hard to believe even a cop's dumb enough to leave you alone on New Year's Eve," he said.

He handed over a glass of champagne. It bubbled merrily. I considered saying something equally cheery but wasn't up to the task.

"I assumed you'd gone back to Chicago."

He shrugged. "Thought I'd take some time to see your fair city."

"Don't you"—I took a sip. It was pretty tasty—"have business back home?"

He laughed. He'd left his alligator boots by the long window near my front door. "I'll let them keep their knees a couple more days."

I was beginning to wake up. "I heard you dealt in livers."

"I don't know how these rumors get started," he said, and finished his drink.

"Wow."

He filled my glass. "I'm slower at other things," he said, and caught my gaze.

I could already feel the first flush of the champagne cruising through my system like sunshine, but I kept my voice steady, my dialogue serious. "What are you doing here?"

"Question is, why isn't there a queue at your door?"

I glanced away. "I'm taking a break."

"From life?"

"From men."

He canted his head a little. "We're not all fucktards, you know."

"That's what they tell me." I stifled a sigh and drank again.

"They who?"

"Men."

He chuckled. "Anyone specific?"

I shrugged and settled back against the cushion. "There's a guy in Edmond Park."

"He good-looking?"

"I guess so."

"Tall?"

"Tall enough."

"Not a fucktard?"

"Doesn't seem to be."

"But?"

"Sometimes I'm not a very good judge of men."

"Who are your other options?"

"There's a guy in Sespe. I think he might be a bazillionaire."

He clicked his glass to mine in a kind of salute. "Looks don't matter squat, then."

I shrugged.

"So why are you here? Alone?"

"I keep wondering if they're planning to kill me."

"Bound to put the brakes on a budding relationship," he said, and filled my glass.

"Are *you*?"

He finished up his wine and refilled. "What's that?"

"Planning to kill me."

"Why would I do that?"

"I don't know. It seems to be a trend."

"The Edmond Park guy try to kill you?"

"Not yet."

"How about the ugly bazillionaire?"

"I didn't say he was ugly."

"Not as good-looking as me, though, huh?"

I drank again, watching him. Donald Archer *wasn't* as good-looking. And probably not as rich. Or as powerful. "Do I owe you more money?" I asked.

He laughed. "Sometimes I honestly don't think you know how cute you are."

I drew back a wobbly half inch. "I'm not cute."

"Beautiful, then."

I felt a little dizzy. "Really?"

"Those damn cops. Never say what needs saying," he said, and kissed me.

He tasted good, sweet like the wine. I drew back a little and watched his face. His eyes were sparkling. Harley was lying in front of the TV. But he lifted his head suddenly and glanced toward the door.

I did the same, heart pounding.

"If he's not here yet, he doesn't deserve you," D said.

I turned back toward him. "I know." I felt a little weepy. Liquor does that to me. Not to mention New Year's. And best friends marrying undersize doofuses.

He kissed me again. "If he shows up, do you want me to beat the crap out of him?"

I was feeling a little breathless, a little aroused. "He's got a gun."

"I've got a black belt."

"Really?"

"Want to see?"

"You've got it on?"

"Under my clothes."

"No kidding?"

He chuckled.

"Oh," I said.

By midnight both bottles were empty. He slipped his arm behind my back and kissed me as "Auld Lang Syne" played with nostalgic moodiness on the television. His body felt warm and tight against mine. His lips were firm, his kiss as slow as summer.

"Want to move back to Chicago?" he asked.

"Not tonight."

"Maybe later," he said, and kissed me again.

After that we talked about family and plans and friends who married outside their species.

When I woke in the morning I was lying in my bed, covers tucked snugly up under my chin. I pulled them aside. I was absolutely, startlingly, bone-jarringly naked.

30

Jealousy. It's a terrible thing. Unless it's someone else's.

—D,
*who likes to stir up the
hive, just to make sure the
bees are still awake*

$\mathcal{D}$ESPITE MY LACK OF A SHOWER and screaming uncertainty regarding what I had done with D, I arrived at Rademacher Funeral Home early, signed the registry, and watched the people. Rebecca Harris was survived by her husband and her son, but the son seemed to be absent. The husband, looking stoic and stiff in his boxy suit, did his best to meet and greet. I felt like a voyeur, but I had been becoming acquainted with the senator's cronies for weeks now and scanned the crowd. Would the murderer feel a need to show his face here? Or was he too savvy for that?

"She was the best."

I jerked toward the speaker, feeling guilty and jittery.

The woman who stood next to me was in her early fifties.

"Faith that could move mountains," she said. She dabbed her nose with a tissue. "I'm Beth Culbertson. I'm in...*was* in..." Her voice cracked. "Her circle at Shepherd."

We shook hands. She waited for me to speak, but I was busy trying to look intelligent.

"Did you know her well?" she asked.

"No. I just..." Words failed me, but probably not for the reason she thought. "We were friends...a long while ago."

"But you know Delbert."

I blinked, mind scrambling.

"Her husband."

"Oh...well..."

"They were well yoked."

I ran that weird image frenetically through my mind, then got raggedly back on track. "I don't remember him from the campaign," I said.

She frowned. "What campaign is that?"

"Becky and I worked for Senator Rivera together," I said.

"Senator Rivera?" She drew back, surprised.

"A long time ago."

"Really? She never mentioned it."

"You were friends?"

"We taught Tykes for Christ together for five years. She never said she had brushed with greatness."

"Greatness?" I gave her a questioning glance, then caught her meaning. "Oh, yes, the senator. Sure. He's amazing."

"And so good-looking."

"Like a god," I said, but before I could swallow my tongue, I felt a presence beside me.

"Ms. McMullen." The voice was dark-rum deep. "Can I have a word with you?"

I turned, and there he was. Rivera, in all his glaring glory, dressed in dark slacks and a navy-blue ribbed sweater with a V-neck. I refrained from passing out. I also refrained from spewing out an apology. I didn't owe him anything, regardless of what I had or had not done on New Year's Eve. But what the crap *had* I done? By the time I got out of bed, D was gone, as were the bottles. The glasses were clean and set in their proper place. I wondered if, perhaps, I was losing my mind.

"I'm rather busy right now," I said, and gave Beth Culbertson my best refined-sugar smile.

"I'm sorry to disturb you," Rivera said, not sounding sorry at all. "But the senator is on the phone."

I turned toward him, baffled. Beth stared at him, agog.

"If you'll excuse us," he said, and, nodding curtly, tugged me away.

"The senator called?" I asked, but he glared me down.

"Sure. Said he wanted to take you for a ride at his rancho," he said, spewing sarcasm. "What the fuck are you doing here?"

"It's a free country, Rivera. What are *you* doing here?"

"I'm a police officer, McMullen." He glanced at the crowd. A muscle ticked in his jaw. "A real one. With a last name and everything."

"What's that supposed to mean?" I asked, and tugged at my arm. He didn't relent.

"So you decided on a thug instead of milquetoast?"

I stiffened, finally catching up. The noise Harlequin

had heard was Rivera at the door. D had left his boots in front of the window by the door. *Holy crap!* I thought, but kept my tone butterscotch smooth. "I hardly thought it would be possible," I said, "but Officer Tavis—"

"Glad to hear the dearth is ended," he said, but he didn't sound glad.

"And how," I said.

His eyes darkened a shade. "So Curly Top lost out."

Anger coursed through me. Anger, and maybe a little madness, but I batted my eyelashes. Innocent as a butterfly. "Why would you say that?"

His lips thinned. "Some men don't like to share."

I smiled. "Some do," I crooned.

For a moment I thought he might explode, erupt like a volcano, but he remained as he was—dark, quiet, and pissed. "I want you to get the hell out of here."

"I'm just asking a few questions." I yanked at my arm again. He tightened his grip more.

"If I remember correctly, you asked a few questions of the last couple guys who tried to kill you," he gritted.

A man passed by carrying a Bible. I gave him a smile. Rivera nodded. If he was any more congenial than that, his head would have popped off. "Why wouldn't Rebecca have told anyone about working for your dad?" I asked.

"Maybe she wasn't as hot for him as you are."

I was far past trying to mollify him. "And maybe she was," I said, and jerked free.

"What the hell are you talking about?" he hissed, but I was already slipping into the crowd.

Despite Rivera's glowering presence from across the room, I examined everyone. Not a soul looked familiar. Easing through the crowd, I offered my condolences to the husband, then studied his face and tone and body language for any smidgeon of guilt, but sorrow and shock seemed to be his only emotions. After a moment he was drawn into another's condolences.

"I don't believe we've met," said a voice from my left. I turned. It was the man with the Bible.

"Oh, I'm Christina McMullen."

He smiled benevolently. "And how did you know Rebecca?"

"We . . . umm . . ." I glanced toward Rivera. He was momentarily distracted. Possibly making some sort of pact with the devil. "We worked for the senator together."

"Oh?" He canted his head a little. "What senator is that?"

"Well, he wasn't actually a senator then. Just a mayor."

He still looked confused. I refrained from scowling.

"Reverend, if I could have a moment," someone said, and he turned away with an apology.

I spoke to four other people. None of them had any idea Rebecca had worked for the man who might very well be the next President of the United States.

I glanced to the right, and Rivera was there, not three feet away. I kept my heart firmly in my chest.

His cheek twitched. "Have you lost your mind completely or do you have some reason to think she had an affair with him?"

I considered refusing to speak to him, but he was so . . . loomy. "Other than the law of averages?"

He snorted. "The woman was a saint."

"Why only one child, then?"

He glared a question.

"Even the Virgin Mary had a bunch of kids, and she was a virgin."

"I'm surprised you even know the meaning," he said.

I stared at him a full fifteen seconds, then cracked a faux laugh and turned toward the crowd, but he grabbed my arm. "Who was it?" he asked.

"What are you talking about?"

"Tell me you didn't really sleep with that damn small-town crossing guard."

I faced him, breath stopping in my throat. "Why do you think it was anyone?"

His brows dipped a little lower.

"You should have rung the doorbell," I said. "As long as you were in the neighborhood."

The world pulsed around us. "I'm not that fond of orgies," he said.

"Too bad," I quipped, and glided back into the crowd.

There was a woman standing alone, watching a little girl twirl like a top in her gauzy black skirt. I approached from a tangent.

"It's unfortunate Becky never had more children," I said.

The woman was short, plump, pretty in a bland sort of way. She smiled.

"The Lord's will, I guess," I continued.

She narrowed her eyes a little. "Or her fallopian tubes."

"What?"

"I don't necessarily believe in God," she said. "But I have a lot of faith in a good healthy reproductive system."

"And?"

She smiled, seeming to draw out of herself. "I don't recognize you. Do you work at Children's?"

"Becky and I worked for the senator together a long time ago." Lying is like most things. Practice makes perfect.

"What senator is that?"

Crap.

"Senator Rivera. Are you a nurse?"

"A doctor. Obstetrics."

Huh. Who would have thought I was sexist.

"Rebecca volunteered there. She also initiated a program to counsel couples with fertility problems."

"Did she have one? A fertility problem? I mean, she seemed the type to want a whole house full of kids."

"She and Delbert tried for years. But endometriosis can be a real bitch. They finally tried in vitro fertilization. Obstetrics threw her a party when they found out she was pregnant with Shane."

"So Shane was her first child." I realized after I spoke that it sounded like I didn't know the deceased from the Parthenon. "We've been out of touch for decades," I said. "I just happened to hear of her awful death."

"Breech. Seven pounds, two ounces," she said. "I was the attending when he was born. She had a lot of Demerol. Yammered like a parakeet. Funny, though," she said. "She never mentioned working for a senator. Or you," she added, eyeing me.

"I'm just one of those people who fade into the woodwork," I said, and, glancing to my right, saw that Rivera was watching me. Eyes dark, mood stormy.

Apparently I hadn't faded yet.

31

Real friends disregard your failures and endure your successes.

—*Brainy Laney Butterfield,*
who was, by all accounts,
irritatingly successful

ON THURSDAY, I did what I do. Psychoanalyzed, watched the SuperSeptic guys do nothing in my back-yard, wondered if Rivera would ever speak to me again.

Laney would be leaving the next day, so she came by that night, but things felt strange. A little strained. I wasn't ready for her to get married. I certainly wasn't ready for her to get hitched to a guy who, if inverted, could be used as a broom.

"How's engaged life?" I asked. We were sitting on my couch, Harlequin between us.

She fiddled with Harley's ear. "I gave the ring back."

"No kidding?" My heart did a little burp, then soared with hope.

"I told him I just wanted a plain band; I couldn't lift my hand," she said, and grinned, knowing exactly what I'd been thinking.

"I don't know why I ever liked you."

She laughed, still the Laney I loved, despite her inexplicable attraction to subspecies.

"Tell me you're not giving back that... *planet* in exchange for a cigar band," I insisted.

"I'm looking forward to babies. Twelve of them."

"What if they look like the Geekster?"

"Ohhh." She lifted her shoulders in a soundless expression of glee. "Wouldn't that be great!"

"You are one sick woman."

"Yeah. *Love*sick."

I rolled my eyes. "You're making *me* sick."

"Marriage will be nice."

"Sometimes it's not, you know." My tone was petulant, but I knew that despite Solberg's irritating habit of being himself, he'd be good to her. That or I'd strangle him with his own entrails.

"We're eloping tomorrow."

"*What!* How the hell—" I ranted, but she was already laughing.

"I almost forgot how easy you are."

"I'm not easy." I might have been pouting a little.

"Tell that to Rivera."

"He'll never believe it. Not at this juncture."

"What do you mean?"

I shrugged. Still childish.

"Have you seen him lately?"

I considered lying, but my heart wasn't up to it. "At a funeral home."

"You've always had such strange dates." She had her legs curled up under her and was drinking some sort of green slop that would probably make her live forever.

I thought about her statement for a second and decided I didn't want to talk about my dates just then. And possibly never. "Why do you suppose Rebecca Harris would avoid telling people about her time as the senator's secretary?"

She shrugged, frowned a little—kept up to speed, I was sure, by Solberg, who needed to tell her everything. "Maybe it just wasn't very interesting."

"Working for Miguel Rivera?" I was skeptical.

"Do you think he came on to her?"

"Is he a man?"

"Do you think she accepted?"

"Donny's father said the senator was excellent at avoiding child support."

"So you think there was a child."

I shook my head. "I don't know. I had convinced myself there was. That Rebecca had gotten knocked up and gone off to bear the baby in shame. But turns out she had endometriosis and couldn't get pregnant without in vitro fertilization."

"Endometriosis? Isn't that . . ." She paused, staring at me as if she should perhaps remain silent, but she spoke finally. "Isn't that sometimes caused by abortions?"

I stared at her for a full five seconds, then launched myself from the couch, scurried into my office, and wrote *abortion* under Rebecca's name.

When I glanced back, Laney was standing behind me in the doorway. "You need a new hobby," she said.

"Well, there are only so many geeksters to reform," I said.

She smiled. "You can't be sure about the abortion," she said.

"No."

"How about the others? Are you sure about their"—she made air quotes—"sins?"

I shifted my gaze over the wall for the thousandth time. "All except Bunting."

She was silent for a moment. "If you're right, they've broken just about every commandment in the book."

"Didn't there used to be more?"

"They've been revised. More sinner-friendly now," she said. "How about you?"

"How about me what?"

"You broken any lately?"

I refrained from fidgeting and went for clever. "I've wanted to, but I've been kind of busy. With the murders and whatnot."

"How about New Year's Eve?"

I put down my marker and returned to the living room. "Asleep by nine."

"Yeah? Who woke you up?"

I turned on her, a little peeved. If she had to be gorgeous, it was her God-given duty to be dumb. "Tell me the truth, do you have spies?"

She laughed.

"Bugs? Little cameras hidden in my teeth?"

"Did Rivera come over or what?"

I shook my head.

"Donald Archer?"

"No."

"The cop?"

I sighed.

"Who, then?"

"Do you remember D?"

She narrowed her eyes and thought back. "The gang-ster?"

"Apparently that term isn't very politically correct."

She raised her brows and stared at me. "Did you sleep with him?"

"No. Absolutely not. That would have been stupid. I'm not stupid."

She stared at me some more. I was beginning to itch.

"I mean . . . I haven't had sex for . . ." I thought back but couldn't remember how many months it had been. Or maybe they haven't invented a number that large yet. "If I did . . . I'd know. Right?"

Solberg took Laney back to LAX. I didn't accompany them, because I don't like to see grown men cry. Well . . . sometimes I do, but that's another story.

Friday dawned, almost cool. Harley and I went for a run before the weather took a turn and tried to kill us again.

I called the senator sometime around noon and asked with my usual tact if he'd had an affair with Rebecca Harris. He flatly denied it. Which meant that she proba-bly didn't have an abortion and was, in fact, the saint everyone proclaimed her to be. Which meant that my en-tire theory was probably nothing more than fantasy.

By the time I returned home, I felt out of sorts. Tomor-row would be Saturday, which, according to my theory, should be the next day for a murder. I wandered into my office to glare at the wall—and my faulty theory. I mean, yes, all the deaths did take place on different days of the week, but not all were consecutive.

Steve Bunting had died on a Thursday instead of on a Tuesday as he should have. Did that mean that Steve's death was unplanned? If that was the case, that left Thursday open for another tragedy. But maybe it was all just my overactive imagination playing tricks on me.

I glared some more, but no new and astounding revelations came to mind, so I had a bowl of ice cream and went to bed early.

I woke up sweating. The house was absolutely quiet, but I could still hear Kathy Baltimore's voice in my ear. Singing. Hymns. I shivered and climbed out of bed. The office called to me. I wandered in that direction. The tagboard was there, scribbled with a thousand seemingly unconnected notes.

Laney said they had broken every commandment, but it wasn't true, of course. As far as I knew, no one had been bearing false witness or creating idols in their basements or . . .

My mind screeched to a halt as my eyes zipped back to Carma. Maybe she didn't exactly have idols, but she *was* Wiccan, which meant she had other gods. Didn't it? I hurried to the wall and scribbled *first and second* under Carmella's name.

Manny had taken God's name in vain. Number three.

Kathy had labored to make sure they campaigned on the Sabbath. Number four.

Steve? Steve! If my theory was correct, he had euthanized his own parents. Which meant he was a murderer. Which put him out of order again. But wait. Killing them wasn't honoring them. "Fifth commandment!" I was muttering frantically to myself.

"Rebecca. Rebecca." *She* should have murdered. Should have . . . But maybe she *had* gotten an abortion, and some considered that murder. Sixth commandment! Which put all the deaths in order.

Not in days of the week, but by commandments. Of course! Why hadn't I seen it before?

Which led me to . . .

I stopped. The marker fell from my fingers and clattered against my desk.

"Adultery," I muttered, and then I was scrambling for the phone, jabbing at the numbers, but all I got was the senator's voice mail. I checked the time—2:42.

I slammed down the receiver and tried another number.

"Christ, McMullen." Rivera sounded tired and angry. "I've had about all the foreplay I can handle. Let's just do—"

"The killer's punishing sinners," I hissed.

There was a pause. "Are you high?"

"Each victim broke at least one commandment."

I heard his mattress creak. "Don't tell me. Harris was coveting the senator's ass."

"Some people consider abortion murder." I felt breathless but strangely vindicated.

There was a moment's pause. "Explain or let me go to sleep."

"First and second commandments, thou shalt have no other gods, before me, and thou shalt not make false idols. Carma was a practicing Wiccan. Third, don't take God's name in vain. Emanuel. Fourth commandment, remember the Sabbath day. It was Baltimore's idea to campaign on Sunday. Fifth—"

His mattress squeaked abruptly. "Where's the one about adultery?"

I paused, barely breathing. "Seventh."

"And there have been six commandments broken."

"Yes."

There was a long pause during which I could hear myself sweat.

"I'll call the old man," he said.

"He didn't answer."

"You try his home phone?"

"Twice."

"Stay where you are. I'll check it out and call you back."

I stayed for about five seconds, after which I snatched my keys from the counter, said good-bye to a droopy-eyed Harlequin, and raced out the door. Pacific Palisades was a forty-five-minute drive. The roads were curvy and crazy. The night was reminiscent of the first time I'd gone to the senator's house. Fog had hung over the roads then, too, a harbinger of horrors to come. Of dead, staring eyes and—

My cell rang, yanking me back to the present with a gasp. I fished it out of my purse and snapped it open.

"Where the hell are you?" Rivera asked. I could hear a motor charging to life in the background.

"Me?" I careened onto the 405, headed west.

"Are you in your car?"

I changed lanes, storming past a compact pickup truck. "Who knew about your father's indiscretions?"

"You get your ass back home."

I was driving with my left hand, swerving rapidly around curves and up hills. "It must be someone from the past. Has to be."

"I kid you not, McMullen. If I see you at the senator's, I'm handcuffing you to your steering wheel."

"Where do you think he is?"

"I'm warning you—"

"Have there been any threats to his life?"

"You're not a goddamn cop!"

"I realize that," I snapped. "I'm a shrink. You're a cop. Your father's in a shitload of trouble. He's going to need all the help he can get to get him out."

He was silent for an instant. I could hear him shift gears. I slipped into the breach. "The senator must have suspected all along that his life was in danger."

"You think?"

I didn't bother to remind him that sarcasm is sophomoric and uncalled for.

"So why did he send the note?"

There was a moment of silence. "What note?"

I scowled a little, taking a curve too fast and gripping the wheel tighter. "He sent a note and a check, saying I shouldn't concern myself with the death. Apologized for getting me involved."

Another silence, then: "How much was the check for?"

"Ten thousand dollars." A sliver of guilt accompanied the admission. "I know I shouldn't have cashed it, but my septic system—"

"Conniving bastard!" Rivera growled.

A convertible zipped toward me around a hairpin turn, missing me by a prayer. I refrained from peeing in my pants and tried to keep my voice out of the upper octaves. "What's that?"

"If he had an ounce of integrity, he would have just put a gun to your head."

I thought about that for a moment while I tried to keep from careening into oblivion. "You think he knew I would take the money and feel obliged to keep investigating?"

Rivera snorted. "The old man's a scheming pile of shit, but he knows how to pull people's strings. I gotta give him that."

I took a deep breath and jumped into the truth with both feet. "He said he didn't want you to get involved because he worried about your safety."

"He didn't involve me because he knew I'd tell him to go to hell."

And yet Rivera was currently speeding to his father's rescue. I scowled at the vagaries of life. "He said he'd had nightmares about seeing you dead on the sidewalk beside Kathy Baltimore."

"And you believed him?" His voice was incredulous.

Despite my Ph.D., I felt a need to explain myself. "Well, to be honest, I had a similar dream, and I thought maybe—"

"About me?" he asked. His tone had changed a bit, still coarse but roughly gentle now.

I felt my throat tighten up. "You're sort of an ass, but I kinda don't want anything to happen to you."

"Go home, Chrissy," he said. His tone was gruff, but there was pleading in it, and worry, and a dozen emotions I had no time to analyze.

"Where do you think he might be?" I asked.

For a moment I thought I felt worry from the other end of the line, but then he laughed. "How the hell would I know? He's probably out whoring."

"If you believe that, why are you breaking the speed limit at two fifty-three in the morning?"

"Go home," he said, and hung up.

I beat him to his father's house by about three minutes.

I was cupping my hands against the senator's window and peering into the darkened house when he screeched into the drive beside my cowering little Saturn.

"McMullen." Maybe his voice wasn't loud enough to wake the dead, but it sure as hell would piss them off.

I scurried through the underbrush toward him. "What'd you find out?"

For a second I thought he actually *might* handcuff me to something, but he just glared at the house instead. "Did you knock?"

"No answer."

"Any windows open?"

"Not that I found."

He nodded, rang the doorbell, and dialed his phone simultaneously. After the third ring, I heard the senator's bass recording pick up. Rivera snapped off his phone and glanced back at his Jeep.

"Could he be with your mother?"

He looked at me. "What are you on?"

"Then where is he?"

"How the hell would I know?"

"You're his son."

"Only by accident." Bending, he picked up a potted fern and slammed it through the window. I jumped as glass shattered in every direction, but Rivera was already tossing the plant aside and reaching between the broken shards.

"Stay behind me," he ordered, and pulled a gun from some unknown orifice.

I followed him, spooked and breathless.

He flipped on the foyer light. "LAPD," he yelled. No one yelled back.

"What about a house alarm?" I rasped.

He glanced toward the little box beside the door. Not a single light was blinking. I could only assume that meant his dad had neglected to set it.

"Maybe he knew he was in danger and left in a hurry," I said.

"Or maybe he's got a hot little piece waiting for him," Rivera said, but his expression was hard as he took a left into the living room.

"Senator?" I called, and, glancing about, took a shaky detour into the great room. The *Los Angeles Times* lay open on the coffee table. One glance revealed it was Friday's edition. He had been there recently. I headed for the curving stairs. But the upper floor was much the same, deserted and immaculate. The master bedchamber showed signs of recent life, and that only by the disturbed bedclothes.

If there were clues I didn't find them. The air seemed breathless as I rushed downstairs. I nearly collided with Rivera at the bottom.

"Christ, the dog takes orders better," he said.

I ignored him. "Is his car gone?"

"One of them."

The house felt still and empty. I skirted him, heading for the kitchen.

The counter was bare. Three half-melted ice cubes languished in the sink. "He hasn't been gone more than a couple hours," I said.

"What are you now, supersleuth?"

"Cocktail waitress," I said, and nodded toward the sink. "It takes three ice cubes six hours to melt at room temperature."

He turned, looking at me as though I'd lost my last marble. "Are you shitting me?"

I opened the dishwasher. "Yes." There were three plates and five glasses. I had no idea what that meant. I moved on to the refrigerator. It was well stocked and neatly organized, hardly resembling a fridge at all.

"Shit." Frustration jerked in Rivera's jaw.

"But he was obviously here tonight. He was reading the paper."

"Jesus," he said.

"Watch your mouth. People have been killed for less."

He swore again, worse this time, then crossed to the phone and checked caller ID.

I watched. "Anything?"

"He got a call at twelve-fifteen a.m."

"From?"

"Unavailable."

We stared at each other.

"Probably a booty call," he said, but his eyes looked as hard as cut amber.

"Whose booty?"

He shook his head and headed into the bathroom.

"Where does he keep his schedule?" I asked.

"You think we're damn pen pals?"

"I don't even think you're human," I said.

He snorted and strode down the hall. I followed him into a room on the right. A sleek state-of-the-art computer system purred at me from a broad walnut desk.

"Wow," I said.

"Nothing but the best." I couldn't tell what his tone implied, but it didn't sound joyous. He sat down and touched a key. It came to life, flashing the presidential seal as wallpaper. I helped him find a calendar. Two notations had been made for Friday. One said *1:00—Aaron.* The other said *4:00—LeeAnn.*

"You know either of them?" I asked.

He shook his head. "According to your stellar sleuthing it doesn't matter. He was home afterward, anyway."

"And alone," I said.

He glanced at me.

"Only three ice cubes."

I was pretty sure he wanted to roll his eyes, but he was too busy rifling through the contents of the senator's drawers.

"Who does he talk to when things are going poorly?" I asked.

He shook his head.

"You *have* met this man before, right?" I said, and reached past him for the keyboard.

But suddenly I stopped. A picture of Salina and Rivera Junior was frozen on the screen. Beautiful, young, and exotically dark, they actually left me momentarily breathless. Seconds ticked away unnoticed.

"Fuck it," Rivera said, breaking the moment, but the picture had already changed to one of high, lonely plains.

"She was amazing," I said. My tone sounded rusty. Awed. And then the picture changed again.

Rivera's jaw looked set in stone. He dropped his gaze to search another drawer, but my wide-eyed expression must have stopped him. My mouth opened. I blinked.

"What?" he said.

I motioned toward the screen.

"What!" he said again, but the photograph was already gone, replaced by an image of the senator holding a child and smiling.

Entranced, I reached slowly out and touched the left arrow.

The former picture flashed back up. Thea Altove was shown in profile next to her father. In the questionable light of Caring Hands, her hair looked a shade darker than its natural gold. Her expression, usually gleefully happy, was also a shade dimmer, and there was something in her eyes...

I stared, blinked, then, breathless and reverent, touched the back arrow several times until the picture of Jack and Salina reappeared.

"McMullen," he said, low and irritable.

I turned to him in stunned silence.

"You don't see it?"

"See what?" Past irritable. Into threatening.

I reached past him, touched the key again. "They're the same eyes."

He stared, snorted. "What the hell are you talking about? They don't look anything alike."

"Not Thea and Salina," I breathed. "Thea and *you.*"

He snapped his gaze back to the screen, stared for one atom-splitting second, then jerked to his feet. His chair spun wildly backward.

"Jesus Christ!"

"Don't—" I began breathlessly, but he didn't notice.

"Jesus H. Christ!"

I only nodded, still staring.

"That fucking bastard!"

"We don't know for sure."

"That fucking, horny bastard!"

I winced.

"She's my sister," he hissed.

32

It'd hardly be worth having a brother at all, if you couldn't smack him in the head every once in a while.

—*Michael McMullen,*
the eldest of the troglodytes

WE STARED AT EACH OTHER, barely breathing.

"What does it mean?" I asked.

He didn't answer.

"Does it mean she's going to kill him?"

"Not before I do." His voice was a growl. He was already punching numbers on his cell. I heard it ring on the other end, then roll over to voice mail. Thea's recorded voice sounded chirpy. He hung up and hit REDIAL, but this time she answered on the third ring.

"Hello?" Her voice was foggy with sleep.

"Thea?" Rivera's tone had lost its hard edge.

"Who is this?"

"Lieutenant Rivera."

"Jack?" Her voice was kitten-soft, feminine.

He stiffened like a boy who's seen his mother's undergarments. "Were you sleeping?"

"Yeah. I think so. What time is it?"

"Listen, honey..."

Honey? Had he ever called *me* honey? Under *any* conditions?

"I'm sorry to bother you, but you haven't seen..." His jaw flexed. "The senator's not there, is he?"

"The senator?" I could almost hear her blink. Could imagine her shoving back her supermodel hair.

He closed his eyes. I could see him deciding not to kill his old man—yet. "Yeah," he said.

"In my *apartment*?"

"Listen, I was just looking for him and thought—"

"Jack?" The bedsprings sang softly under her nonexistent weight. "What's going on?"

"Nothing. I—" he began, but my gasp interrupted him. He shot his dark gaze toward me like a javelin.

"Her father!" My voice was raspy.

His brows lowered.

"Theo Altove," I said. "He must know."

His jaw bunched and flexed. "Hey, your dad didn't say anything about meeting with my old man, did he?"

"Dad?"

"Yeah."

"Jack, why—"

"Listen, Thea, this is pretty important. Do you know where your father is?"

She delayed an instant. "He's out of town," she said. "San Diego, I think. For the weekend."

"Do you know where you can get a hold of him?"

"I could try his cell phone, but—"

"What service does he have?"

She told him.

"Number?"

Her voice faded, but I knew she complied, 'cuz he was scribbling indecipherable numerals onto his father's blotter.

"Does he keep it on at night?" he asked.

"Usually. He likes to stay in touch with—"

"Call him," he ordered. "Use the land line. I'll hold." He turned to me, not bothering to cover the receiver. "McMullen." Using the same pen, he wrote another phone number on the nearly blank sheet. "Call the captain."

I flipped open my phone, punched in the number.

"Ask for Kindred."

I did, then waited while Thea came back on the line.

"He's not answering," she said.

"Have you noticed anything strange lately?" Rivera asked.

"Strange?"

"Any unusual behavior?"

"Jack." She sounded foggy, scared. "What are you talking about? What's going on?"

"I'm not sure. Listen, I have to go. I'll call you as soon as I know something."

"Just—" she said, but he was already hanging up.

"Captain Kindred here."

Rivera took the phone from me. "This is Lieutenant Rivera. I need a favor," he said.

"Do you know what fucking time it is?" His voice was little more than a ground-level rumble from the other end of the line. "There better be a life hanging by a fucking thread, Rivera."

"I think there is, sir."

There was a pause, a sigh, deep and long-suffering. "Well, it damn well better be someone I like."

The muscle ground in Rivera's jaw. "It's the senator."

"The hell—" he began, then softened his voice, speaking to someone in the room with him before redirecting his attention to the phone. "What do you need?"

"A trace. T-Mobile," Rivera said, and rattled off the number.

He hung up in a minute. His eyes were black-granite dark and getting darker. "Any idea who the old man's been cozying up to?" he asked. "Besides you?"

I shook my head. Out of ideas and too nervous to take offense.

Rivera turned away to rummage through the rest of the drawers. I rambled through the house, looking for something, anything that might shed light on the senator's whereabouts, but everything seemed perfectly in its place. No SOS messages written in seashells. No clothing strewn about the house in some strategic manner. Shoes perfectly aligned in the closet. Caps hanging in a row.

Rivera's cell rang. By the time I reached him, he was already striding out of the kitchen. Someone was rambling off numbers too fast to understand, but I thought I caught the word "century" before he snapped the phone shut.

I barely avoided colliding with him. He caught my arms to steady me.

"What'd they say? He's here, isn't he? In Century City. Theo Altove."

He stared down into my eyes. "It looks like you were right, McMullen."

No one was more surprised than I. "What's going on?"

"He used to keep a gun in here. Check that middle cabinet."

"Altove's not in San Diego, is he?" I asked, and turned shakily away, but something snapped around my wrist. I jerked. Rivera was already attaching the other end of the cuffs to the cupboard handle.

"What are you doing?"

"Stay here!" he growled as he strode out. "And stay the hell out of trouble."

"Rivera!" I screamed after him, but he didn't stop. The door slammed in his wake. I yanked the cabinet open, but it did little good.

Outside, I heard his Jeep roar to life.

I strained at the cupboard, stepping into the doorway and screaming his name again, but he was already squealing onto the street.

The house lay quiet around me. Everything in its place. Everything...And then I saw it. The hat rack with the antler prongs. Minus the cowboy hat. Only the two caps remained.

Holy crap! The senator was at his ranch. I reached for my phone, but I'd given it to Rivera.

I swore then, long and unimaginative, but I was already stretching toward the drawers. There were no screwdrivers within reach. But I finally managed to snag a butter knife.

Five minutes later I found my phone on the senator's desk. I snatched it up and ran to my Saturn, already dialing, but Rivera's line rolled over to voice mail. I swore and dialed again.

"Babekins." Solberg's voice didn't even sound sleepy.

"I need directions to the senator's ranch."

"Oh, babe, I don't think—"

"Alba Rojo. Now!" I snapped, and screeched onto the 27 heading north.

I don't know how long it took me to reach my destination. It seemed like a lifetime, but I was finally there. I turned into the driveway, heart pounding, and there was the senator's car. The house was absolutely dark. I had made it in time. Altove was still in Century City. All I had to do was get the senator out of there and all would be well.

I slammed out of my car, galloped up the veranda stairs, and pounded on the door.

"Senator! Senator!"

No one answered.

"Miguel, wake up! Please."

A light switched on inside. Footsteps padded across the floor. I held my breath in my throat, my Mace in my right hand, but the senator finally answered.

"Who's there?"

"It's Chrissy. I need to talk to you."

"Now?"

"Immediately."

He opened the door. Light streamed out. The senator was fully dressed. So was Theo Altove. He stood with his legs slightly spread, a pistol extended at arms' length and pointed directly at Miguel's back.

"Come in. Close the door," Altove said.

For one panicked moment I considered bolting, but he spoke again.

"Come in or the good senator dies where he stands."

I stepped inside, heart hiccuping in my chest.

"Who are you?" Altove asked.

I tried to speak, but my mouth failed.

"She's got nothing to do with—" the senator began, but Altove stopped him.

"You will sit and you will be silent."

The two men stared at each other, but finally the senator took a seat on the nearby couch. He looked worn and old.

"The police know," I said, forcing my lips to perform.

Altove turned back to me. He wore glasses. His hair was thin, his skin pale. But his hands were steady on the pistol. "What is it they know?"

I tried to breathe, but it was hard. "Thea's not your daughter."

His mouth twitched, but he didn't move.

"She's his," I said, and nodded toward the senator. My neck barely moved. "Rivera knows you—"

"Yes." Altove's voice was steady. "My wife—she was beautiful." His voice had gone dreamy. "Lips like scarlet cord, but she was..." He paused, cleared his throat, seemed to come back to himself. "He seduced her. I knew that. But it ended. She said it ended months before the pregnancy. And she gave me a daughter. A daughter that was everything her mother wasn't. So devout. So decent. She adored me. 'Daddy, may I. Daddy, please.'" He smiled. The expression made me shiver. "Do you have any idea what's it's like to learn it's all a lie? That she had sprung from another man's loins?"

"Why did you kill the others?"

"They also sinned."

"Dear God!" Rivera jerked to his feet. "I thought you were my friend, Theodore. A man of God, a—"

"One move and her death will be on your conscience, Miguel." The world ticked in silence. "If you have a conscience."

"You killed Kathy." The senator's voice was hoarse. "Rebecca. You bastard."

"Sit down," Altove ordered.

He sat. I felt faint, but I spoke again. *Keep him talking. Keep breathing.*

"You called the governor," I said. "Told him to make sure Kathy's death went uninvestigated."

"In fact, I reminded him that she had worked with the good senator here. We certainly didn't want to muddy the waters when Miguel would soon be announcing his bid for the presidency, for he would surely remember his friends when he entered the Oval Office. Kathleen's death had already been determined an unfortunate accident, after all."

"She broke a commandment," I said.

He didn't respond.

"They all broke commandments," I said. "But how did you do it? There was never a sign of struggle. Never—"

"No man builds granaries without first figuring the cost."

"What—"

"I planned, Ms. McMullen. I planned for years. Oh . . ." He shook his head. "I didn't truly intend to follow through, but it was soothing to think about laboring in the Lord's fields. I dreamed of reaping one death on each day of the week according to their sins, then resting on the seventh day after Miguel's demise." He smiled wistfully. "It was naught but a dream. But then Thea..." His lips twitched again. "Thea felt she was being called to work in Los Angeles. And I knew—all those months, ago, even before she told me she'd met Miguel—I knew their paths would cross." He shook his head, eyes somber. "It was a sign from the Almighty. A sign that I must not let him corrupt others. Corrupt *her*."

"Theo." The senator shook his head, eyes beseeching. "Surely you don't believe I would touch her. Not my own daughter."

In the distance, I heard sirens.

Altove pursed his lips. Resignation showed in his eyes. "No. You won't," he said, and twisting toward Rivera, he snapped off a shot.

"Don't!" I screamed, and lifted the Mace.

Altove swung the gun back toward me. I could feel his intent, could see him pull the trigger. Thunder echoed in the room. Something struck me. I was slammed to the floor. Pain tore through my shoulder. The senator grunted and rolled aside, smearing blood across the hardwood, but he dragged himself upright, sitting brokenly in front of me, shielding me.

"Kill me, then," he rasped. "But spare her, for God's sake."

Emotions streaked through Altove's eyes. Confusion, fear, remorse. He stood, frozen, horrified, and then he placed the muzzle in his mouth and pulled the trigger.

33

Dating is my second-favorite hobby. My first is being audited.

—*Donald Archer,*
rich and single

I WOULD LIKE to take this moment..." The room fell silent, faces turned expectantly. Senator Rivera stood surrounded by a hundred or so of his closest friends. The Sapphire Room of the Mandarin was filled to overflowing. "...to extend my heartfelt appreciation to each and every one of you." He smiled, charismatic, calm, controlled. The left sleeve of his charcoal Armani suit looked a bit tight, doubtless because of the bandages, but there were no other indicators to suggest that, less than twenty-four hours before, a bullet had plowed a path through his upper arm, missing his aorta by a handbreadth. "My family, my friends..." He paused again and glanced around the room. His eyes gleamed with sincerity, and suddenly it seemed that the room was smaller, more intimate. As if he spoke to me alone. "You have supported me when I needed it most. Guided me when I lost my way and made me proud in more ways than I can mention. But today . . ." He lifted his eyes from mine. "Today I have called you here to announce that I will be leaving the political arena."

There were gasps of shock and disappointment.

He raised a calming hand. "I realize that many of you had hoped for different news. For better news, perhaps. But in light of recent events, I feel it is time for me to focus exclusively on personal issues.

"My family, for instance." He glanced toward Rivera, smiling gently with his ever-wise eyes. "Lieutenant Gerald Rivera—thank you, my son. You are my greatest accomplishment."

Ten feet away, Rivera showed no emotion whatsoever but for, perhaps, a slight stiffening of his musculature.

"And his inamorata, Ms. Christina McMullen." He clenched his fist against his well-dressed chest. "You shall forever be in my heart. You are like the daughter I always wished to have.

"And you others . . ." He lifted both arms like a benevolent demigod. I couldn't help but wonder what it cost him in pain and dry-cleaning bills. Surely the wound was seeping. "You have cheered for me in the good times, mourned for me in the bad, and, perhaps most important, forgiven me my mistakes. Of which, sadly, there have been many." He looked solemn and earnest.

"But good comes even from mistakes." He drew a deep breath. "As you may have heard, there was a terrible tragedy at my ranch. My good friend and longtime confidant, Theodore Altove, who had been battling depression for some time, took his life." He paused again. The crowd murmured, bubbling with the need to gossip. He lifted his hand and Thea slipped out of the crowd, graceful and solemn. How he had convinced her to be there so soon after Theo's death was beyond my imagination. But there she was. "His beautiful daughter, Thea, will have to carry on without him. And for that I feel terrible sorrow. But together..." He took her hand, lifting it high. "She and I will be founding a broad-reaching charity in East L.A., a wonderful program that will help end the suffering of our fair city's urban poor."

There was enthusiastic clapping, perhaps initiated by shills, and he smiled. "I am thrilled with your response," he said, "for I shall certainly appeal for your individual support when the time is ripe. But until then, please—enjoy the hospitality of this fine establishment. Eat, drink, and remember to live life to the fullest, for only God knows the number of our days."

With that, he turned and disappeared, taking Thea with him.

I slipped outside a few minutes later. The parking lot was well lit and my Saturn stood close to the door. I popped the locks and reached for the handle.

"I suppose I should thank you."

I glanced up with a gasp. Rivera stood on the far side of my car.

"For saving the bastard," he said.

I shrugged. The last twenty-four hours had been rather trying. The senator had been rushed to the hospital. Altove had been declared dead, and Rivera hadn't said more than ten words to me.

"Shouldn't you be in there answering questions?" I asked.

"I'm sure the good senator can explain everything away. He's an expert at talking while saying nothing at all."

I couldn't argue. It seemed as if I'd had endless conversations with him, each one leaving me more confused than the last.

"Besides," Rivera said. "I don't think they want to hear that the old man's an ass."

The night air felt soft against my face. Strange how a near-death experience can make one appreciate even the feel of the air. "He apologized."

"Six people are dead," he said. Despite the darkness and our distance, I could feel the anger in him. "Because of him, because he can't keep his dick in his pants."

"Why didn't you out him, then?" I asked. "Tell them the truth."

He shook his head, jaw set. "Thea's life is going to be hell enough without having to admit she's the old bastard's illegitimate daughter."

He looked tense and hard. But it was a tension I had missed. A hardness that touched me in ways I couldn't explain. "At least she knows," I said.

He snorted. "The senator gracefully agreed to tell her that much."

I wondered if that meant there had been no bloodshed.

He drew a deep breath, rounded the bumper. "What about you?" he asked.

I could feel his approach like the advance of a storm

and lifted my chin against the onslaught. "What about me what?"

"You okay?"

"Sure."

He glanced away, close now. "I'm sorry."

I savored his words for a moment, knowing it might be the last time he ever said them. "For . . . ?"

He stared into the distance, then shoved his hands into the front pockets of his jeans and propped the heel of his shoe on my hubcap behind him. "My temper." He exhaled, making the apology seem physically painful. "My bad judgment. My genetics."

"I believe you've met my family."

He smiled a little. A teaspoon of tension seemed to drain from him. "I'd trade half a dozen old bastards for three crazy brothers and a father with a flattop."

"Even if he called you Pork Chop?"

"God." He shook his head. "It's a wonder you're as sane as you are."

"Gee," I said, "I don't think you've ever said anything quite that nice to me before."

He chuckled, turned toward me, and suddenly his arm slipped around my waist. "You're not half ugly when you get cleaned up."

"Stop it. I'm blushing." The sad part was that I might truly have been. We were standing pretty close, and there was something about him . . . something indefinable and alive.

Running his hand up my arm, he brushed the hair away from my face. "I had a dream about you," he said.

"Yeah?" I didn't manage to say more. Dreams had started this whole debacle, and I couldn't help but wonder if his was the death-on-the-sidewalk kind or the steamy-shower kind. I have to admit, I really prefer the steamy-shower kind. Especially if they come true.

"You were naked," he said.

"Oh?" My chest hurt a little. I wondered vaguely if my heart was about to pound its way through my rib cage and grab his ass. "Was I still alive?"

"You were screaming my name." He slipped his hand behind my neck. His skin felt hot and rough against mine.

"Because you were trying to kill me?" I guessed.

"Because you hadn't had an orgasm for a millennium." He moved closer still. I could feel his erection against my belly. "You hadn't forgotten how, though."

I swallowed. "It's probably like riding a bicycle," I said.

"Christ, it *has* been a while for you, hasn't it?" he asked. "Tell me the truth . . ." His breath felt warm and hopeful against my cheek. "Those other guys . . ." I could see the muscle in his cheek tighten. "Do you have feelings for them?"

There were so many things left unresolved. Ramla's sister. Micky's son. My stupid septic system. But at that moment the world seemed to narrow down to Rivera's whiskey-dark eyes.

I wanted desperately to kiss him, but I stayed as I was, nearly as desperate to refrain from stupidity. "Which ones specifically?"

"Are you intentionally trying to make me crazy?" he asked, and pulled me closer.

"Don't blame the physician," I said.

He almost smiled. "Pretty clever how you made sure I was there every time you were cuddled up to a different guy."

"You're delusional," I said, and he kissed my jaw.

"You saying you didn't plan it?"

"That's exactly what I'm saying."

He slipped his other hand behind my neck. "So you're just irresistible?"

"You seem to have been resisting pretty well."

"Hardly any damage at all."

I raised a brow.

"From spending the nights beating my head against the wall."

"It was probably a real hardship spending your time with the supermodel with hair."

"She's my *sister*," he said.

"Well, it didn't look like you were feeling too brotherly when I saw you at Caring Hands."

He narrowed his eyes at me.

"The senator had asked me to meet him there the day you and he had words," I explained.

"The senator . . ."

I nodded.

"Asked *you* to go there."

"Yes."

He inhaled deeply. "He asked *me* to meet him there."

"At the same time?"

"Two o'clock."

Weird. My mind clicked over that fact. "He must have been trying to get us together."

Rivera shook his head. "He was dead set against me meeting Thea. I didn't understand why until yesterday."

"Then why would he want us there at the same time?"

"Did he call you in person?"

I shook my head, remembering back. "His secretary."

"A guy named Rick called me for him. Said it was urgent. How about dinner at Vegas?"

"What?"

"The night I saw you with Curly Top. What made you choose that restaurant?"

"I got a coupon," I said.

"One night only?"

"How'd you know?" I asked, but he was shaking his head.

"Fucking bastard."

"You don't think your father set it up."

He snorted, but just then a shadow stepped from the shadows.

I jerked.

"Miss Chris." D sauntered toward us. His cowboy hat was gone, but his sunglasses remained.

"D!" I straightened abruptly and glanced at Rivera, who had eyes only for the supermobster.

"What are you doing here?" I asked.

He shrugged, grinned. "The senator makes a rousing speech. If I hadn't known he cuckolded old Altove, I would have been pretty moved."

"How did you know—" I began, but Rivera interrupted me.

"You know a lot of things, don't you, Dagwood?"

Their gazes met and clashed. D was grinning a little. Rivera was as serious as a hangover.

"I know she's too good for you," D said.

"But not for you?"

D laughed. He looked loose and amused. "Archer's a nice guy. Drinks a little too much, maybe. On the other hand, that small-town cop hardly drinks at all, but he's got some issues. Celibacy being—"

"Holy crap!" Understanding hit me like a falling house. D had set it all up. Every seemingly accidental meeting with Rivera and each time I had been with a different man. The restaurants, Caring Hands. I scowled.

"What about the meeting at the dog park?" I asked. "Was that just a coincidence?"

Rivera was glowering. "I got a call from an informant," he said. "Asked me to meet him there."

"But he never showed," I surmised, and shifted my eyes to D's.

His were laughing.

"A little competition's good for the soul," he said.

"Who do you think—" I breathed.

"You one of them?" Rivera asked.

D turned slowly toward him.

"My competitors," Rivera said. "You one of them?"

D smiled. "Miss Chris," he said, not facing me. "Tell the lieutenant here that I'm a sixth-level black belt."

"Listen, D, I—"

"Tell your mobster I don't care if he's a damn junkyard dog."

D smiled. "Is your lieutenant suggesting he would like to fight me for your honor?"

My heart clenched tight in my chest. "No," I said. "No, he's not."

"Bare fists," Rivera said.

I turned on him with a snarl. "Don't be stupid," I hissed.

"Good to see he's got some balls," D said.

"First man down is out of her life," Rivera said.

"Rivera." I felt breathless, shaky. "Don't be stupid. He's—"

"What?" Rivera turned toward me, eyes burning. "A felon? A lying bastard?" His face was sharp-edged and earnest. "Not good enough to say your name out loud?"

"Dangerous," I breathed.

"Thank you," D said. "But I say the last man standing gets to take our girl Chrissy to bed."

"Don't even think about it!" I hissed, but D smiled as he made the first strike.

Rivera was somber as he blocked it. I swore at them both, scared and frustrated and madder than hell as I pulled out my Mace. . . .

About the Author

LOIS GREIMAN lives in Minnesota with her family, some of whom are human. Write to her at lgreiman@earthlink.net. One of her alter egos will probably write back.

Check out her website at www.loisgreiman.com.